D1637857

MRS WINCHESTER'S
GUN CLUB

A NOVEL

BY

DOUGLAS BRUTON

SCOTLAND STREET PRESS
EDINBURGH

Published by Scotland Street Press 2019

2 5 7 3 12 9 7 5 9

First published in Great Britain in 2019 by

Scotland Street Press
Edinburgh
www.scotlandstreetpress.com

Cover design by Angus Henderson

ISBN: 978-1-910895-24-5

Typeset in Scotland by Theodore Shack

Editorial Note:

This is a novel written by a Scot set in America in times gone by. In accordance with this quaintness, American spelling has been used throughout.

For the late Helen Lamb for telling me this was good enough to put 'out there'.

And for Daniel and Holly who first told me about the Winchester Mystery House.

Prologue

One day there was a message from my dead grandmother. I knew the crack and clack in her voice, and I passed what she said on to her daughter, my mother. It was a small arrangement of words that made no sense to me, but when spoken to my mother caused such a pain in her. She said I was a wicked child to say such things and she shut me in the airless dark beneath the stairs and all there was in that space was the voices crowding round me – my grandmother's and a thousand more besides.

I learned from that day to keep them from my mother, the voices, and I understood then that she did not hear them the same as I did. I now know that no-one else hears them – but to me they sound like the wind when it moves through the trees, like leaf-whispers and those leaves never still. A hundred voices sometimes there are and all speaking at once.

I used to think my mother heard them, too, but with her it was just pretend. A part of the act it was and all for show. What she did was read people. Sharp as a pin or a razor she was with her reading, so she could tell what was what just by looking, and the people pressed silver dollars into her palm for the things she told them, things they knew already but having my mother tell them made those things somehow more true.

It was not like telling lies, she told me. She gave them what they sought and there was some small comfort in what she told them. It was not really like lying, she said, not when she did some good in the world, when she gave the people something that would help them get through this day and the next, helping them to carry some burden of loss or grief.

My mother taught me all the little tricks. How to read in the lines of a face a broader history of a person's life; how the way that a person held themselves betrayed them; how the look in their eyes, or the quickness of their breath, or the words that they spoke gave away their secrets. She taught me the questions to ask and what to look for in the answers that were given.

When she was dressed all in black, with dark kohl to line her eyes, and her hair in plaits and loose tails, the ends tied with strips of colored cloth, and rings on all her fingers, and her voice all lilt and music, then they'd come: women who held a knot of suffering cradled in their empty arms, or their hearts broken and broken so they were closer to the grave; or stooped and shrunken figures of men who had lost their mothers and the guilt for something they'd said or not said was too big a weight for them to bear. They'd come to my mother and ask for her help, their voices shrunk small as a child's. Then my mother would pretend.

She pretended she could hear the dead talking and she tilted her head as though she was listening, like a bird when it thinks it hears something of some meaning or threat but is not sure. She tilted her head and she half-closed her eyes and she held her breath, one hand raised to still all other noise in the hall. The people listened and could hear nothing. Some felt as though they were watched and they thought it must be that the dead were there with them; but it was my mother who was watching, searching for clues in them, looking for the question she must ask to draw their story from them.

Then, from the few or many words that they gave up, my mother would piece together enough of a picture of their lives that she could pretend she spoke with a near relative on the other side, or a child that had passed from this world to the next, or a loved one who could not yet leave for there was business still to finish. She measured the grip of their hands, or the crook of their bodies. She made calculation of the catch and choke in their voices. And there'd be a message at last, once the silver had been passed from their hands to hers and quickly secreted in the hidden folds of her dress. A small enough message it was, something without particulars or voice, something that was resonant with meaning, and this or that might be easily inferred from what was said. Whatever it was, there was a truth in it that was recognized and a truth that was looked for so that hearing it brought forth tears and sometimes more silver.

On the poster out front, it said that Madame Cora Price could talk with the dead and the show gave truth to that lie. But my mother never did hear voices, not like I heard them. Always there have been voices, all wanting to be heard and sometimes all talking at once so that my head hurts and sleep is the only thing to make them quiet, or drink now I am older, or music played loud and dancing taking me over.

They would have remained hidden, those voices, except that I soon discovered there was money to be made by being in touch with the dead, really in touch with them. So it is that I now do what my mother did before me, but I do it better. Days and nights I sit in darkened rooms or halls, a tin-whistle music blowing through the place, and curtains pulled on strings as thin as hair and not seen, and those curtains made to flap and flap, and the air made artificially cold as though the dead are near. All this is a lie to make more believable the truth I have to impart. I give the people what they want to hear and sometimes what they don't want, and all I do is tell them what the dead do want me to tell.

I see the looks in their faces afterwards, all softened, and smiling through tears, like God has touched them and in that touching has made their world a sunnier place to be walking around in. It's a sort of healing, what I do, like I am a surgeon cutting away some painful lump in them so that their lives can be lived again. The people I have healed may be counted in the hundreds and those hundreds stack into small thousands and thus I am not short of dollars in the bank.

But though the voices continue and do not give me rest unless I am sleeping or drunk, there is one that I would talk with and he does not come. I do not think he ever will, and I would give all the dollars I have if such a gift would let me hear his voice once again. Be that as it may, it is not the substance of what I have here to tell.

There arrived another day in my story, a day that must be marked out from the rest for the reason that *she* did come to me on that day. She had not more years on her than I, though her skin was softer and more pale. I knew her at once, though she used some other name than her own and wore a black lace veil that she lifted only briefly at our introduction. I should have known her from the newspapers that had made report of her life over the past few years, her picture tucked into their pages and the picture of her lost husband and her lost child there, too. I should have known her for the ring that she wore on her wedding finger – much had been made of it once. I should have known her for the grief that was on her, a grief that I recognized and understood. But if truth be told, I knew her for some other reason: there was a voice in my head that did name her, a hundred voices, all speaking at once, all shouting, as the Jews must once have shouted at Pilate's door for Jesus to be the one that was crucified, and all the shouting voices saying the one thing over and over, and that one thing was her name.

She came to me or was brought, leaning on the arm of a sister or a friend and further supported by a man who was more than a brother and less than a husband. Though her hair was not yet grey nor her face lined by anything more than grief, yet there was something akin to age upon her, for she did not seem able to move without that her two companions did move with her, carrying her almost. I recall she wept throughout our consultation (see how my language does make comparison between what I do and what a doctor does – a 'consultation' I call it!) and her gloved hands were knotted as though she was a woman who had been too much with her needle and thread and now all her joints were tied in pain. It was her lady companion who spoke for her at first, who told the story of the woman's loss and her hurt. I do not think I heard what the lady companion said; it did not matter, for I knew the woman's story almost as well as I knew my own.

It was the untimely death of her husband that had brought Mrs Sarah Winchester to me, though her grief was doubly deep for there had been an infant child some years before and her name was Annie and she had met an early demise also, through some illness or other. It was not an unusual story and there was no difficulty in reading the need in Mrs Winchester. I made some sympathetic comment on her loss and promised to connect her with her child and husband.

Mrs Sarah Winchester gestured to her lady companion. She said she wanted to be alone with me and her words were broken breathless whispers. She waved the lady away and her footman too.

I saw then that Mrs Sarah Winchester was dressed plainly, as though she did not wish to be known. She slowly and with some difficulty removed her hat and her gloves and the black lace veil. I could see that grief had marred her as it had marred me, though the newspaper reports were old news now and it had been some months since her more recent loss. I ordered tea and, while we waited, made polite comment on the weather and the time of year and said something inconsequential about death and the ways of God being beyond all human understanding and something about rewards in Heaven awaiting us.

She was impatient. She tapped her crooked fingers on the back of a chair and remained standing. I took my time in pouring the tea and adding the lemon and the sugar. The noise of my spoon against the china was a further irritation to her and so I stopped. Then I cleared my throat, and asked her once more to be seated, a little more metal in my voice.

'You wish to know why?' I ventured.

'Both taken from me,' she said, 'with no explanation. All the doctors confounded. Is there some wrong in me? Something I have done?'

I made a show of listening, just as my mother had taught me. I tilted my head, and took pause with one hand lifted to put a stop to her speaking. I could see her, Mrs Sarah Winchester, through half-closed eyes. I could see her fright-faced like a caught fish on a hook.

I told her there were many voices on the other side, which was not any word of a lie. Not just the voice of her daughter and her husband, I said, but others, all wanting to have their say. There was a rent in Heaven and in Hell, I said, for a great wrong had been done and the voices of the dead were lifted up as one and all in protest.

'What says my daughter? What says my husband?'

I held up my hand again and made as if I was listening as before. Then I said that her daughter and her husband were together and that they spoke with a single voice, their twin lips giving shape to just the one word, but saying it over.

'What do they say? Tell me.'

I told her that her daughter and her husband said that they were sorry, that 'sorry' was the only word that they spoke. She was moved by that, but not satisfied. She said that *she* had a message for them. She asked if it was possible for that message to be passed back to them or if they were there in the room and could hear what she said. She thought it might bring her some small peace to say it.

I did not give heed to her question but went on to explain to her that there was some sort of a curse set against her family, a curse for the wrong that had been done. I said that the blood of thousands was on their hands, the hands of her husband in particular, and by association her daughter and still on her. I said that there was a price to be paid, to which she responded by placing a purse on the table before me. I recoiled, as though stung. I told her that there was a greater price to be paid, a greater price than money, and that all the voices of the dead had been raised against her, like dogs in a pack that have rounded on a lone elk.

She asked if there was something that could be done. She was in earnest and I understood that I could have asked anything of her then and she would have given what I asked. She reached out for my hand and held it in hers and her claw-like grip was fast.

'There is something,' I said. 'I do not understand, but there's something you can do.'

She pleaded to know.

'The spirits are telling me that you must go from here,' I told her, 'far away. You must go west, as far west as ever it is possible to go. There you must build a great house, a place for the spirits to find rest in, a house of many rooms. For as long as the house is under construction then so long will the spirits give you leave to live.'

I do not think she was surprised. There was no shock in her, none that I could discern, not in her features or in her breath nor even in her grip of my hand. She merely thanked me for my time and for the tea, which she had not touched. 'Thank you,' she said, her voice steady and sure. She patted the back of my hand and kissed it. She got to her feet, the paper-rustling of her dress the only sound, pushed the purse across the table towards me, bade me good morning and left.

There was more money in that purse than I might make in a busy month or a three-month. I should have been the happier for that. I should have been drunk that night and for many a night afterwards and in such drunkenness there would have been rest and a sweet silence that others enjoy and which is solace to the soul, for in silence might be said prayers. But the money was tainted. There was blood on the money, I felt sure, and the voices, clamoring, confirmed it, and so I gave it all away to a destitute whose bowl was empty, one I had been directed to by a voice that had once been his mother's.

There were fewer and fewer reports of Mrs Sarah Winchester in the morning papers after that day. I did discover somehow that she had gone west as I had instructed her to do and that was all I knew till much later when the years had caught up with me and with her.

CHAPTER ONE

Where do the years go? It seems like only yesterday that Annie was in Sarah's arms and song and singing was in every room, and laughter and stories too. William was the giant pursuing a brave cowherd-Jack who had taken his magic hen; and William was also Jack, climbing down the beanstalk to escape the giant who wanted to grind his bones to make bread.

'Bread from *bones*?' says Annie.

'Fie-fi-fo-fum, I smell the blood of an Englishman.'

Annie curls into her mother's body, the pretend-fright making her shake and laugh at her father's voice sunk deep as a growl, as he lumbers about the room like a bear or a great ape.

'I want a hen that lays golden eggs,' says Annie when the giant is felled.

Sixteen years since then, though it seems scarcely possible. Sarah moves from room to room, listening for the smallest noise. Like she did before in the game that they played when Annie hid from her mother under beds, in cupboards, behind curtains. All these years later Sarah searches all the known places and the unknown, and listens as keen as listening can, sharp as pins or pinches, for held breath and heartbeats and soft slippered footsteps.

'Help me, William. Help me find her.'

Sixteen years since Annie lay small and pale in her mother's bed, all the best doctors in attendance, the best that ever money could buy, and they shook their heads and scratched their beards and looked for answers in their black books and looked for solutions in their black bags. Annie was ever restless in her sleep, and Sarah sat with her and cooled the child's brow with cold wet cloths, held Annie's limp hand and begged for her to be allowed to live through this night and the next.

'You should rest, Sarah. You should get some sleep. I'll sit with Annie.'

Sixteen years she has slept and each time she wakes it is the same hurt that she feels and each new morning she loses Annie again so that the day, every day, begins in tears and with a pain where her heart should be.

'Help me, William.'

But William is lost, too, now. One minute he is with her, holding her arm, as they move in step from this place to that place, and sometimes he calls for his daughter, as Sarah does. He searches behind curtains, under beds, in the dark corners of cupboards.

'See, Sarah, she is not here. She's gone.'

One minute he is with her and then suddenly William is in the same bed and the same doctors are scratching the same beards and the pages of their black books are blank and their bags are empty, and Sarah does not sleep this time for there is no-one who dares counsel her to do so. Instead, she watches the breath taken from her husband, slow and slow, watches for the moment when there is something so small and then nothing, and she whispers in his ear: 'Jack, brave Jack, eschew the hen and the harp. Bring back a little girl called Annie instead, for the giant must have her shut in a cupboard or hidden under his bed or stood behind a curtain.'

Now William is gone, his bones ground down to make a giant's bread, and all that is left is the hen laying golden eggs, hundreds of them, and Sarah Winchester, widow and childless mother, with nothing to spend her great fortune on.

'Be he alive or be he dead.'

William was laid in the ground soon after, laid next to Annie, and Sarah was all tears and grief. And where do the days, weeks, months all go, for there seems no time since then and now, and she has not yet grown accustomed to waking up alone. Indeed, some days she wakes and just for the shortest time she thinks she hears William and he is laughing and Annie is running from his bear and his great ape and Sarah holds open her arms so that an Annie might curl into her and not be frightened any more, even though she never was and it was all just pretend. Just for the briefest moment on waking, everything is as it was. Then Sarah sees her arms are empty and a space is beside her in the bed and no sound to be heard save her own snatched breath when she realizes, and there are tears then.

Her sister visited some days and she threw wide the curtains of Sarah's room, and all the rooms, opened the windows of the house, and chattered like a bird about things of little consequence, chattered without cease. Sarah thought she heard voices then, underneath the voice of her sister. She thought she heard Annie and William and they were reading together, the singsong voice of reading, the lilt and leap of his words and the dancing after of hers. It was a memory that played over so often that it felt like it was more than just remembering.

'It is not seemly or decent to be so much abed,' her sister scolded, though there was no spit or spite in her scolding.

Sarah put a finger across her lips.

'There's someone I wish you to see,' said the sister, giving no heed to that finger and Sarah's call for hush. 'A woman, and she is by reputation remarkable for she gives readings and it's said that she talks with the dead. Maybe she could talk with William and Annie. Maybe in talking with them, a way might be found for you to move on from this darkness.'

Sarah heard only broken bits of what her sister was saying. She heard 'William' and 'Annie' and she heard something about how 'maybe she could talk with them'. She asked her sister to say again what she had said and this time Sarah gave her sister's words a greater portion of her attention.

So it was arranged and Sarah drew strength from what her sister had told her, and each day she rose from her bed, and she picked over a small breakfast, and she dressed, and with the help of a stick or her footman's arm, she walked from her bedroom to the front door and took a turn once around the garden. The color returned slowly to her cheeks and an excitement she had known when she was younger overcame her. She set her house in order once more, and flowers were brought into the rooms, and the fires in the house were lit, and food was taken at table.

She also re-discovered letters William had sent her when she was a girl, letters she had bound up in blue ribbon and which she'd kept in a wooden box beneath her bed. Hundreds of letters there were and she began reading them again, in the order in which they had been written, and it was as if she was reading them for the first time and every page was a surprise and a new delight.

There were pictures folded into some of the pages, too, pictures of William Wirt Winchester, dashing in his frock coat and cravat, and standing in front of the factory of the Winchester Repeating Arms Company. Some of the letters talked of the work he was about and the details in the day-to-day managing of the company and the sales of this or that rifle to this or that buyer. Others talked of their last meeting, Sarah and William's, and how lost for words he had been and how he had wished himself braver that he might have asked for her arm or her hand. In one letter there had been a silver and sapphire necklace, and earrings the same and a bracelet, and William Wirt Winchester hoped that he did not trespass beyond the limits of good taste in saying that when he had seen these items he had thought only of her.

Sarah relived William's extravagant year-long courtship, and in three weeks she was wooed again and won, and maybe it was this that gave her back her color. Even her sister remarked on it and the footman, Jack, made so bold as to pass comment also that she did look well. Paler and paler she should have been for there approached a darker day than all the rest of the year, the anniversary of the first loss and the greatest. But this year Sarah had resolved to call on the spiritualist at this time, and to speak with her alone, and in that resolution she found strength and a reason to go on.

Then, one hopeful morning and before they were cold, she wiped the waking tears from her cheeks, ordered strong coffee, instructed the maid to prepare her dress, the black one with the veil, and a carriage was called for and her sister fetched.

Beyond the gates of her house, the world was about its business and the world little knew that the one-time 'Belle of New Haven' was again parading through its streets, less of a parade perhaps and more of a stealing – like thieves steal and they do not wish to be known so their collars are turned up and their faces covered. Down the dark back-roads they travelled, turning this way and that, and doubling back, and always looking over their shoulders in case they were followed, for the eyes of the press were everywhere. Then at last to an address that was out of the way, a small house with shutters on all the windows and a door painted black.

Sarah felt a weakness overcome her and had to lean on her sister's arm and her footman's for support. The steps to the house had to be taken one at a time, resting between steps. 'There is no hurry, Mrs Winchester,' said the footman. Sarah almost turned back. The door was open before they had to knock and they were led through the gas-lit dark of the quiet house to a room in the back. The air was chill in the room and a woman waited there. She was dressed in black too, but had colored rags in her pleated hair and thick-crusted rings on all her fingers. When she moved she seemed to glide, with no sound save that of the jingle of small bells.

Sarah's sister made some brief introductions and Sarah did not recognize herself or her sister in the names that were used. The woman nodded as if she understood the lie that was in every word she had been told. Then something more true: an account was given of the loss of a child and afterwards the loss of a husband, and that was all the reason why they were there and it was asked if the lady-spiritualist thought she might help and if some message might be looked for and found.

The lady-spiritualist nodded and said something mannered about how sorry she was for the loss, and something about the difficult to bear it must be. Her voice was seeming-sincere and all her movements slow and gentle. She said that she was sure that she could speak with Annie and with William; and that a message could be passed from their world back to ours, of that she was certain.

Sarah brought forth from beneath the folds of her skirts a heavy purse and held it out for the woman to take. She gripped the woman's hand and would have spoken, but there were not the words in her. The woman leaned in close, kissed Sarah's cheek and whispered something. Then Sarah's sister and the footman both left, with assurances that they would return in due course when the transaction was completed.

A table had been moved into the center of the room and the lady-spiritualist made to be hospitable with the offer of refreshment. Sarah was impatient to be talking with William and with Annie. She did not know how it would be, if she would hear their voices in her head as they spoke, or if their words were to be spelled out on the table before them, or if the words were to come out of the woman's mouth so that it would be the woman's voice she heard even if the words spoken were William's or Annie's.

Sixteen years of grieving and Sarah could remember the day of her loss as though it was yesterday, and she did not know where all those years had gone; now, an interview that would afterwards be counted in minutes, seemed to stretch beyond enduring. The lady-spiritualist made tea and took her time with each step in the process. Sarah lifted off her hat and her veil, not so that the woman should better know her, but for William and for Annie. She peeled off her gloves, too, and laid them aside. Then she paced the floor and wrung her hands and tried to control her breathing.

'You wish to know why?' the spiritualist said at last, and it was as though she had read Sarah's thoughts – though Sarah's thoughts, such as they were, were not so very hard to read.

Sarah took again the seat she was offered and she leaned into the spiritualist and would have spoken then but the woman held up one imperious hand to command silence.

The air in the room fizzed and sparked and was at the same time chill. Sarah felt a presence, as though she was in a greater company, as though the room was crowded and everyone in it was talking at once. She felt a little dizzy and held onto the table to steady herself.

The spiritualist let fall her hand and took in a deeper breath, sucking the air through her teeth. Then she said that she had spoken with William and with Annie. She said there was a message in one word, and they both said the same, said it as one, or almost as one, like William reading to Annie and Annie tripping after with the same words. 'Sorry,' was all that they said and in that 'sorry' was to be found a whole world of meaning if the looking was hard.

Then, without taking another breath, the woman went on to talk about a curse on the family and a hundred spirited voices all raised against the name of 'Winchester' and how the curse would be visited on Sarah next unless the spirits could be appeased, 'for their blood is up and they would have their revenge on your family.'

Many were now dead, the lady-spiritualist said, dead and too-soon in the next world in consequence of the Winchester family and their business, so there must be some account settled. The woman said that it was up to Sarah. She said that Sarah should go far from the city, as far west as it was possible to go. There she was to build a great house and all the troubled spirits would find room there, and peace perhaps, and so long as this house for the dead was still under construction then the spirits would not exact further vengeance. When the house was finished, though, the spirits would take from Sarah's life yet again.

Later, after the coach journey home and several days had passed without notice, Sarah turned over and over what the woman had told her. She took all the woman's words and found new ways to say them, new configurations and even new words, and the more she thought of what was said the less certain she became of what was and what wasn't. She considered returning to the spiritualist's house a second time or instead asking that the woman visit the Winchester family home to talk of what had passed between them. Sarah wrote things down and crossed things out and tried to get back to what was actually said.

Then, as though in a dream, it was all clear again and as if it was her own idea. She woke up without tears for the first time in sixteen years, called the servants and announced her determination to move west, to stay with her niece at first, in California, and then to build a new house of her own. She promised them employment, if any wished to follow her there, or some sort of pension if they did not. Then she set about arranging the packing, for now she was resolved, she was in haste.

CHAPTER TWO

Days of lists, and pages on pages of all that was in the house, from thimble to chandelier, and everything documented and written down. Some things were to stay, for Sarah did not think that this was all certain, the moving west and the not returning. Dust-sheets were to be thrown over the furniture and the beds, books packed in boxes, and clothes and bed linen wrapped in camphor against the small sharp teeth of moths.

Sarah gave some things away, to friends and to neighbors, but she did not explain to them why. She did not want the extravagance of their goodbyes and their tears. She made no fuss of her giving, but pretended a fey madness borne out of a small recovery from grief. Even her sister was kept uninformed and excuses were made to put off her visits to the house, put off so that she might not see the boxes stacked on boxes, the rooms shrouded and shrunk, and the servants weeping behind closed doors.

Annie's room she kept as it was. Not a thing was disturbed, not the dresses in the wardrobe or the dolls on the bed, not the books lying with their pages open, not the slippers tucked just under the bed. From Annie's room, Sarah took only a small purple velvet box that contained a lock of her child's hair and inside the box she imagined she could still sense the fading smell of her lost child. All Sarah's last days in the great house were spent in Annie's room and every small detail was taken in so that no part of the room would ever be lost to her or out of the reach of remembering, and so whenever she closed her eyes she could, if she chose, see just as clearly everything in its place.

Tickets for the train were purchased in secret – she did not want the fuss of her story reported in the newspapers and such was her importance that this would surely happen if it was known. Her footman, Jack, said he would accompany her till she was settled in California and then he must, begging her leave, return to his family and his home. Sarah wrote wordy letters of recommendation for all in her employ and in her writing showed that each was known and valued. Some she gave directions as to where they might find further and immediate employment, though how she knew of such vacancies after having been so closed away and for so long was a mystery to them.

Only when the shutters began to go up on the windows did news leak out, and then rumor tumbled through the streets like an acrobat flipping head over heel, and growing wings and a tail in the retelling. Sarah was ill or dead, they said; or she was going to Europe to take the waters at Lourdes; or was enamored of a charlatan magician who had brought the dead daughter and the dead husband back from the brink; maybe she was finally mad and her sister had consulted doctors who had committed her to a local asylum; or she had removed herself to the one room at the back of the house where there were no shutters and there she had resolved to pass all her hermit days retreating into childhood once more. No-one came close to the truth, except that a woman in black with her hair in plaits and scrap ribbons was seen in the street one day and she nodded as if she understood and she smiled quietly to herself and turned away.

Come the day of her great departure Sarah's sister made the journey with her to the station, for by then she had been let in on the details of what was afoot. Much of what had been packed was kept in the house awaiting later instructions to follow Sarah out west. Jack carried what was required for the journey and saw to the two packing trunks that held sufficient for Sarah's immediate needs at her niece's home in California. The servants made their tearful farewells in the hall of the great house and Sarah touched the arm of this girl or shook the hand of the gardener or kissed the cheek of the maid below stairs. Such a fuss she made of everyone and something personal to say to each of them, even those that till then had thought themselves unnoticed.

At the station, aside from the come and go of the other passengers and their relatives, it was a much quieter affair. Sarah was settled in her carriage and Jack spoke with the conductor that he might know who was traveling on board the train that day – yes, Sarah Winchester of the Winchester Repeating Arms Company and mistress to the greatest of fortunes. Sarah's sister was unusually silent and every time she made to speak her words gave way to tears and she shook her head and held a lace kerchief to her cheek and to her nose. Sarah smiled and gave assurances that this was the right thing, her going, and that her sister might visit, and that California was not so far away as might be imagined.

Time collapses in such moments, or folds, and looking back it is hard to put things into the order in which they occurred. There were silences, and then the lowered voices of people used to being loud and now, in the proximity of strangers, reduced to whispers. On the platform, lovers hung onto each other to the last, like the survivors of some natural catastrophe, not daring to let go lest they be cast asunder. Children hid in the folds of their mothers' skirts and some dared not look at the day that was happening and some hoped that this was all dream and they blinked as if by blinking their sight might be corrected and every part of the dream turned to everyday and normal. Sarah's sister would not leave the carriage till she was certain of the imminent departure of the train, and even then thought to go a small part of the way with her sister. Jack had to help her down from the train; on the platform, he called for a porter to assist her to the waiting hansom that would take her home again.

The train shrieked and choked and jerked as though sudden and startled life was in the solid metal. Steam burst forth, billowing and white, like clouds had fallen over everything, turning the people on the platform into angels. As the train pulled away there were tears even for Sarah, and they were the last tears, and the whole of her sister's goodbyes and her lace handkerchief waving like a flag, and a dog barking somewhere on the platform, and a glimpsed woman in black with rings on all her fingers and her hair in pleats, and travel cases and trunks pushed from one end of the station to the other, and men in dark coats with shiny buttons consulting waistcoat timepieces, and the station clock with its outsize hands raised in the air in hallelujah, all that and everything dissolving into dream or fancy. Then nothing but the feeling of being now alone and cut off from the world that had been before and the fear of what lies in front.

Sarah pulled down the blinds on all the windows of her carriage and tried to go to sleep. The endless clickety-clack of the wheels on the track and the scrape of metal against metal prevented it, as did the holler of men filled up with their own importance, and the cries of children and mothers scolding. Instead, Sarah sat with her head against a pillow and her eyes closed and she heard voices in her head: the spirit whispers of the dead or the voices of simple memory – if memory is ever simple.

Two nights before the journey, Sarah had slept and dreamed. In her dream she had seen a house, not so small or so grand, but a house that was not yet finished. A young man was taking her from room to room and pointing out all its features: the size of the rooms, the number of the windows that let in such a light that filled the space, the height of the ceilings that gave to the house a sense of grandeur. Sarah let go of the man's hand, not aware till then that she had been holding it. Then she was alone in the house, and outside a cloud must have drifted across the sun for the light faltered, and there was one small room that she was drawn to, smaller than all the rest. On the front of the door to the room was a number, the number one. Sarah did not know why a room should be numbered, unless it was so that the servants would know.

Sarah pushed open the door and stepped into the room and the air was chill and still and thick as cloth. It was dark, too, darker than night and darker than cupboard dark. Sarah found it hard to breathe. She put a hand to her throat to loosen her collar. She was not alone. There was a woman in a corner of the room, small and dressed all in white as though in her undergarments. She stared at Sarah, as though she was looking for something in her.

Sarah could not move. She wanted to call out for the young man to improperly take her hand again, but she had no voice. She wanted to give comfort to the woman, to reach out to her, for she sensed that comfort was needed, but somehow she also knew that there was no comfort she could give. All Sarah could do was bear witness to the woman and to what she had to say. Words were suddenly adrift in the air; or not adrift exactly, which may be like snow falling and something light and soft; instead, the woman's words rushed out, as a wind that bends trees before it or moans or whistles in tight spaces.

When Sarah woke, the dream stayed with her. She was in Annie's room and the curtains were not drawn and the sky was a blue-black blanket and stars did not allow the room to be dark. Sarah sat up and she looked to one corner, expecting that there she would see the small woman in white and her mouth moving and her story being whispered over and over.

Now in the shuttered dimness of the train carriage, with her eyes closed and the everywhere screaming and coughing and crying, and the world dimming, fading into dream, Sarah heard again the small woman's story and it is the first story, the first of a hundred and more stories from The Winchester Gun Club and the first of a hundred and more rooms in a house that was yet to be built.

Room 1

The Winchester Gun Club

When the day was a darker place for him, he'd walk out back to be alone. He'd arrange old cans on the paddock fence, a measured space between them. Then, thirty paces back from the fence, and he'd turn and start shooting, sending the cans one after another into the air, and a quick movement of the lever action of his rifle and the can in the air hit again and spinning this way or that to land at last somewhere in the blue grass. And this was my husband.

The sound of those shots echoed back off the hills, and birds kept their distance, and cattle added a plaintive moaning to the music of Howie's shooting and the small thunder of stamped hooves, and the startled hares scurried to be far from the house, the air all shook and shocked, and the whole world knew then that Howie was upset or angry or hurt. Or maybe he was just drunk, as often he was when the darkness came on him, though he was as keen a shot whether he was drunk or not.

The rifle was an old Winchester 1873 that Howie had got from his Pa when he was a boy and it was his Pa who had shown him how to shoot cans or bottles, or rabbits for the pot when there was no beef, or redwings when there was no rabbits. There's a black and white picture of Howie's old man, grey in his tangled beard and one eye shut like he is squinting at the brightness of the day, though the day in the picture is grey and grim; and the old man holds a rifle across his middle, his finger on the trigger as though he might shoot the unseen photographer if the picture doesn't turn out just right. And Howie in the picture, too, knee-high to his old man then, a Winchester in his hands also, the boy a copy of the man and one eye pinched shut the same. The picture hangs on the wall next to the fire, the pins fixing it to the plaster all rusted and bleeding onto the paper. Maybe it is there still. I like to think that it is.

And Howie, I hope he is there, too, not so deep in his cups that he don't remember what he done. No, I hope he sits in front of that picture some days and weeps and curses. Howie's old man was laid in the ground three years back, half the man he was, shrunk with age and illness and Howie looking down on him and not knowing what to say to his crumpled Pa at the last. I hope he curses his old man now.

Maybe he should have cursed the old man then, for schooling him in all the small things Howie had to do to keep his Winchester 1873 clean. How to load the 15 rounds into the tube magazine, because Howie's Pa used to boast he could keep a can in the air for all 15 shots, the can like a kite pulled in all directions by a gusting wind or a child tugging and tugging on the string. That man should be cursed and his own Pa before him, for maybe it was Howie's grandpa who bought the first Winchester rifle and passed on the lessons handed down from father to son and father to son.

I hope he remembers the day he'd wish to forget. I hope Howie remembers, and in his remembering I hope he weeps and cusses and spits into the fire and calls his Pa all the names under the sun, all the wasp-names that are filled with spite and sting and black bile. And I hope Howie shrinks before the memory of that day he wishes never was.

Started the same as any other day. Leastways, in my head it did. Rising early to light the fire, collect the eggs, get the once-risen bread to rise again and cut the ham into thick steaks. Howie turned in his sleep and that was the same, too, same as a hundred days before and a thousand days before that.

I don't know what it was that made that day different. Three years past to the day since we'd put his Pa into the ground and a stone with his Pa's name cut into it and no money for beer for a six-month afterwards on account of the bill from the mason. Howie talked about it at first, about his Pa and all the good that was ever in the man and the bad too, for the old man had whipped the boy when he was small and Howie still bears the scars. But Howie just laughed when he remembered those days and shrugged and said it was nothing less than he deserved for the boy that he was. Howie rose same as he always did, and the first words in his mouth were for me and they were not unkind, I remember, not as they could be if his head was still thick and sore with the drink of the night before. No, the words on this day were soft and kind. Something about the light in my hair and the eggs on his plate and the smell of new bread hanging everywhere, and I thought he might be found singing sometime later in that day.

But something there was that snatched the song out of him and I don't know what that could be – and I play over what we spoke about over breakfast and maybe I mentioned the pretty that the boy Tom was who had served me in the grocery the day before, and maybe that was all it was. Maybe I laughed when I spoke of that boy, and touched my hair, playing the ends through my fingers. Maybe that was enough even though it was nothing.

I was hanging out his washed shirts later in the morning and the sheets from our bed and towels and a dress that had once been my mother's and with small alterations was now mine. There was a playful wind that lifted the sheets and made them like clouds in front of my eyes and through the gaps in the clouds I saw Howie coming up from the house. He was carrying the Winchester 1873, carrying it like *he* was now the old man in the picture by the fire and his face grim the same and his eye squinting against the day.

I don't know what was in his head at that moment. It makes no sense to me even now. It all happened so fast, the surprise blast of thunder in a dry sky and the hole in the sheet, the edges torn and burned, and I felt no pain, just the wind taken from me, punched from me, again and again, and a darkness falling over everything and Howie standing over me, his fingers pumping the lever action of his Winchester rifle one more and one last time.

Maybe there's a man somewhere who sold Howie's Pa that rifle, and a man who put the parts together, and the designer pushing his pencil across the paper plan of that rifle, and someone with money to set up the business and that person making his money back and more than that, grown fat and rich on what was sold to Howie's Pa, and I curse them all, and Howie should do the same when he sits in front of the picture of his Pa holding his own Winchester rifle and the boy a copy of the man, and Howie should weep too, as I do.

CHAPTER THREE

There were other voices on the train, in the moments when Sarah did manage to sleep. There were other stories told and she should have remembered them on waking, all of them, except she was so exhausted by the days of the journey and the nights which were never so quiet as nights should be, so exhausted that her mind was a whirl of broken thoughts and half-remembered incidents.

The footman, Jack, saw to her every need, in so far as that was possible. When the train stopped to take on water and coal, he woke his mistress and led her from the train so that she might take in the air, and walk off a growing stiffness in her legs and her back, or even just to stand and to appreciate the act of being still and not moving, and so to regain something of herself.

Evidently word had spread amongst the passengers concerning the important personage with whom they travelled. Men tipped their hats to Sarah and wished her a good-day, and women nodded, and dipped and curtsied, and smiled, and made comment on the weather and the time of morning or evening, and asked after her good health as though she was known to them and not just a name that they had read about in their morning newspapers.

Jack brought her tall glasses of cool lemonade before she asked for them, and small pastries wrapped in cotton napkins that might be easily consumed, and fruit – apples and pears and plums – pared into neat quarters, and plates of steamed white fish or roasted lamb or beef. In this way might her strength be kept up, he told her, but Sarah did not feel much like eating.

In the morning while she breakfasted, or made some show of it at least, Jack laid out clean dresses for her, and the instruments of her toilette – and filled a bowl with warm water from a jug that had stood on the small wood-stove in the cabin. He laid out her undergarments, gloves, scarves, hats and shoes, all that she might have some choice in how she was attired and might go about the day in the normal way.

At night he turned the lights in the carriage down low and he stayed alert in case she called, which once she did but when he knocked on her door there was no reply and so he calculated that she had merely dreamed and was still in sleep and not in need of his services.

Sarah, when she was not sleeping, or making plans on railroad paper, made endless lists of things she had to do, or elaborate drawings of the house she had dreamed of, the one with the white woman telling her story over and over, or writing long letters back to her sister complaining of the dirt and the smell and the weariness of the journey, letters she never sent, instead posting off shorter notes of forced cheeriness – when she was not taken up with such things as these, she stared out of the window at the unrelenting flatness of the land and the small two-bit dirt-towns or homesteads that littered the way, and she wondered at the decision she had made to move west, and she did not conclude that what she was about was remotely sensible.

Once, the train slid to a shrieking halt in the middle of nowhere, and Jack was dispatched to find out why. He reported back that there was a dead animal on the track, a steer or a horse, but that they would not be long in having it removed and starting on their way again.

Sarah saw something, in that waiting time, in the time between Jack being gone and being back beside her, and at first she thought a boy had climbed down from the train and was engaged in some light exercise as was the habit whenever the train stopped. The boy, almost as tall as a man, and almost a man himself, stood outside her window and he was talking, on and on without rest, though his words could not be heard from behind the glass and only his lips moving told her that he was talking.

There was something strange in the boy, Sarah thought. Maybe it was the color of his skin, pale as milk, as if he had been kept from the sun for a long while; maybe it was the look in his eye, all sharp flint and grey steel, and fixed on her as though Mrs Sarah Winchester had done him a wrong and he bore her a heavy and a hard grudge for it; maybe it was seeing the gun in his hand, held so tightly his knuckles showed a whiter strain, and Sarah thinking that he wanted to use it against her or against somebody.

Then Sarah noticed that there was blood on the front of the boy's shirt. She clasped her hand over her mouth. The blood was wet and the stain spreading outwards as from a new wound. The boy did not seem to be aware that he was hurt and was still talking, his mouth making the shapes of words on the other side of the glass.

Sarah called for Jack to see to the boy, to attend to the boy's needs and his injury, and to see what he wanted with his endless talking, but the footman couldn't see any boy anywhere and the story Sarah told seemed fanciful and the product of an exhausted imagination. The footman offered her a mild sedative and said she should try for sleep again.

The train pulled itself forward and so suddenly that everything shook and the thoughts in Sarah's head were muddled again and the boy by the side of the track forgotten. Jack shut the door of her bedroom and he tiptoed away and he made a note in a small black leather-bound book of what had transpired – the train delay, the horse slumped heavy on the track, and his mistress tired and imagining she saw things, the story she had told him of the boy with blood on his shirt; he also made record of the medication he had given her.

Sarah slept fitfully, and the rest of the sun-shot day was spent in tossing and turning, and chasing after the suffocating comfort of sleep and the brief and briefer oblivion that came with it. In such a state of disturbance she returned at last to the unfinished house, which had seen rooms added to it since her last dream-visit. The man had her hand again. She could not see his face or who he might be. He was leading her beyond the great hall with the high ceiling and further into the house. He held aloft an oil lantern in his other hand and his shadow and hers trailed behind them, dancing crooked up walls and across floors, and before him was a smaller and a lesser sun.

'I saw a boy by the train track,' she said to the man and there was no reason for her saying it except that her dream and her reality were somehow mixed together. The man made no reply or gave any other sign he had heard her.

They passed rooms on either side with their doors closed and numbers on the doors as there had been on the room with the woman dressed all in white. The numbers did not follow any sequence that she could see, as though they had been dropped into a bag and the bag shaken and shaken, and all the numbers tipped out again and selected without heed to their usual order, but only to the demands of chaos, and the whole universe stood on its head.

Sarah was breathless and stiff and the pull of the man's hand was harder and harder until his grip broke and the man disappeared and the light went with him. She tried the first door that she came upon in the corridor of numbered doors and with heavy heart stepped inside room eleven of The Winchester Gun Club, dark as before, and cold and with a smell of camphor, strong and pungent and making her want to sneeze.

Then, her eyes becoming accustomed to the dark, she saw the boy from the train tracks and the gun in his hand and the blood wet on his shirt like before, and his stare as hard as hate.

Room 11

The Winchester Gun Club

So small a hole. No bigger than an Indian head penny. No bigger and yet all of life can leak through that hole. I saw it happen once up close and it was a terrible thing.

Curtis was explaining to Maisie how it worked. Showing off, pretending he was older than his years. I don't blame him for that. Maisie was the prettiest girl in school, prettiest girl in the whole valley and for miles around, and all the boys following her about and all of 'em throwing down cartwheels and headstands for her attention. And here was Curtis alone with her in our Pa's barn, 'cept he didn't know I was hiding there and I saw the whole thing.

Curtis was making like he was teaching her. He showed her how to hold it and he was standing behind her with his arms hugging her and his face level with hers, so close he could smell her hair, so close he was almost kissing her cheek. And he was saying how she should tip her head a little so she could see along the barrel of the rifle and that way she could better fix on her target. Her finger was on the trigger and he whispered into her ear that she should grip the rifle firm and just squeeze the trigger, slow and with no extra movement.

I heard the empty click and she laughed and Curtis said she'd done good. Then he explained about the kick there'd be if there was a bullet in the chamber and the noise of that bullet leaving the gun and the small smoke that followed. And he showed her the lever action and he let her work it, though it was a little stiff from being idle and needing oiled.

Then they was kissing, standing there in the barn with the rifle between 'em and they was kissing and making the noises a puppy makes when it is happy, the small moans and sighs, and all breathy, too. I didn't think I should be still watching, but I'd never seen a boy kissing a girl before, not like that with his hand touching her tits on top of her dress, squeezing, and Maisie not pushing him away, not angry or hurt.

And there, in the middle of their kissing, it went off. Sudden as waking is when Ma smacks and smacks the bottom of a saucepan with a metal spoon and she hollers up the stairs that we'll be late for school if we don't drag ourselves lickety-split into the day. Sudden as thunderclaps or dog barks, and smoke thinning to nothing between 'em, between Curtis and Maisie, so as I didn't know at first, didn't know till I saw the blood like an opening flower spreading on the front of her dress and she cried out then and fell to the floor, sinking like she was in water, still holding onto my brother's arms.

And when he ripped the cloth of her dress from her wound, I could see that tiny hole, and Maisie was weeping and her breath coming in short gulps like she was snatching at the air. And I watched as the life leaked out of her and her grip on Curtis loosened, though he begged and begged her to stay with him.

Now there's a hole in me that is the same, a Winchester bullet hole. No bigger than an Indian head penny. And men shooting over my head and no-one is begging me to stay. I think of Curtis and the time he had afterwards, after what happened in the barn, and how he could never forget what happened on that day. And I know that was what made him drink so hard, till he was drunk and blind drunk, and that was the only way he could close his eyes and not see Maisie dying in his arms, over and over.

I watch the blood as it soaks my shirt, and everything slows down, like seeing it all through smoke or mist, and all sound muffled and faint, and it's like falling into heavy sleep.

CHAPTER FOUR

At the station there was such a commotion and a fussing over everything that Mrs Sarah Winchester stayed on board with the blinds of the carriage pulled down and she waited for some quieter time to arrive. She was packed and ready to leave and she sat on the edge of the bed, and she waited.

It was a rougher place where they were now, a rougher place than Connecticut; even the sounds coming from the platform told her as much, the voices all cuss and splinter and punch, and everywhere so hot that the air was sucked dry. She flapped a handkerchief loosely before her face for coolness, removed her shawl, and might have also divested herself of one of her petticoats if she had thought it seemly, which she did not.

The footman was busy making arrangements for her luggage and ordering a horse and cab to transport her to the house of her niece. So Sarah was alone. Her mind, still tired and not straight, turned over the events of the journey and the events that had preceded it. She thought of the lady-spiritualist with her voices from the beyond and her injunction to go west and to build a house where the spirits of those who had been wronged might find rest. Even in her muddled state Sarah was not sure that it made sense. Miss Sarah Lockwood Pardee, a society beauty who had once caught the eye of Mr William

Wirt Winchester, of the Winchester Repeating Arms Company; now, Mrs Sarah Winchester, widow, and share-holder in the company, and inheritor of a greater fortune than might be dreamed of. And all the wrong that she saw in that was that her child and her husband had been taken from her and not love nor all the money in the world had been enough to keep them with her.

She thought of the woman in white and the boy by the train tracks. She replayed their stories in her head and she was moved again to tears by what they had told her. She wondered who they might be, these troubled spirits that had followed her westwards. She wondered what their stories had to do with her. And the man in the dream who held her hand and led her from place to place in the unfinished house, she wondered who he might be also.

'Is there something the matter, Mrs Winchester?'

Jack had returned to escort his mistress to the waiting cab. He had come upon her unawares and there were tears on her cheek and she was staring into the distance as though she was not where she was, but transported to another place. Aside from her initial report on the boy standing by the tracks when the train had stopped for the dead horse, Sarah had not shared any other detail with her footman, not a word of her dreams or her reasons for moving west.

'I was just thinking of my sister,' she said, and she wiped away the tears and got to her feet.

'The cab is ready, ma'am,' he said and he offered her his hand, which, being a little unsteady on her feet, she took.

'My niece?' she said.

'I have sent word to her that we are arrived,' the footman replied.

This was no answer to the question she had intended. Sarah expected that her niece would have come to meet her from the train as courtesy demanded. Indeed, the footman was more than a little surprised to find that she had not.

'No matter,' she said.

The cab was stuffy and smelled of horse and hay and smoke. The road was long and rutted so that they made slow progress and Sarah had to hold onto the sides of the cab to prevent herself from being thrown about and being so taken up she had not the time to take in the land about her. The footman made too frequent his apology for how things were, as though he was somehow responsible.

'It is another place,' said Sarah to her footman. 'We must accustom ourselves to the differences here. It is no matter.' She held her handkerchief over her mouth and her nose and breathed through the cologne-scented cloth.

The niece, Mrs Marion Marriott, had made some preparations for the arrival of her rich aunt. The front rooms of the house had been cleared and cleaned and transformed into a bedroom and sitting-room to accommodate her. A smaller room, also at the front of the house, had been made ready for the footman. All this had followed the request of her aunt made through a short correspondence some weeks before. A money order had also been enclosed with the last letter and the final instructions so that the niece and her family might not be inconvenienced beyond the giving up of several rooms; the result was that the front rooms were grander now than they ever had been before, but not so grand as might be imagined by anyone from the East.

Sarah Winchester had made some stipulation as to the size of the bed, and the quality of the sheets and the curtains, and the arrangement of tables and chairs, and the general ornamentation of the rooms. Indeed, she had included drawings in her letter, sketches of how she liked things to be.

Mrs Marion Marriott had done her best to comply with her aunt's wishes. However, this was California and the state was still new and there was not the fine cloth that her aunt had made mention of, nor the design of chairs or the fitments and fittings. Mrs Marion Marriott might have sent orders east for such as her aunt had desired to be in place, but though there was money enough for such a course of action in what her aunt had enclosed, there had not been the time. Everything moved at a different pace here and it was only by chance that a carpenter was found who could fashion a bed to her aunt's basic outline.

The oldest boy had been bound by threats of hell to pay if, standing at the highest point of the farm and looking out over the foot of the dusty drive, he missed the approach of his mother's aunt – his own great-aunt. He peered into the distance for some small sign that she was near. He had been made to put on a clean shirt and the collar chafed his neck and he blew curses into the blue sky against this day and his great-aunt; he had also been forced into a coat that had been purchased with some small part of the money that the aunt had sent, and his shoes had been given a shine as though they were new – a shine they had since lost under the dust of stepping out to take up his position as lookout.

Then she was there.

With just such a fuss as Sarah Winchester had left her house in Connecticut, so did she arrive at last at the more modest home of Mrs Marion Marriott. There was much holding of hands and kissing of cheeks and stroking of hair and asking after the trials of the journey and after her aunt's health. Indeed, manners were forgotten for a moment and Mrs Sarah Winchester was kept waiting in the open air before she was invited to step inside.

'You must be tired?' asked Sarah's niece. 'Or in need of some refreshment? Or a wash?'

For so long had Mrs Marion Marriott been out of decent society that she had forgotten the common rules of propriety. Sarah waved away her niece's many questions and asked if she might be shown instead to her rooms.

'Yes, of course, aunt.'

Her luggage followed her into the house and for a moment it was as though everyone had crowded into the sitting-room where Sarah was to reside for the next two weeks, and everyone talking at once and far too loudly to be heard other than as a combined noise that quickly brought to the fore a headache that Sarah had been nursing since waking: the boys in their uncomfortable-looking coats, and a girl with her ribbons all askew and dirt on the hem of her trailing skirts, and the niece whose skin was dark by being too much in the sun as might be the case with a gardener and his men. There was no sign of Mr Marriott and that also showed a want of good manners.

When Sarah and her footman were alone, he made further apology for how things were and asked if there was anything that he could do for her.

'I shall lie down for a while, I think. Perhaps something cool to drink might be found and a bowl of water and some soap.'

The bedroom was not to her specifications at all. The curtains were a heavy and rough cotton and plain as the day is long. The floor was unpolished wood with no square of carpet to soften the tread of one's step. And everywhere she looked, Sarah met disappointment in the furnishings and the ornamentation. Only with the bed did she find something resembling satisfaction. She undressed and slipped between the sheets and she set her head to the pillows and slept.

The rest of the house stood to attention waiting for her to wake. They talked in whispers and listened at her door for the smallest sign that she was about. They looked to the liveried footman for report on how the aunt fared and each time he assured them that she was well, that she slept and that the journey had been particularly taxing on Mrs Winchester's energies.

The horses in the barn were restless, sensing that things were different. They stamped their hooves, kicking up a small thunder; and the hens in the yard kept a distance from the house and Emily Marriott knew there would be fewer eggs in the morning and she was a little irritated at that thought; and the dogs took to howling and would not be quieted, not by treat or by scold. Still the aunt, Mrs Sarah Winchester from back east, slept.

She slept soundly at first, through a day and a night, only waking to slake her thirst, wet her head and neck and drip cologne onto the pillows. So soundly did she sleep that dreams did not break in, and the stamping horses and the nervous crowing of the rooster and the howling of the dogs were nothing to her.

Not till part-way through the second day, when her niece began to worry and talked of doctors and asked the footman if she might check for herself that her aunt still lived, not till then did Sarah begin to surface and a lighter sleep was on her then and dreams came, too, fleeting and snatched and broken.

The man was holding her hand again and Sarah knew this was not her husband for the hand was calloused and rough and not like a gentleman's hand at all. And yet it was a warm hand and he was leading her like before, through corridors that were dark at her back and lit up yellow in front, and the air smelling of camphor, past rooms bearing numbers on all the doors and the murmur of voices behind those doors and Sarah and the man hurrying past as though there was some purpose to their hurrying.

'How many rooms are there here?' she ventured to ask, her words all breathless and rushed. 'How many?'

Then his lantern was held up to one door in particular and the number fifteen was on the door and Sarah could not discover any significance in that. She reached out for the handle, which was cold against her palm, and she turned it, and the door opened easily into dark. She looked to the man, wishing that the light of his lantern might be better directed and so thrown into the room, but he was gone and she was clutching at air where before she had clutched his hand.

Somewhere a dog was howling, far off, and the sound of that dog was faintly in the dark of the room. She stepped inside.

Room 15

The Winchester Gun Club

There was a dog howling out back. Night after night, it was the same. The noise of that howling dog broke my sleep and I lay in the near-dark, cussing and spitting, and my fingers in my ears could not shut out the noise, nor cloth, nor bread dough.

At breakfast there were no words that were soft. Not from father or mother or from any of us. Everything as sharp as thrown stones or jagged as broken glass, and the clatter of dropped knives and forks on all our plates, and the complaint of chairs scraping the floor when we got up from table.

It was the same for every house in our street, I should think. Even old Thomas, who was deaf in one ear and who once boasted he could sleep through the thunder of cannon fire or the bells of church, even he was like a bear that is disturbed and it does not know why it is angry, and he kicked at the dirt when he walked and growled at every 'good-day' that was called out to him, and those 'good-days' were fewer and fewer.

I could see that Julia had slept little, too. There were blue-grey shadows under her eyes and her brow was crumpled like cloth before it meets the heat of the iron, and her hair was all mussed up, and she kept yawning, and did not smile once. Bad enough that our nights were all itch and clutched fist, now Julia not smiling and all our days were spoiled too.

'It's that fucking dog,' hissed Julia.

I'd never heard her swear before. Not once. None of us had. Julia swearing was like a blasphemy yelled out in church.

'Someone ought to do for that damned dog,' she said.

Then and there, a plan hatched in my head. Maybe in the heads of all the boys who were listening to Julia complaining and wishing for something sweeter and warm and holy.

So that night I fought sleep, and I lay awake listening to the house cracking and creaking and father and mother tossing and turning in their bed and the scritch-scratch of mice under the floor somewhere and cricket song coming in through the window. The night was long and slow as molasses falling from a spoon, and there came a time when I felt that I could fight no longer, and sleep was winning me over; then it was that the dog out back set up with his moon-yelling and I was spark awake again.

I crept from my bed, quick as creeping can, and I slipped my feet into my boots and made my way downstairs, keeping to the crouching shadow of the wall, tip-toe slow and feeling my way through the dark to the kitchen and a string of sausages hanging in the pantry. It seemed a small sacrifice just so that Julia might smile again and all her swear words made to sweet words once more.

The porch door groaned on its hinges and I held my breath and waited to see if I'd been heard.

Outside, the air was warm and still. My feet made no noise as I crossed the patch of garden behind. It wouldn't have mattered if they had. Nothing could be heard above the yowling of that devil-dog.

I saw that there was a light on in Deaf Thomas's house and a light on in Julia's house, too. Lights on in all the houses in our street, and maybe there were other boys creeping through the night to quieten the dog that dared to break Julia's sleep. Then the dog was there, right in front of me, moon-pale and sitting on its back legs with its head raised to the sky and a long drawn out moan against loneliness and longing and darkness hanging on the air.

A window was suddenly jerked open someplace and a man's voice raised against the dog and all dogs, and the sound of a Winchester bullet pushed into the chamber and maybe the rifle pointed in the direction of that howling dog in front of me, and the crack of gunfire, sharp as a thunderclap, a single shot, loud enough to wake the dead if they were sleeping that night – and then nothing.

CHAPTER FIVE

The days following Sarah Winchester's recovery from the train journey west were a blur to her. She woke hungry and with a new impatience to be doing, for in doing she could forget the things she had lost. First, she ate two meals, one after the other and, like a dog when it eats, she did not seem to taste what she was eating but merely chewed and swallowed until she was replete, which was most unlike her.

Then she called for paper and ink and she made further additions and amendments to the lists she had started on the train. She talked to her niece only in so far as she needed to know how things might work in the place she now was, how things might be ordered from back east and the time it would take for such deliveries to be completed. Mr Marriott she saw only briefly and was courteous enough to give thanks to for his hospitality in rendering the front of his house for her use. She made clear to him that she would stay only for as long as was necessary and for any discomfort or hardship he was put to she reassured him that he would be fully recompensed.

To her great-nephews and her great-niece she gave not a word or a nod of recognition, no more than she would the urchins in the streets back home. But she left small gifts of money with their mother so that they might also be in some way requited for any awkwardness suffered by them due to her presence in the house. From four in the afternoon until seven she did ask that they be kept quiet so that she might have peace to think.

Much of the day, every day, Sarah was out and it was so for almost a week and a half. From an early start until late in the afternoon, about the time that she required of the children that they be silent, Sarah was out inspecting the territory about her. She was accompanied on her journeying by her footman and, whenever they stopped, he made enquiry on her behalf where she might find property that was for sale or land that might be built upon.

Sarah Winchester made brief notes on everything that was to be discovered: on the weather and how the winters fared and what trees might grow in the fertile soil in this valley or on that steeper slope; on the craftsmen responsible for this or that house; on the roads, such as they were, and what lay in the next valley and what people were in the area, their names and their families; on the price of food in the stores and on the gathering of the names of those that might at some later time be made useful to her.

Returning from such excursions, she excused herself almost at once from the company of her niece and her niece's family, and she ate alone in her sitting-room with her papers spread before her showing drawings of the house she saw over and over in her dreams, a house which had recently grown wings and several floors, and turrets sprouting at the corners, and balconies added to several windows.

When the light began to fade on the day and a candle or a lantern was required to dispel the gloom, Sarah took up one of her books and pretended to be occupied in reading. Then, as the day's exertions crept up on her, she prepared for bed.

So the days, those days, were a blur, each one like to the other and little to differentiate them. She kept a diary, but even here she did not distinguish between night and day or between this day or that day. Its pages were a record of the names of the people she met, and a list of questions for which she needed answers, and here and there a brief reference to something dreamed.

However, towards the end of this period there is a day that is picked out from the rest, given a date and a time in her diary and it begins with 'I have found it.' Sarah had been out as before, journeying further afield than her niece's farm and its immediate environs. The two rooms of her niece's house had begun to feel small and uncomfortable and she was overcome with a growing impatience to be gone from there. Some twenty miles they had shifted and running down from a slope into a shallow valley she came upon a doctor in his shirt-sleeves and not about a doctor's business, but occupied rather in directing workmen on how they might proceed building the house before them.

'I have found it,' she exclaimed to her footman, Jack, and not a word more, not for some several moments. Sarah sat in the cab and she looked at the house under construction, and she measured it against the drawings she had made and against the picture she held in her head – a picture that was everything she had seen in her dream – and it was indeed something the same. And there was a feeling in her, too, that she could not explain except to say that it was a little like the feeling of coming home, and if she had put it into such words it would have made no sense to her at all, but it *was* a feeling and maybe that was what had made her exclaim that she had found it.

The doctor made to approach the carriage and offered his greetings and was mannerly and polite. Sarah made note of this for it was not, in her brief experience, the usual way in these parts. Her footman interceded and made known to the doctor the identity of his mistress and enquired as to whether she might be given some small tour of the house as it stood.

The doctor apologized, but he was already late for an appointment. 'Neither birth nor death will be kept waiting,' he said. He consulted the sky as if reading the time of the day from the position of the sun. Then he rolled down his sleeves and made to go without intimating whether it was a birth or a death that he was to attend on.

'Another time, perhaps, unless one of my workmen would show you round and this would suffice.' The doctor pulled a card from his waistcoat pocket and proferred it to the footman. Then he bowed somewhat stiffly and with an almost military air, and departed.

It was one of the workmen who took on the duty of escorting Mrs Sarah Winchester through the empty rooms, and he was somewhat loquacious for a man of his standing. He pointed to the craftsmanship employed in this or that feature, rubbing the ball of his thumb over the neatness of a join or the fluted decoration of a sill or a shelf, and as he did so it was as though he was overtaken with a great pride and an undisguised joy in what he had produced. He made observation of the number of the windows and the way the light played across the floors and up the walls; he indicated how some of the rooms led one to the other, and the height of the ceiling in the hall which gave the building its grandeur, and the arc of the great staircase that led upwards. That is what he showed her, and for Sarah Winchester it was like in the dream.

Then he took her past a closed door and she stopped him and asked after what might be behind it. Just a small room, he told her, a cupboard really, where would be stored files or medicines or any such tools of the doctor's trade, and he opened the door so she might see inside, though it was dark and there was not much to be seen.

Sarah stumbled, for the floor was in places not yet complete and a little uneven and littered with offcuts of wood and discarded bent nails. The workman reached out to save her and his hand held hers, just for a moment. She thought she recognized the hand and its calloused palm and the warmth and the strength in his grasp. She afterwards wrote about it in her diary and so it must have been important.

'This is room number one,' she said, as though she expected him to understand.

He made no reply and so she took it that he did.

When the tour was over she asked for the workman's name and where he might be found hereafter. His name was Mr John Hansen and he was to be found in no other place but here since he was employed by the good doctor to work on his house until completion and everything finished inside to the doctor's expectations, which was estimated to stretch across several months still.

It was later discovered that this was the same man who had fashioned the bed in Mrs Marian Marriott's house, the one that conformed with Sarah's written instructions sent from Connecticut and which was the only source of satisfaction in the small rooms where she was presently housed. That discovery and the greater coincidence decided it.

A meeting was hastily arranged with the 'good doctor' and the next day a price was offered for the house that was still a long way from being finished and a price also for all the land surrounding the house. Sarah Winchester was rich enough that she did not know what it was to not have what she wanted in this world – not if it could be bought. At first the doctor was not for selling the property, and he was polite in his refusal, but when a second figure was written down on a piece of paper, and that paper passed via the footman across the table for the doctor's inspection, it had the precise effect of taking the wind out of him, just as a strong-armed punch to his stomach might have done.

The workman she had spoken with was duly informed of the change of circumstance and assured that he would be still be required to see out the completion of the building, although with some proposed changes and additions the length of his employment might take him beyond the planned several months.

Within a week orders had been sent east for fine furnishings and bolts of rich cloth and furniture of the very best manufacture and chandeliers made by Tiffany for the great hall. Within a week further a part of the house on the ground floor was made ready enough that it could be occupied and Mrs Sarah Winchester took up residence, and the house of Mrs Marian Marriott was her own again and the children hung up their coats and their stiff shirts were put away and Emily's ribbons returned to her top drawer.

The bed that had been Sarah's bed for the time that she had been in her niece's house, she did, with her niece's permission and all costs covered and paid in full, have transported to her new house and though John Hansen suggested small improvements that might easily be made, Sarah kept it as it was – save that she did in time replace the mattress and the sheets and the blankets and the pillows, all for greater comfort.

The small room that might be called room number one of the Winchester Gun Club was the first to be furnished. Though it was little more than a cupboard that might be walked into, it was dressed out in the finest ornament and luxury, and everything to the highest degree of comfort, and a low trestle bed moved into one corner, and damask curtains hung where a window might have been but where there was just blank wall. When it was finished, Mrs Sarah Winchester ordered that the door be removed and the room sealed and never more referred to.

Mr John Hansen carried out the lady's orders to the letter and without question and so a partnership was begun. Other workmen were quickly hired and the work continued apace and the house spread beyond its original conception and rooms appeared that were given numbers in no sequence and like the first they would be furnished and decorated, with money no object, and then sealed up or the doors bolted fast.

On the first proper night in the new house, Sarah Winchester ate a meal with her footman and with her head foreman. She had by this time employed a cook and a girl to help her. At the meal she made a toast to the house and to the people in it and what she said then gave everyone to think that there were more than just themselves in the house.

Room 18

The Winchester Gun Club

I came across him in the barn. He was sleeping in his clothes and with his boots on and horses blowing through their noses and stomping in their stalls and the day already up and already bright and warm, and he was sleeping. *Like the dead,* my daddy would have said. I could hear my daddy's voice in my head, *sleeping like the dead.*

I had the point of my rifle on him and I kicked his feet to wake him and he moved real quick, snake-bite quick and grabbing for his Colt pistol – only I had taken it from him and thrown it into the back of the barn and the tangle of hay to hide it.

'You is trespassing,' I told him. 'This here is my barn and my land and you is trespassing, mister.'

He didn't say nothing. He just looked at me, his eyes narrowed and his mouth set. Looked me up and down like he was figuring out who I was. Like he was calculating what kind of a puzzle was set before him.

Shoot first, ask questions later. That was the voice of my daddy in my head then. *Shoot first.*

'And you been in my henhouse, too,' I says to the man, 'and stealing my eggs and they don't belong a you.'

They should cut off their hands, that's what they should do with thieves. Cut 'em off at the wrist. I heard they do that some place.

My daddy had strong opinions on everything.

The man in my barn didn't move save to settle hisself where he was, like he was just getting comfortable, and like he didn't fear the point of my rifle aimed straight at him.

'Maybe you has reason enough for doing what you done,' I says to him. 'Maybe there's a reasonable explanation and I prides myself on being a reasonable man so you got a little time to be telling me before I start shooting.'

The stranger spat in the dirt, the sound of a pea snapping, and he removed his hat and he ran his fingers through his hair. He cleared his throat like he was preparing to make a speech, which he was.

'Name's Walton,' he said, 'and you gotta know I done bad things in my time, real bad, and maybe you should just shoot me heres and now, because if you don't then I sure as hell will shoot you.'

His words came out from between gritted teeth and mostly they was little more than a hiss or a growl and I had to lean a little closer to get all that he said and there was menace in what I heard.

Don't give a cornered dog a second chance.

'But it don't have to be that way,' he says. 'It's all up to you. I could just walk out of here, slow and easy, and you letting me, and at the end of the day you ain't lost no more than a half dozen eggs and that seems to me to be the best course of action for a boy in your shoes.'

He called me 'boy' and that irritated, but he was right, too. I can see that now. But then my daddy's voice was in my head, taunting, and daddy calling me a *fool* and a *coward* and saying how I *wanted for some real backbone* and I should *just pepper the bastard with holes* and *no-one to blame you if you did.*

The man replaced his hat, everything slow and careful, and he was smiling like he knowed something that I didn't and he sat up like he was meaning to get to his feet.

He who hesitates is lost.

Then quick and sudden as a horse kick he has my rifle in his hands and I'm laying on my back in the straw and the hay and he's laughing at me and I don't like the grit and the grimace in his laughing.

I hears Janet and the boy then and they's calling for me and they's asking if everything is OK.

The trespass-stranger shoots me, jamming the Winchester lever action back and forth, back and forth, and not once or twice he shoots me, but three times to be sure.

The last that I hears is Janet at the wide-open door of the barn and my daddy's voice in my head and he's saying something about how I never did listen to what he said.

CHAPTER SIX

Things began arriving at the station. Every week there was something and more than something, till in the end a special siding had to be laid at San Jose to store all the crates brought for Mrs Winchester. Freight trucks took days to unload and everything was documented and signed for and taken by horse and cart across wide open spaces to her new house.

Improvements were made to the road so that even when the rains came there was always something moving between the station and the house.

Mrs Winchester got a good reputation and men eagerly volunteered to work for her, even for a day, for the pay was generous and a man could earn enough in a day to feed a family for a week. She paid on delivery, no waiting around, and that earned some respect.

One day she took delivery of a safe and several men were required along with ropes and pulleys and the cart had to be strengthened for the journey and a team of four strong horses harnessed to pull it. The safe was manufactured by the Hall's Safe and Lock Company and weighed over a ton. The workers who moved it speculated on what Mrs Sarah Winchester would keep locked in her safe; it was soon known in those parts that she was the inheritor of the Winchester fortune and though they each made wild guesses as to her worth, in the local bars and deeper in their cups after a day working for Mrs Winchester, and each time going beyond what they could imagine in their estimates, yet they none of them came close as to the extent of her worth or to what she kept in her safe.

In the safe, Sarah Winchester stored only her most personal possessions, most important of which was the small purple velvet box that contained the lock of her lost daughter's hair.

Mr John Hansen oversaw all movement on the Winchester estate and all transactions were carried out through him. Mrs Winchester met with him in the early morning and the day ahead was mapped out on paper and every page was filled with scribbled annotations and reminders of what had been discussed pertaining to this or that delivery.

Her footman, who had not made a decision on when precisely he would move back east to be with his family again, looked after the domestic arrangements and it was his job to ensure the efficient running of the house – and it was soon a house that needed running for the builders worked apace. The footman also oversaw the employment of appropriate housemaids and personal maids and kitchen staff as and when they were required.

'You must always knock, do you understand? She is not to be caught unawares, and do not ever look at her, not unless she orders you so to do. Look at the floor and curtsey on arriving and on leaving. And she is Mrs Winchester always and nothing more or less. Your more general orders will come from me, but she may make alteration to the particulars.'

Some girls passed the test; some were sent home within days but were well paid for their brief employment.

As to the development of the house, every morning Mrs Sarah Winchester woke with some new idea and she sketched it down on paper before she got out of bed and that morning's scribble would be the basis of the meeting with Mr Hansen over breakfast. After lunch

Sarah Winchester took the time to review the work on the house and Mr Hansen gave her a tour, pointing out what progress had been made since the day before.

'I feel I am watched, Mr Hansen. I feel there are eyes on me all the time and outside there are people spying on me and what I do here. What goes on in this house is my business, you understand, and I would not have any details of what I do leak out to the world and their newspapers. They might make much of it and yet not really make sense of it. Indeed, I fear they would make nonsense of it.'

Mr John Hansen was not used to being the recipient of such a confidence and he gave some quick assurance that what could be done to keep people beyond the line of her fences was being done and that, as far as it was possible to do so, her privacy was one of his priorities, next to the building work.

'I think there must be trees planted around the house, at the front to begin with, or a hedge, something thick and easy to maintain. Maybe we should seek to employ a gardener or a team of gardeners. Could you look into it?'

Before her on the table there were pattern books showing ornate ironwork designs both for the exterior decoration of the house and for the interior. There were sample books too, showing the latest cloth patterns and wallpaper patterns. Rooms were laid aside for the storage of Tiffany glass windows designed to her own specification, and great bronze inlaid doors imported from Germany and ornate bathtubs all the way from Switzerland.

'I think the building work progresses too slowly, Mr Hansen. I desire that you employ another team to work through the night. There is much to do here and I have added further to the plans as you can see.'

At no time did Mr Hansen ask why Mrs Winchester had need of so many rooms added to her house. There were no guests at the Winchester home in that first year and visitors were few. Even when Mrs Marian Marriott called, perhaps as a mark of courtesy, she did not stay for above an hour and took only tea in the English style and no arrangement made to call again on her aunt.

On one occasion, Mr John Hansen did experience something out of the ordinary. Room 23 had just been completed. It was a room that could only be reached by means of a tight staircase so that furniture for the room had to be hoisted through the window space before the window was fitted. It was Mrs Winchester who referred to it as 'Room 23' though it was not the twenty-third room in any way shape or form.

The floor of the room was an elaborate parquet of rosewood and white ash, which had required to be relaid when the pattern had revealed a slight imperfection in the cut of one single piece. Mrs Winchester had shown her impatience then and she asked that Mr Hansen take charge of the floor himself and that it not be assigned to some junior craftsman. She placed a hand on his arm and almost beseeched him. There was an agitation in her such that Mr John Hansen had not seen before, except once in a girl who had been taken for mad and had soon enough proved herself so in the taking of her own life.

'It must be done tonight. I have promised him it would be ready and I do not know what form his displeasure might take if it is not.'

She did not, however, make any more reference to who this person might be that she talked of and for whom the room was to be ready.

Mr John Hansen did as was requested of him. He sent word to his wife and family that he would not be home and, by the light of four oil lanterns that made the air thick as a blanket, he completed the relaying of the floor.

Mrs Winchester did not sleep either but paced the lower rooms beneath the staircase, checking every hour on the progress of the work. When it was done, some several servants were pulled out of sleep and the fitting of the room was undertaken, the laying down of a small carpet, and the making of the bed, and paper and pen and ink set on the oak wood desk, and a bottle of fine wine and a bowl of fruit on the table.

As a final touch, Mrs Winchester left on the nightstand beside the bed a solid silver William Ellery fob watch and chain from the American Watch Company in Massachusetts. She made sure the watch was wound and set to the right time before closing the door behind her.

Once the servants were returned to their beds, for it was not yet morning, she ordered Mr John Hansen to dismantle the staircase that led up to the room so that by such could the room no longer be approached nor by any other means. Only when this was complete did the agitation leave her.

She thanked Mr John Hansen for his work and asked that he might take her apologies home with him to his wife and family. Then she pressed some gold coins into his hand and forbade him entry to the house for the next twelve hours.

'We shall manage without you for this day, Mr Hansen,' she said.

Then she retired to her room and after a glass of water and a small time at her desk making further annotations on a plan she had earlier started, she took to her bed and slept till the breaking of the next day.

Room 23

The Winchester Gun Club

Twenty-two years and some I've worked for the bank, white starched collar and cuffs, and a plain black suit and a tie, and everything all carefully balanced and not a penny short or a penny over. Twenty-two years and I know everyone that comes in here and I know to the dollar and the cent how much they have in their accounts and how much they owe on their farm or their shop or their home. It's a position of trust that I have and Mr Wilson, the manager, tells me over and over how much he values what I do.

Mr Wilson has almost thirty years service. They give you a silver watch when you reach twenty-five. Mr Wilson wears his on a heavy link chain attached to his waistcoat and the watch folded into a small pocket. He's always taking it out and pretending that he's checking the time. He said maybe I'd get one, too, in a few years, if I stayed with the bank.

I sometimes pretend that I have such a watch, and I pull it from my waistcoat pocket on an imaginary silver chain and flip open the lid and I look at the face of the watch and the hands shifting time. It is a nice feeling.

They must have been watching the place for some while – from the outside. Weeks, maybe months. They knew stuff. They knew the days when the money was collected from the safe and the days when there was a little extra locked up in the bank, the takings from Marty's bar and Ben Grundy's 'All You Need Emporium' and Kittley Wilkes' dress store. They knew all that; but they didn't know how everything worked *inside* the bank – if they had known this then things might have turned out different.

They were not from hereabouts, even with their masks I could tell that. They were young, too. Just boys, and they were nervous and their fingers itchy on the triggers of their guns. One of them held a Winchester rifle. They waited till it was quiet, and maybe they had seen how Wednesdays before ten were when the bank was empty. Mr Wilson took his coffee out front then and he kept looking at his watch knowing that Mrs Hart and her six-year-old daughter, Emma, would be along about ten past the hour, regular as clockwork.

They kicked their way in, making more noise than they needed to and they grabbed Mr Wilson and put a gun to his head. He dropped his watch and I could see it still attached to the button of his waistcoat by the heavy silver chain and swinging like a clock pendulum that has lost its rhythm.

They shot Mr Wilson first, to make the point that they meant business, and that was their big mistake. You see, we had an arrangement, me and Mr Wilson, to do with the safe. It was a Marvin Safe Company model with a combination lock, and Mr Wilson knew the first two numbers and I knew the second two. That way we both needed to be there to open it. It was like extra security that Mr Wilson had put in place. Only they'd just shot him.

There was maybe sixty dollars in the drawers behind the counter and maybe six hundred in the safe. I tried to explain but they thought I was just messing with them. They thought I was playing at being employee of the year and that I valued my position in the bank more than I valued my life. They held the point of a rifle to my head and they ordered me to open the safe. I was crying and I pissed my trousers and I begged them not to kill me. I pointed to Mr Wilson's silver watch and one of the boys snatched it up and examined it. Mr Wilson's name was engraved on the back and the dates of his twenty-five years of service. The boy flipped the lid and he could see that it was ten past the hour.

The door to the bank opened then and Mrs Hart entered with Emma leading the way and chattering like a bird. Mrs Hart has twelve hundred and forty-two dollars and sixty-two cents in a savings account; Emma has fifteen dollars and thirty-four cents. You see, that's the kind of stuff I know.

The boys were caught by surprise and they panicked. There was shooting then, so much shooting, and when they were done they'd killed Mrs Hart and Emma, and me and Mr Wilson. All for sixty dollars and a silver fob watch on a silver link chain.

CHAPTER SEVEN

'She's mad. Has to be. On account of the money she has, I reckon. Millions they say, enough to turn a saint into a sinner, and enough to make someone ordinary into mad.'

Mary-Anne worked in the kitchen. She chopped vegetables and washed dishes and scrubbed floors. She had no reason for her idle chatter and no reason to be so against Mrs Winchester. She'd been in the house for more than three months and she, herself, had more money now than ever she was used to.

'I had an uncle was mad,' she said. 'Leastways they said he was. He kept talking to his hat and he put his shoes on the wrong feet and his shirt on backwards. I caught him one day, just standing under the apple tree in our backyard, and he was looking up at the apples that were not yet ripe. I did not know what he was looking at, so I asked him. He said he was just counting apples. When I asked him why, he said so he could check they was all there the next day.'

Mary-Anne was talking with Cassie. It was Cassie's job to set table and to polish spoons till her face smiled back at her from the surface, and knives and forks the same; and she took out the washing twice a week: the cotton sheets and the lace petticoats and the linen tablecloths. And she had to keep the birds from the washing as it dried and there was a wooden rattle that she shook for that purpose and it made a sharp clack-clack like repeating gunfire.

'I ain't never seen Mrs Winchester counting no apples, and her shoes is always on the right feet and I don't think she does wear shirts backwards or frontwards,' said Cassie.

Mary-Anne laughed and she poked Cassie in the arm thinking she was just making fun.

'No, it was the way that he said it is what I was meaning. My uncle really meant it. He really was serious about those apples. He said that if they wasn't counted they'd just disappear, like it was his counting them that held them to the tree. It didn't make no sense. And it's the same with the Missus – mad as hatpins or brushes or moonbeams. Well, she has John Hansen building rooms that she just closes up again soon as they're done and she don't say why or for what reason. That's a little mad, don't you think?'

Cassie shrugged. It was not for her to say and she understood that.

'And there's a flight of stairs in the back of the house and if you follows them stairs then you comes to a blank wall and must turn back and step down them stairs again. Where's the sense in that – stairs that go no place 'cept up and down again?'

Cassie was ironing the creases out of one of Mrs Winchester's best petticoats. It took all her concentration not to burn the lace or leave any mark on the fine cloth. She lifted the iron from the petticoat and paused to consider what Mary-Anne had said.

'Maybe she just changed her mind. The mistress can do that if she pleases and if she's a mind to. F'rinstance, a week past Tuesday she wanted chicken and corn for supper, only when it came to it she asked for eggs and toast instead. Cook was mad as hornets, I can tell you, but I don't think that makes the Missus mad.'

Mary-Anne laid down her knife and set aside the carrots and potatoes she was chopping. She breathed onto the blade of the knife and began rubbing it with the grey cloth that she held. There was a small knit of irritation between her eyes and she bit her bottom lip and her breath came short and quick and blowing.

'Well,' said Mary-Anne after some thought, 'I heard her talking to herself this one time and there was no-one near her to be talking with. She said how she was sorry and she said, 'My child, what can I do?' She did have a child once, so I heard, a girl, only the child died and Missus still talks to her lost child when she is alone. But I heard her and that I think is something like mad — when someone is talking only to no-one.'

Cassie did not think so. She thought sad is what it was. 'There's a brother I should have had, only my mammy lost him soon after he was born. She gave him a name anyways, so's he might be taken up to Heaven and sit with Mary and Jesus. His name's Billy, and once a year we all goes to his grave at the farthest reach of our place. There's a pile of stones there and underneath there's Billy. We says thing to him on that day, how we misses him and how we hopes he is with the Lord and that he is safe. I don't think that's being mad.'

Mary-Anne's bottom lip was all pout. She didn't like to be wrong, not ever, and she didn't like Cassie telling her she was. They'd been to school together, before Mrs Winchester was looking for kitchen maids, and in school Mary-Anne was always smarter. That's what Mr Brendan, the teacher, said, and the apples Mary-Anne brought him were, he declared, the best apples in the county, and thinking about that now she was not sure that their being the best was not on account of her mad uncle counting them.

'I ain't saying there's anything wrong in being mad,' Mary-Anne started again. 'Shit, I was mad as a bag of sticks when Saul Milner said I kissed him at the back of church on a Sunday. Saul Milner can go kiss a horse's ass or a jack-rabbit's. Sometimes there's a reason for being mad and Mrs Winchester has reason enough with what her life has been. She lost her husband, too, after losing her daughter. If she ain't mad, then she oughta be.'

The cook came back in then. She'd been out for air and a glass of lemonade and just for the peace. She overheard what Mary-Anne had said about Mrs Winchester being mad. She flew at the girl with a soup ladle and might have beat her till she was blue and screaming but only scolded her sore for being so disrespectful, and the cook's scolding was maybe worse than the ladle, and Mary-Anne crying hard as hailstones, and so hard it brought the footman from upstairs.

A brief report was made of what the cook had heard and Cassie kept quiet on the matter and only nodded her confirmation of the cook's account of what had been said. Mary-Anne, through her tears, said she was sorry and how she should never have said it and how it was just kitchen talk and it didn't mean nothing, not nothing at all.

Mary-Anne packed her things and returned to her mother's house with three months' pay and a pocketful of rue. The footman gave no report to his mistress other than that the girl's work had been in some way unsatisfactory.

'It is not for me to meddle in what happens below stairs. I trust to your judgment in that, Jack. But I think it is only natural that there will be things said and people speculating as to what is going on in a house that grows arms and legs and runs in all directions,' Mrs Winchester said. 'I do not think that to have a chit of a girl dismissed for the silly talk below stairs does solve anything. There is little enough harm in what she did, I shouldn't wonder, and she was always respectful when she was with me. I hope I make myself understood.'

That was all that she said on the matter. The footman left everything as it was for three days, so that the girl might learn a lesson from what had happened. Then he sent word to her mother that she was to return at once to her duties in the kitchen and he cautioned her that perhaps a greater care might be taken in holding her tongue from thenceforth.

Mary-Anne made the most of her second chance and there was no further talk of madness in the kitchen, or her uncle checking apples in an apple tree, or stairs going no place but up and down. And certainly nothing about Mary-Anne's mad-as-a-bag-of-crickets grandpa and how when he was near the end he believed he could see through walls and he knew what was what in a room before ever he entered it and he could tell what a person had said when he wasn't even by and maybe what they was thinking, too. And that was a thing that could not be rightly explained and so it was called mad and Mary-Anne did never speak of it to no-one and certainly not to Cassie polishing spoons in the Winchester kitchen.

Room 30

The Winchester Gun Club

'What would you risk?' says Snooks. 'What would you be prepared to risk just for one look?'

He's talking about Linnie and how there's a place just across from her house where you can see right in at her window, clear as day when she's got the lamp lit, the room all yellow like the sun sleeps there. Only it's Linnie's room and Linnie sleeps there in a metal-framed bed.

Linnie's a girl at our school. Not just any girl. She turns boys' heads when she walks by, and the teachers look at her all soft and shy too. Sometimes I don't think she knows how beautiful she is; sometimes I think she must. I wrote a poem 'bout her once. I bet more than me has done the same. But there ain't the words, not in my head. I watched her for a whole class one day, from behind my work, watched the way she chewed the end of her pencil and how her hair fell across her cheek, and a small knot at her brow when she was thinking and that I wished I could untie and smooth away.

And Snooks says he sees her some nights and she doesn't close the curtains in summer and what he sees is something close to perfect. 'Like looking God in the eye and all of Heaven's angels are held in His glance.' That's how he says it. And he describes how Linnie undresses there in her room and her not knowing she is seen. 'Down to her slip some nights,' he says, 'and once down to nothing.'

Snooks says how she moves slow as dancing and her small tits lifting and falling, and her hips swaying, and Snooks licks his fingers when he tells us, like he can taste something sweet and sticky, and he rubs his fingers and thumb together like he's feeling the slip of fine cloth.

'So what would you risk?' he says again. 'For just one look?'

The minister says God is terrible to look upon. That no man may do it and live. That God makes himself known through mysterious ways. Like the burning bush that Moses beheld and the word of God carved in stone tablets, for if God had spoken then all the world would have shook and all the men in the world made deaf and blind and the women and children too.

'I'd risk my very soul,' I said, and my words came out all hushed and whispered, small as prayer words.

Snooks would accept nothing less than four dollars and a slice of pumpkin pie filched from my mamma's pantry. We shook hands on the deal and it was set.

It was everything that Snooks said it was: Linnie's curtains open and the room lit up yellow and Linnie dancing to music in her head. I watched her brush her hair and twist it into a plait the end of which she bound with a white ribbon. Then she unbuttoned her dress and let it fall to the floor before retrieving it and draping it over the back of a chair. I couldn't breathe.

In just her slip she stepped from one end of the room to the other, her shadow thrown behind her on the wall and her shadow stepping something the same.

'Like looking into the eye of God,' said Snooks, and he laughed and his hand was fiddling down the front of his breeches; I wished then that my four dollars and slice of pie had bought me something more private, just me and Linnie and the darkness between us.

'Fuck, yeh,' said one of the other boys behind Snooks. And he said it loud as a cheer and I think she must have heard for she turned to face where we were, and she smiled and tossed her plait over her shoulder.

I don't know if it was a sin what we did. I can't think of the ten commandments that Moses brought down from the mountain. Not all of them. And what I do recall has nothing to do with watching Linnie undress from the secret dark. Something about not stealing, or killing, or worshipping false idols. 'Thou shalt not covet thy neighbor's wife,' comes closest, and I don't know what 'covet' means but Linnie was no-one's wife so I do not think it applies.

More than Linnie heard that cried out and hollered, 'Fuck yeh'. Her damned father heard, too, and he fetched his Winchester rifle and fired into the dark where we were. Warning shots they might have been, but they came close enough and closer so as I'll never look at Linnie undressing again nor anyone else.

CHAPTER EIGHT

A little over a year after moving into the house, Mrs Sarah Winchester made an excursion into the nearby town. She travelled in a closed carriage and she wore a veil. Her visit was in response to a petition made to her by a group of church ladies who had come to the house for the express purpose of winning her charitable support. Though they had not gained admittance to the Winchester House, they had been able to transmit the import of their visit to Mrs Winchester via the footman.

The carriage progressed at a sedate pace from one end of the main street to the other and then, on reaching the furthest end, turned and travelled back again. It stopped once, in answer to Mrs Winchester's tapping of the roof with a stick.

From the closed window of the carriage, Mrs Winchester observed a girl at play. She was maybe ten or eleven and wearing a yellow and green pinafore dress and green stockings and heavy leather boots that made her feet look too big for her legs. Her hair was tied back from her face, though there was a want of a ribbon, and it fell in untidy flaxen folds across her shoulders. She did not at first know that she was under scrutiny. She held a piece of wood cradled in the crook of her arms and she was talking to it and fussing over it as though it was an infant child or a pet.

The carriage at rest attracted the attention of local shopkeepers who soon understood that the much talked about Mrs Winchester was come to town. They brought out samples of their most expensive wares and made to show them to her by parading them in front of the carriage window.

The young girl, becoming aware of the dark-veiled woman in the carriage, set her crude doll aside and stood below the window peering in to see what might have occasioned the fuss being made by Mr Carlton the milliner and his three female assistants, who by this time were smiling so hard it hurt and were engaged in making much of dresses in the latest fashion.

Mrs Winchester tapped the roof of the carriage and the horses pulled away.

It was all the gossip of the town for a week afterwards and the story of her visit grew fat in the retelling. In one she reached out and fingered the cloth of one of the dresses; in another she stepped down from the carriage and shook Mr Carlton's hand and even entered his shop; or she made a fuss of his three assistants and enquired after their names and some smaller details of their day. What was missed in these stories was the little girl in the yellow and green pinafore dress.

Mrs Winchester discovered by discreet inquiry that the girl's name was Lizbeth and she was from the orphanage. That had indeed been the substance of the petition made by the church ladies on that rare visit made to the Winchester House, that there was an orphanage in the town in need of financial support and the ladies were about the business of collecting contributions from the local population.

Mrs Sarah Winchester thought of all those children who had lost their parents and all those parents who had lost their children. She had thought in her isolation that she was the only one.

At the end of a month after the incident of her visit to the town, Mrs Winchester sent a porcelain doll to the girl called Lizbeth and a sizable donation was made to the running of the orphanage, though conditions of secrecy were attached to the money she gave.

The hedge at the front of the house was something of a success. The gardener had suggested cypress for its speed of growth and it afforded Mrs Winchester some comfort in her need for privacy, though it had to be broadened as the design for the house spread beyond the edges of her paper and far beyond what was originally conceived. Indeed it was already described as a mansion by those who passed by and the number of its rooms was a matter of conjecture even amongst the workmen who labored there day and night, and the windows were beyond counting.

Mr John Hansen continued to take coffee with Mrs Winchester every morning at nine. They talked of the house and what might be achieved in the month ahead and what problems had been thrown up by the addition of this or that feature and how the problem might best be solved.

'I find that my way to the dining-room is a somewhat circuitous one and I wonder if a hidden passageway might be constructed. I have designs here for the installation of a sliding panel and a narrow corridor that takes me more directly to the place.'

Mr John Hansen inspected her drawings and nodded and made small alterations for their improvement and then set about ordering materials to facilitate her requests.

'And the room on the third floor, number seven, how does it progress?'

There was no rhyme nor reason why a room at the top of the house should bear such a low number, not as far as Mr Hansen could see, but he made reply that the room was almost finished and he offered to take her there and to show her.

'The view from the window, tell me about the view.'

Mr John Hansen described the view. He was not a poet or a wordsmith, but there was in his description something of both.

'The whole of the north of the valley can be seen, and the road, so that nothing might approach without it being known to any person standing at the window. And all the changing weather can be witnessed there, the rains sweeping in off the ocean and the winds bending the trees and the sun setting the far away hills a-glinting. I have to mind the workmen employed in the room for they are some days drawn to the view and stand for an hour sometimes, their hammers and awls at peace, and just looking.'

Mrs Winchester nodded and drank her coffee and was satisfied.

'I have been thinking lately, Mr Hansen, of installing a bell in the house. Not such as might summon a servant or a maid, but a proper bell. I have completed preliminary sketches for a tower and made enquiries after the casting of such a bell. Please look over what I have so far envisaged. You have such an eye for the smaller detail. See what you think.'

At half-past nine precisely, as though a bell had been rung or a clock had chimed, Mrs Winchester retired to her bedroom for a short rest. At this time her own spirit was often low and she thought of her daughter and her husband. There were photographs displayed on the walls of her room and in silver frames by the bed and on tables and bookshelves. She flitted from one to the other, picking first this and then another and having some conversation with her family, as though they lived and as though they might hear what she had to say.

'There is a girl in the town. She is called Lizbeth and I think she would make a gentle playmate for you, Annie. I have determined to invite her here for you to see. William, I do believe you would like her, too. She reminds me of… I do not know what exactly. But something in the color of her hair and the softer contours of her face; it is as though she is known to me.'

At ten o'clock the first carts from the station pulled into the front of the house and work began on unloading the orders. A list was brought to Mrs Winchester's room and she took the time to check everything off, comparing the delivery sheets with what she had already written down in a large leather-bound black ledger, and thereby ensuring that what she had sent for had been duly delivered. An embroidered cloth from China might be her particular interest one day and, seeing it on the list, she would immediately require it to be brought to her room and unfurled across the floor in all its wonder and splendid color; or a cabinet made by a blind craftsman in Italy in which every joint was as smooth as a caress and every small drawer moved as if oiled and moved without ever making a sound; or a fireplace sculpted from a single block of Carrara marble and with such detail as might make you think the carved birds could shake their feathers and fly to the ceiling, or fly out of the window if ever it was open; or a lamp fashioned in colored glass and small jewels by an Austrian artist, and when the light was on it a room would be transformed into a magic cave and almost there was music in such colors so that all the shadows danced.

'Jack, I have need of a piece of straw, straight as a rule and clean and yellow and dry. I leave it to you to find suitable samples for my inspection.'

Her footman was accustomed to the strange and stranger demands of Mrs Winchester. He showed no surprise at what she asked of him, but simply bowed and assured her that her request would be carried out forthwith.

Late mornings she slept. It was often the hottest part of the day and ice was placed in enameled basins situated about her bedroom as she lay in a state near to undress on the top of her bed, the bed that had been made by Mr John Hansen, and she slept. Indeed, this was the best of her sleep, for it was the least troubled. She had read somewhere that there were certain hours when the spirits were abroad in the world and at other times they were not. She supposed from the peacefulness of her midday sleep that this was a time when the spirits were themselves at rest and did not trouble her.

In the afternoons she wrote letters to make such orders as had occurred to her, and to her bankers she wrote, and to the other shareholders of the Winchester Repeating Arms Company on matters of business – though increasingly she was silent on such affairs.

And sometimes she wrote to her sister:

'Dear sister and best,

I fear I must again add delay to the date of your intended visit. Not only is the season uncomfortably dry and the air hot as candle grease, but the house continues to be in turmoil. I have changed my mind about the design of the floor in the main hall and Mr John Hansen, with all the patience of a saint, has agreed to have the floor relaid to my newer specifications.

I would not wish you to see the place as it is and so I must beg your further forgiveness in once more putting off your journey west. Perhaps I might come east instead. It is something I am considering and these plans may come to flower in due course.

For now, let me tell you about a girl I have seen, in the town. She is the sweetest little doll you ever saw and I am given to think of Annie when I do see her and the girl Annie might have been had she not been taken from me. Her name is Lizbeth and she is an orphan, a lost child.

Do you remember what it was to be a child and everything consumed you and one minute you were hot and the next minute cold and there was no reason for the difference? I recall you once loved a boy who brought books from the library and his name was George and you never read so many books in your life as you did in that one year. Then one day it was not George who was the center of your thought, for you had lost interest; then it was a dress you had seen in a shop window that took your attention, or a necklace, and George was forgotten and you stopped reading.

I have ordered a bell for the house. It will be cast by the London firm of Lester and Pack. The same company that cast the Liberty Bell that was rung when the body of the late President Lincoln was carried in procession by rail

through all the country and did, you will recall, stop a while in Philadelphia
where it is now housed.

Dear, dear sister, I hope that we may be together before too long, but not
until the house is presentable or until I am able to be released form my duties
in supervising construction.

Ever in my thoughts,
Sarah'

The footman knocked on the door to her room precisely on the
stroke of four.

'To let me sleep longer would have been a waste of the time that is
given to me.'

The footman carried in his arms some small sheaf of cut straw
for her perusal. This was laid out on the table and Mrs Winchester
appeared and made her selection, taking such a care as though she
might be selecting a precious stone to be set in a necklace about her
own neck or the neck of her dear sister.

'Thank you, Jack,' she said, and she waved the discarded straws away
with him.

Later that evening she made inspection of room number seven at
the top of the house, how the walls had been papered and the windows
polished so that the whole of the valley was in perfect view, and the bed
made fit for a gentleman. She fussed over an arrangement of books in
one corner and a cup and dice on the table and a cask of beer fitted
with a wooden tap and set on an ornate ironwork stand.

At the foot of the bed she laid a pair of new boots, all spit and glassy
in their shine, and threaded through the buttonholes of the left boot
she put the straw that her footman had found for her.

All that done, Mrs Sarah Winchester checked the hour on a timepiece
that hung from the waist of her dress and she pulled the door closed
and turned the key in the lock, a heavy mortice lock and the key with
iron teeth. And nevermore did she or anyone else enter the room.

Room 47

The Winchester Gun Club

I don't rightly know what purpose is served by a man dying – nor a hundred men, or a thousand, or more. I don't know what it 'mounts to in the end. Maybe in years to come they'll put what we done into song or write all our names down in a book and tell stories of what happened that day, campfire stories and school-hall songs. Maybe they will. But that won't make no sense of all those men dying like they done.

I ain't an educated man; not book educated. I had to tie a straw to one boot so's I could learn my left from my right. And I cain't sign my name with nothing more than a cross. That didn't matter none to them. They'd see me right and give me all the training I needed. That's what they done told me, all smiles and nodding their heads, and calling me soldier even 'fore I'd joined.

I could already shoot straighter than most on account of the rabbits we had for the pot back home, rabbits to shoot when there was no beef or venison. I soon knowed my way round the single-shot breech-loading standard-issue Trapdoor Springfield, a .45 caliber.

'You treat her like she is your lady wife,' the sergeant said. 'By which I mean you treat her nice – real nice – and you keep her close, and she'll do you right.'

We all of us laughed when the sergeant said that. We was expected to laugh. We laughed at his joke about 'doing us right' and some scratched at their crotches to add sauce to the sergeant's fun, or stuck out their tongues like they was big-licking the air. But a few of us, though we laughed, we din't think there was a whole lot there to laugh 'bout. A single-shot rifle, no matter how much we loved her, was no match for the Henry repeater or the Winchester, and we'd heard as that was what we'd be up against.

We'd have followed him anywhere, the General. That was our boast and his. Loyal to the end. Into the jaws of death itself if that was what was asked of us. It's what was expected and everything we'd been trained for, insofar as we was trained. Our spirits was riding high on that June day in the Big Horn Valley when five companies of the 7th rode into oblivion.

I seen a man die once before, right in front of me, his blood staining the dirt where he lay and his breath coming short and quick and a scared look in his blue eyes that was faraway. I sees him still just as I closes my eyes for sleep. It ain't easy. And on a sunny June day, the thought of so much killing and so much dying – well I still don't see the why or the what for.

We was outnumbered in the battle and that's the undressed truth and it should have made us scared, but we wasn't – or at least we made as if we wasn't, which the sergeant says is the same thing. More of them than anyone had figured, all whoop and holler and shriek, and we stood as bold as no never-mind. And it all happened so fast. Quick as a dry thirsty man takes to tip back two fingers of gimcrack whiskey and no longer. Men fell to my straw-left and my right, so many I could not put number to them, and the Indians came so close I could see the wild and uncomprehending fright in their eyes and I could see that killing was no easier a thing for them as it was for us.

And in that hill-top end, all the wide valley laid out so we could see, the General was among the last to fall. I saw him, his yellow hair like a shook flag, and a bullet to his chest.

I followed soon after, my own blood spilling in the dirt and the sky as blue as faraway and my every snatched breath feeling like my last; my final thought was not understanding what purpose was served on that day by so many men dying.

CHAPTER NINE

Mr John Hansen thought the bell might be a Sunday bell and the ringing of it might be something to do with church and a call to prayer. The only bell he knew was the church bell in town and that bell had been ringing through all the years of his growing into man.

'Our Father, who art in heaven.'

Sometimes, in the matter of a wedding or a death, the church bell would be rung, either dancing or slow-tolling as befitted the occasion. Hadn't his own father had the bell rung for him just days after his passing and now he is laid in the churchyard with a new stone at his head. Charlag, the stone mason, had made a grand job of cutting the stone and the inscription was something the teacher, Mr Brendan, had helped with, to get the words right and few enough they would fit on the stone and not be wandering all over the churchyard.

'Hallowed be thy Name.'

A roof was constructed over the stone so that it might have protection against all weathers, the wind and the rain and the blistering sun; and flowers were laid at the grave and it was Mr John Hansen's wife, Martha, who saw to the flowers, and it was the prettiest grave in the churchyard, and people who were new to the town stopped to mark who was buried there. In such a way was the man, who had been Mr John Hansen's father, remembered, his name at least.

'*Thy kingdom come.*'

A new stone followed the arrival of Mrs Winchester. The old had been rough and just bore the father's name and nothing more and, though there were flowers then as now, there was nothing of notice in that stone. Then the job on the Winchester House began to pay and it didn't look like it would ever stop paying, and Mr John Hansen went up in the world, as is the saying. He bought dresses for his wife, shoes for his children, and a horse and a cart so that everyone would know of his new standing in the community, and an addition to his own house so that there was a room for everyone in the family and one room that was his father's room and Mr John Hansen gathered all his father's things into that room and it became a place of quiet and thought and peace in the house.

'*Thy will be done.*'

Hadn't that been the father's last wish? On his death-bed, hadn't he said that he feared the nothing of the grave and not being remembered and his body food for worms and nothing more? 'Please let me be thought of now and then, and remembered. Do this for me, son.' And so there is a room in Mr John Hansen's house, and it is his father's room though he sleeps in the grave, and there's a finer stone erected in the churchyard and the flowers for remembrance.

'*In earth as it is in Heaven.*'

He'd had plans, the father, fanciful dreams for what could be in this world if he had but the time and the money. He was used to stand at the end of the yard and just stare into the blue at the furthest reach of his sight, his imagination all aflame and muttering to himself, and there were tears on his cheeks then and a heaviness in his heart borne of the frustration of being poor for all his days of working and turning the soil and herding cattle and setting down roots. One day he spoke those dreams out loud, and his voice ringing as clear as any bell, as clear as the church bell, and he told his son what he wanted for the future and what the son could do to make a Heaven here on earth: trees planted, cherry and apple and pear, as far as the eye can see, and fields of corn reaching for the sky and a bountiful harvest that would be shared with the whole town.

'Give us this day our daily bread.'

Those plans were taking shape now Mrs Winchester was lining the son's pockets. There's an orchard begun at the end of the yard, just where the father had stood that voice-ringing day, and there will be apples soon, and a yellow field of corn beyond, smaller than the father's imagining, but bigger this year than last and three men to work the fields and Mr John Hansen pays them well enough from what he makes at the great house.

'And forgive us our trespasses.'

It is known in these parts that at the Hansen place there's a hot plate of beef for anyone who is down on their luck, as the father had been once and it had been the church that had fed him then, though there had been cussing against God in the father's mouth and he split the door of the church with his fist one drunken night and he said the church should be always open and God should be always there in the hour of anyone's need.

'As we forgive them that trespass against us.'

Easy to forgive when the belly is full and the wolves are kept from the door, as they are now with Mr John Hansen. And he shakes hands with Tom Carpenter these days, and he has reason enough to spit at Tom's feet for the things Tom said to his wife Martha. Indecent things and lewd and he laid a hand on her hip and would have done more had not the younger boy come into the kitchen at just that moment. And now Mr John Hansen shakes the man's hand and makes a place for him working on the Winchester House, for isn't Tom Carpenter the best man for measuring wood and cutting it straight as a sunbeam?

'And lead us not into temptation.'

Easy to forgive when one has tasted temptation oneself. There's Missy Claire and she bakes the best pumpkin pie on this side of the county and didn't he stop in on her once, and for no reason he understood, and Missy Claire laying a hand on his chest and Mr John Hansen standing so close he could breathe in the scent of her and it was all flowers and soap and sweet. And didn't Mr John Hansen waver then, and maybe he kissed her and maybe he didn't, but there was a temptation he had to be led away from and maybe it was God that made him do the right thing, though there's nights still when Mr John Hansen turns and turns in his hot sleep and all his dreaming thoughts are of Missy Claire's kisses.

'*But deliver us from evil.*'

And so the bell that Mrs Winchester has ordered, all the way from London, England, which is further than imagination can picture and further than hell, this bell he thinks might be a Sunday bell and something like a church bell and prayers might be said at the Winchester House and with such prayers might Mrs Sarah Winchester be delivered unto peace. That's what Mr John Hansen thinks when he makes calculation of the height of the proposed bell-tower and inspects the drawings for its design and decoration.

'*For thine is the kingdom.*'

But he is mistaken in believing he has the measurement of Mrs Winchester's thinking, for here is a woman who has turned her back on God, whose heart is hard against the taking of a daughter and then a husband. 'What manner of God is this?' is what she would say, what she does say when the minister from the church thinks to call and extends forth an invitation to her to attend the church in town. No, the bell will serve another purpose at the Winchester House.

'*The power and the glory.*'

For there is a greater power at work. That is what Mrs Sarah Winchester believes. A power that must be assuaged and made room for and made comfortable. That is all the glory of her house and its stairs leading to nowhere and the sliding panels and hidden passageways that bring her unannounced to stand behind servants at work so that she might watch what they do and know that she is well-served by the people in her employ.

'For ever and ever.'

The bell is intended for a night-time ringing. Once at midnight and then again two hours after, and that, it is believed, is the spirit-time, the hour of their arrival and then the hour of their being gone again. Between that time, some other room is closed off from this world, never more to be discovered, and a spirit is at peace then, one more spirit, and there is some small comfort to Mrs Sarah Winchester in that. With one more voice made quiet, she thinks there will come a day, a day at the last, a final day, when there will be such a quiet in her sleeping dreams that the voices of Annie and William might be heard at the tolling of the bell.

'Amen.'

Room 56

The Winchester Gun Club

Maybe it was wrong what we did. But at the time it didn't feel wrong, not altogether. It was something natural; that's how it seemed to us: the spread of civilization. Taking our good manners and our good values to wild and savage places, untamed places, like we were bearing gifts, and that's what we thought it was.

The land of plenty and everything there for the taking – that's how they sold it to us. A place where a man could put down roots and by the sweat of his own labour amount to something in this world and something in the next.

Of course, it looks different now. Nothing is so black or so white. It was *their* land before it was ours, I can see that now, but then we just rode in and took it, staking a claim that was backed by papers bearing the seal of government. We just took and took. Because it was easy and because we thought it our right. We were making the West a better place, and not so wild, and God was on our side. That's what we thought. But now I'm not so sure.

Sometimes we did a trade with them, talking in gestures more than words, beads and bracelets offered in exchange for animal skins. Then we gave them whiskey, and guns and Bibles. Only they were different from us, in ways we could only guess at. They had their own gods and their own manners and places that were sacred to them, none of which we showed respect to. Instead, we called them 'heathen' and 'beasts'. It was soon nasty between us, and we fought bitter wars against them and so many women and children are dead because of what we did in God's name. Men dead, too, and good men at heart.

There were losses on both sides. Heavier on theirs at first, but then with the guns we'd given them, we began to pay a price above the value of buffalo hides. That's when I lost Agnes. A raiding party burned to the ground the house I'd built, and Agnes, heavy with our first and our unborn, was inside. I was filled up with hate and hurt in equal measure. I laid her body deep in the ground, so deep the earth was cold and dark, and I swore to Heaven that I'd get revenge for what they'd done. And I did.

Hot-headed and stupid – that's what I was. It's what we all were. None of us stopping to make sense of it all and if we had then maybe the losses would have been fewer on both sides. I was made a little braver by drink on that day, gut-rot whiskey drunk straight from the bottle, and I rode like one crazed, right into the Indian village, shooting without fear and without thought, not counting the men, women and the children that fell. An eye for an eye, a tooth for a tooth, and God have mercy on their souls – and on mine.

One I remember, just a boy. He stood unflinching in the path of my horse with a Winchester rifle aimed at my head, and maybe there was a god on his side, too. And I saw the flash and flare of smoke from the barrel of his gun, not once but twice, and everything all out of focus, and the crunch of his bones as his body was trampled underfoot and as I fell heavy from the saddle.

And in the dark place where I am now, I try to reach some understanding of everything, and I see it all different now, and the right and the wrong is not so easy, not so clear as words written in a book or on a government paper. There was wrong on all sides is what I think, but more on ours, and I wonder how God – our God or theirs – could have let that happen. And I weep for Agnes and our never-to-be-born child; and I weep for the Indian boy who died under the iron hooves of my horse, and for all the men and women and children that fell on that day of wrath and vengeance; and I weep for all the wrongs on both sides.

CHAPTER TEN

At night Mrs Winchester took to wandering the corridors and back-passages of the house. She rang the bell at midnight and then it was a catch-me-if-you-can race around the house until the ringing of the bell again at two. With Mr John Hansen's help, she had devised ever more clever ways of avoiding the spirits she believed trailed her then. The house was becoming a maze of hidden staircases and dead-end corridors and doors that gave no access to anywhere.

The bell woke the servants at first, as once did the fall of night-time hammers and the chatter of workmen sawing wood at all hours, building walls, laying floors, and fitting windows and doors; but as time advanced, they became accustomed to the bell's ringing just as they adjusted to the work going on in the house round the clock, and they turned over in their sleep without waking. Some said they heard footsteps behind the walls, small and skipping, and so stories of lost children or the ghosts of children came to life in their dreams.

'I trust that you slept well,' said the footman overseeing the serving of breakfast, as Mary-Anne looked at the floor and pretended not to hear the lady's answer.

'I slept as well as may be under the circumstances,' said Mrs Winchester, but she did not make any plainer what those circumstances might be. 'I slept well enough, Jack, thank you.'

At two in the morning, or a little after the second ringing of the bell, Mrs Winchester returned to her private sitting-room and resumed work on her designs for the house and the grounds. Or she made plans for the annual children's picnic that had become a feature of the Santa Clara Valley these past five years and an event looked forward to by the younger women of the Winchester House for the laughter and play it brought to the place. Or she wrote serious letters to the Winchester Repeating Arms Company on matters of cold business, or letters to the Society for the Poor in Santa Clara with a small donation enclosed and that letter not signed except by the words 'from a well-wisher', or letters to her sister making further excuses for not visiting and excuses for not having her sister yet visit Winchester House.

Some nights, when sleep just would not come, she crept to the music room and sat at the piano. There was a time when she would have played the piano. She had played for William before they were married, tripping little dance tunes and, though with less expertise, more sweeping romantic pieces brought from Europe, modern pieces by Chopin or Liszt or Mikhail Glinka. She had played for Annie, too – Annie kicking inside her and Annie lying naked on the bed; and she'd sang then also, the whole house brought to a smile when she was singing. Now, without Annie and William, she simply sat at the Collard and Collard drawing room grand piano and read the sheet music and her fingers hovered over the keys or the rosewood finish without ever playing a single note, except what might be heard playing in her head.

'I want there to be more trees,' Mrs Winchester announced one morning, having slept later than usual. 'Annie liked trees, so I would have more. I believe, Mr Hansen, that you have the beginnings of an orchard on your own property. Apples, if I am not mistaken?'

How Mrs Winchester came by such details of his life and, indeed, of the lives of all her servants, can only be imagined by those that served her. Some said there were spies in her pay, known only to her and not even known to Mr John Hansen, but that is just fancy. The truth was probably plainer. She was a regular visitor to the town by this time, talked at length with the merchants, and passed pleasantries back and forth as is the way when there is a wealthy client to be courted. And she talked with children in the street, lost and found children, and children do so easily give up any secrets they have; and sometimes Lizbeth, no longer so small a child, sat with her in her carriage and they took a turn or two together around the town and Lizbeth was breathless with so much talking when she stepped down again into the street and lighter for having rid herself of so much chatter.

'Yes, we have apples and a good crop this year, more than can be eaten by the Hansen family, big as it is. I have given the greater part of our harvest to the orphanage and to the church. It is what my father wished for.'

Mrs Winchester nodded as if approving of his goodness and his charity. 'I would follow your example and have trees. Here, I have been reading and with some small understanding I have laid down plans. I think I should talk with the gardener before the day is much longer and see what he thinks. I have a yearning for apricots and plums.'

The gardener, who still continued to manage the cypress hedges much to Mrs Winchester's satisfaction, and who had broadened his own duties to include expansive flower beds and sweeping lawns and some straightforward landscaping, was excited at the prospect of a meeting with the lady of the house. He had plans of his own which he was so bold as to think he might set before her for he too had been reading and was well informed on the horticultural fashions of the day.

'I would have orchards,' she said, wasting no time in introductions and no time in commenting on the weather or the season or asking after his health. 'I understand that the soil is rich and so I think that apricots and plums might be grown. I have purchased the land to the west of the house and I would have orchards there. I appreciate that this will take time and that further laborers must be employed and trained. Mr Hansen may be consulted on this matter, when he has a moment free from his duties in overseeing the house and its further construction.'

Either the plans that the gardener had dreamed up chimed so well with the plans laid before him by Mrs Winchester, or at the last moment he lost all the boldness he thought to have had. Either way he simply nodded and said something about the plum varieties he was familiar with and how he knew nothing yet of apricots.

'I will leave the matter with you for your greater consideration. Perhaps we might meet again later in the week.'

An hour was set aside each day for the closer scrutiny of the account books. Every small purchase had to be documented and the price recorded and the figures set down in columns and made to add up. Some days a ten dollars or a fifteen hid from her on the page and she would not rest or give leave for her book-keeper to rest until the monies were found and the books set straight again. Then on the rediscovery of the hidden dollars, she would cheer and it was almost as though it was a game and the money was not money but children hiding from her.

And, of course, there were her day-time wanderings about the house and the workmen she stopped to observe, and the maids about their business, and orders for dinner and supper to be communicated to the cook, and by this and that meeting was Mrs Winchester kept busy and all the hours of the day brought to some account and, it was said, her greater loneliness pushed at an arm's length away from her.

There were times, however, when everything became too much. Sometimes whole days passed when Mrs Sarah Winchester was not to be disturbed, when work on the house almost shut down and hammers and chisels were softened and the silence grew so deep that even the creeping of spiders could be heard. On such days she kept to her bed and the curtains were drawn against the sun and 'No, a doctor need not to be informed'. She would remove her purple velvet box from the safe and stroke the lock of Annie's hair, holding it close to her nose to breathe in the scent of her daughter, or imagining that she did, before crying herself in and out of sleep.

These were her black dog days – that is how she described them, and she barked and snarled at every small intrusion into her grief. Once, a girl in the kitchen was sent home for dropping a knife onto a plate, making such a noise that it carried up to Mrs Winchester's room. The girl was brought back a short time later, when Mrs Winchester was recovered and all the house was in a flurry to make up for the days that had been lost.

Only Mr John Hansen was exempt from Mrs Winchester's coldness in these times, and not even her loyal footman could say that. Mr Hansen brought her apples from his trees, so many that the sweet smell of them filled her rooms; and he sat beside her bed and he talked in whispers of all that was going on in the house, and what was what in the town, and sometimes what was happening in the wider world beyond their 'way out west'; and Mr John Hansen sometimes made small confession of the things he loved – the smell of new-cut wood, and apple blossom when it falls, and staircases that go nowhere. And Mr John Hansen's laughter then was something of a tonic to Mrs Winchester.

The years passed one into another, and one day the house moved towards room fifty-nine, or sixty, or sixty-one, or sixty-two, or out of all order and room a hundred-and-four or a hundred-and-twenty-four; and there seemed no end to how things would be and no end to the money that paid for everything.

Room 62

The Winchester Gun Club

They picked 'em real mean. Eyes as hard as stone and a snarl in every word – that's what they wanted. Men who'd seen heavy days and made hungry and bitter by them. Men as weren't afraid of nothing or no-one. Ice in their veins, some of 'em.

What they got when they picked 'em was somethin' less than men. Not upright or straight but bent in the wind of their growin' up and twisted all unnatural. Beasts, or not much better than. The worst of what could be, yet pin a cut tin-plate star badge on their shirts and they were lifted up higher than the law. An oath of sorts had to be sworn and guns to be issued and then it was all official.

They was supposed to make the world a better place. A new broom to sweep the streets of Floresville clean, the streets of every town in Texas. They was the big sticks to make all men good and woe betide those who crossed them. That was how it was supposed to be. Only the choosin' was all wrong and those tin stars made 'em untouchable and they knew it.

His name was Brewster and with a drink in him he was a devil and the town shrank back in fear and good men did not feel any bit safer. He'd shoot off a few rounds just so he could smell the fear of honest folk and he'd laugh at the shakin' in a man's hand and the pale in a girl's face. Hearin' the snap and snap of his Winchester repeater, curtains twitched and lights was dimmed and doors was quickly shut and bolted, and the Drovers' bar emptied and men went sooner to their beds.

We looked the other way at first. We all did. When he was about some dirty business, we pretended that he weren't doin' nothin': making lewd comments as he fingered the dress of a respectable woman or teachin' the minister to dance to the music of his shootin' or takin' meat and bread and hens' eggs from the town grocer without offerin' to pay. We looked the other way and kept our complaints to ourselves, and our children we brought to hush whenever they asked why we didn't do nothin' and why there was one rule for Brewster and a different rule for all the rest of the world.

Then there was a day that was somehow different. Sun came up same as usual, and clouds runnin' skittery across the sky, and the smell of new-baked bread hangin' in the air, and bacon fryin', too, and eggs. Kids was slow to rise from theys beds, and that was no different, and there was few words at breakfast and the clock on the mantle shifted too quickly towards the start of another day.

Brewster was out on Main Street and he'd an early drink in him, and that was nothing new neither, and he was in ill humor, snarlin' at the smallest thing, and he kicked Douty's dog and it shoulda knowed better than to get in Brewster's way. He had his Winchester rifle attached to a leather sash and hangin' from a saddle ring at his side, and his tin star had lost all its gleam. Not anythin' out of the ord'nary in any of that, but today was soon to be a different day from all the rest.

Brewster touched the front of his hat and made a slurred and cheery good-day to me and my wife. There was mockery in what he said and what he did and I wondered what I might have done to cross him. He took Lizzie's hand, actin' all gentl'manly, and he said she looked pretty as a flower and he said how I was a lucky man. I did not in that moment feel lucky, not with Brewster givin' me and Lizzie more attention than we wanted.

Behind Lizzie's skirts was our Jim and he looked up at me as if he expected me to do somethin', as if there was somethin' I should say to this tin star ranger who was making so bold with his mom and my wife.

'I hopes he be treatin' you good,' Brewster says to Lizzie, and by 'he' Brewster means me, and he winks when he says it, and he does not let go of Lizzie's hand though I sees she'd rather he did. 'And if'n he don't be treatin' you right, you just whistle and I'll be there to make it better between yous.'

He leaned in to Lizzie, his face level with hers. And maybe he was just wantin' to whisper some further pleasantry in her ear and maybe he was goin' to kiss her cheek, there was no way of tellin'. Jim was still lookin' and I could see fear and disappointment and shame do some sort of struggle in that boy's face.

And there it was, all the difference that was in the day, all that would mark that day out from the days before. I spoke out when I shoulda been silent and noddin'. I spoke out and I said somethin' 'bout the badge that Brewster wore and somethin' 'bout goodness and law and somethin' 'bout takin his hand off Lizzie. And I reached for my Colt without thinkin', reachin' fast as blinkin', and everythin' after that is all rush and blur and smoke, the blasted air shriekin' and more than just the air, and when everythin' settled there was Jim cryin' over his mom and his outspoken pa layin' in the dirt next to the tin star ranger, and not a breath to share between us, between me and Lizzie and Brewster.

CHAPTER ELEVEN

Some doors led nowhere, only solid wall behind them, and the servants sometimes were lost with so many doors to choose from and some of them just doors and not entrances or exits. There was no way of telling either, except to take the handle and try for an opening.

A junior footman was temporarily employed, promoted from another position below stairs, and one day he strayed from the corridors he knew and wandered for the better part of a day until he was found standing in a room at the center of which was a grand wood fireplace carved over with angels and musical instruments and fruits and flowers.

It was Mr John Hansen who found the boy shaking and he could not put his words back together for an hour or more. He was taken to the kitchen and the search called off. Mary-Anne, under the watchful eye of the cook, fed the boy two small spoonfuls of imported French brandy in an effort to restore him to himself.

He sat in a stiff-backed chair and only after some time had elapsed did his teeth stop their chittering and an alertness return to his eyes.

'There was something in the room,' he said, when his wits were about him again.

But he could not explain what that something was, except to say it was strangely cold in the room where Mr Hansen had located him. And a sound, he said, like whispering or the floor being swept with a besom broom and the shush and shush of it.

No-one gave heed to what the boy said for he was known for a leaping imagination, seeing words in the configurations of geese in flight or pictures in the clouds or messages tucked in the music of the birds that had nests in the cypress hedge.

Once, there was a bee caught on the inside of a window, and again and again it rushed at the glass as if glass might be caught by surprise and a tumbling way found through to the other side. The boy opened the window and set the bee free, saying how the bee had spoken to him and asked after its own freedom. So now no-one gave any credence to his talk of besom whispers and the cold touch of fingers on his cheek and the vision of a boy in breeches and his hair all this way and that, and everything else that he described and said was in that lost room.

Mrs Winchester came upon the junior footman, seeming to creep up on him, appearing from a solid-looking wall, and the junior footman was telling Cassie in the kitchen and she was polishing a fork and seeing her face in the silver handle and not really giving ear to what the boy was telling her.

Mrs Winchester made her presence known and the boy gave a start and was shaking once more and afterwards kept looking over his shoulder as though he expected he was followed – and it was so with him for the rest of the week.

'The boy in breeches, tell me about him,' said Mrs Winchester when she and the junior footman were alone.

'Begging your pardon, Mrs Winchester, I do not know what you mean.'

Mrs Winchester tapped at the table with her fingers as she might were she waiting for something that was late in its delivery; as she had when the arrival of a Winchester rifle was later than expected, the rifle a model 1873 with an ornately engraved brass plate to her own specifications.

'I mean the boy you saw in room seventy-six, when you were lost, and there was a grand carved wood fireplace and angels holding up the mantel, and there was a cold to the air that was strange for the day was hot as ovens.'

The junior footman shifted his weight from one foot to the other, uncomfortable with his own words being fed back to him in this way, and he looked at the floor as he had been instructed always to do and he shrank back from her closer examination of him.

'I tell stories,' he murmured.

'Stories?' said Mrs Winchester.

'Just stories. I always has. Sometimes the stories is a little near the mark so that I has sometimes seemed to foretell what's yet to happen; for some example, the birth of my youngest brother and the death of my grandfather both falling on the same day. They just come to me, the stories. I don't know where they come from. Sometimes I don't even know the end of the story when I has begun to tell it. My mother said I was a liar and I should take care with the things that I spoke. It was just a story, about the boy in breeches.'

Mrs Winchester stopped her tapping and she got up from her chair and walked to the window. Outside, they were unloading another cart that had made the journey from the station. The horses were hot and one of her stable-hands held a bucket of water to their thirst. Mrs Winchester was expecting a carpet from Persia, red and black and yellow with a white fringe, and a homespun quilt in the flying geese design with stars and stripes.

'Tell me the story,' she said. 'I should like to hear it.'

The boy looked over his shoulder as if he suspected that he was not alone. Then he looked back at the floor again.

'There was a boy in the room,' he began. 'Thin as air he looked, and pale as mist. He was sad and angry at the same time. He was hurt, too and he said it was *his* room that I had wandered into and I shouldn't have trespassed there. I thought at first he was angry at me, but he wasn't. He was angry at you, Mrs Winchester, and he said I should tell you that.'

Mrs Winchester waited for him to continue, but there was nothing more. Without turning from the window and her overseeing of the unloading of the carpet and the quilt and sundry other items, she thanked the junior footman.

'Could you bring to the attention of Mr Hansen, if he is not already aware, that the last items for room seventy-six have been delivered and I should like to see the room finished before the ringing of tonight's bell. He will understand.'

The junior footman turned to go.

'And if you have any more stories, I should gladly hear you tell them.'

'Yes, Mrs Winchester.'

Then he was alone in the corridor. This time he was more careful in his way back to the kitchen and quicker on his feet and almost running the last few steps. There was a change in him after that day. He was quieter and had no stories to tell Cassie or any other of the kitchen girls whose attention he would have enjoyed.

Later, under the direction of Mr John Hansen, the Persian carpet was laid on the polished floor of room seventy-six, and the flying geese quilt draped over the bed. In one corner was a plain oakwood writing desk with three drawers, the top one of which was locked. On the desk was a wooden box inlaid with ivory and precious stones; and inside the box was stored black leaf tea; and hidden in the tea, almost at the bottom of the box, was the small brass key to the locked desk drawer.

Mrs Winchester inspected the room after Mr John Hansen had left for the day. She checked the tea in the box and felt around for the key. She unlocked the drawer and was satisfied that all was as it should be. Then she pulled a chair across to the fireplace and climbed awkwardly and stiffly onto the seat of the chair, all her movements slow and careful. From two solid brass hooks above the wood-carved angels and the wooden fruit and wooden musical instruments, she hung a

Winchester rifle, model 1873 with an ornately engraved brass frame and a richly polished rosewood stock. That completed the room.

She climbed down from the chair, wiped the mark of her shoes from the seat and repositioned the chair by the desk. Then she left the room with the door thrown wide as an invitation to enter. Until the bell was rung at midnight, Mrs Sarah Winchester kept to her own room, and she sipped at a glass of lemonade and looked out at the dark beyond the cypress hedge and wondered how the gardener was progressing with the laying out of the second orchard and the third. And she thought, too, of the junior footman and his story, and wondered whether he had overheard her talking with Mr Hansen about room seventy-six, or talking to herself as she was wont to do when she thought herself alone.

Room 76

The Winchester Gun Club

It hung above the fireplace in the front room. I'd sit at the table doing my letters for school, Ma fussing over Miriam's hair, unplaiting it and brushing it straight, and Pa doing the accounts beside me, his lips giving shape but no sound to the numbers that would not stay still on the page in front of him. I'd pretend I was thinking over a difficult word and turn my head so I could see it. Some days the light from the window fell on it and it was like a message from God. Other days it had its own light.

On Sundays, Pa would lift it down from its place on the wall. He'd lay a cloth out on the floor and then he'd set to cleaning the rifle.

'It's a Winchester repeater,' he'd say, like we didn't already know from all the hundreds of other Sundays he'd told us, like we could forget that small detail. 'It's the 1873 model,' he'd say, and my lips followed his, the shape of his words without the sound. It was like his voice was my voice then. 'The gun that won the West.'

Then he'd launch into a story about his own Pa, our Grandpa, and how he was one of the first settlers hereabouts. 'Nothing more than the breeches he stood up in and his Winchester repeater and a cloth to polish it with.'

It was the same rifle our Pa held in his hands. The exact one. Pa held it like it was a holy relic. Like it was something in church, the bone of a saint's finger or a wooden piece of the cross, and Pa talked in hushed whispers and brooked no interruption to his story. Not that we ever would, though we'd heard the same story a hundred times before, more than a hundred.

'They didn't call it the Wild West for no reason. No, sir. And your Grandpa carved a life for hisself, here where there was nothing before. Built the very walls of this house, stone by stone. Turned the soil where our corn now grows. Dug the well out back. And his rifle by his side every moment of every day, just in case.'

He told how his Pa had killed an Indian once. A savage with an axe in his raised hand leapt out of the dry grass where he was hid. And the snatch and grab of Grandpa taking up the rifle and the jerking of the lever and the quick shot he got off and how a dead Indian lying on top of him was such a heavy weight.

'Saved his life. Wouldn't be here myself if it wasn't that he shot that Indian, and you'd not be here neither. Stands to reason.'

Still, a part of me couldn't help thinking of the Indian, dead, and the loss he must have been to his own family.

He'd tell of his Pa seeing our Grandma's girl-picture in a newspaper and the rough letter Grandpa wrote asking her to join him in his stone-built house and promising her all manner of impossible things just so she'd come be his wife. And I'd watch the way our Pa's fingers handled the gun and the quick rub and rub he gave the metal parts and the wood, how he'd look down the barrel shaped like the single hole in a honeycomb, looking to make sure it was clean, holding it to the light like he was using a telescope and seeing into the future or the past.

Some Sundays he let me hold it and he showed me how and I got to pump the mechanism that reloaded the gun, except the chamber was always empty. Pa kept the bullets in a locked drawer in the kitchen. The key to the drawer he hid in the tea-caddy on a high shelf. I don't know how I knew all this, but I did.

Then one day Pa was gone and there was just Miriam and me and Ma. He'd got sick and it was a day's ride to the doctor and by the time the doctor came there wasn't a breath in Pa. Ma was all tears and Miriam held my hand and held it tight like she feared I might go after Pa and be gone just the same.

The doctor said he was sorry and he hugged our Ma and patted Miriam's head, and he shook my hand saying I would have to be the man about the place now. He meant it kindly.

My thoughts, when I was alone, turned to the Winchester repeater hanging above the fireplace. I lay in the hayloft pretending I held the gun in my hands, polishing it like Pa had done, and the words that I spoke were his words, the story of his Pa and the one-shot-dead savage, and the words when I spoke them were a little strange for now they had the sound of my voice in them, and the sound of my Pa's voice was missing.

News spread fast. Like fire in the dry brush when a wind is up. Neighbors from miles around came to pay their respects and we had a gathering to lay our Pa in the ground out back. The minister said prayers and kind words and afterwards there was pie and potatoes and cornbread.

Then, days upon days later, there was a man came calling. Every other day he was there, asking after our Ma. He winked at me and at Miriam and I didn't like that wink. His name was Brooke. He brought dead rabbits he'd shot with his own rifle. They were a present for our Ma. He sat in our Pa's chair some days and our Ma fetched him bottles of beer and he held our Ma's hand and said she was still pretty and didn't she think that the place had need of a man to help make ends meet.

I passed our Ma's room one evening, late, and Brooke was there in her bed, and he was lying on top of her and I thought of the dead Indian lying on top of my Grandpa. And our Ma was making a sound like she was hurting. I went down to the kitchen and I climbed on a chair so I could reach the tea-caddy and the key to the drawer inside. I opened the drawer and picked out six bullets. They made a clicking sound in my hand, like pebbles picked out of a clear river. In the front room I lifted down the rifle and I loaded the gun like Pa had showed me, only this time I loaded it with more than imaginary bullets.

I climbed the stairs then, pushed open my Ma's bedroom door and I took aim at the savage beast that was lying on top of our Ma. And I shot him. Twice I shot him before he got off our Ma. Once in the leg and once in the arm. Holding the gun was not so easy as when Pa showed me all those Sundays in front of the fire, jerked in my hands and kicked hard against my shoulder.

Brooke rolled off our Ma and reached for his own gun by the bed. I never saw a man move so quick and he turned and shot without looking to see what he was shooting at and before I could get off a third shot.

His was a Winchester 1892.

CHAPTER TWELVE

Why would Cassie report it if it was Cassie who was to blame? Spoons were missing from the drawer in the kitchen where the cutlery was kept. She didn't notice at first, when it was just one or just two. On the last Friday of the month everything had to be checked, laid out on a broad white cloth and inspected and counted; she'd have noticed then. Only it wasn't the last Friday, it was a week before, and Cassie had the cook's ear, and she told the cook that she thought there was maybe spoons missing.

'I ain't so good at counting. Mr Brendan, the school teacher, he said as such. But I knows there's spoons missing. I been polishing them for years now and my face fat in every one of them when I is done. But I ain't done yet, and there's spoons missing, I swears there is.'

The white cloth was laid out like it was the last Friday and all the spoons and knives and forks were arranged as if for inspection. Cassie was found to be right, and not only spoons, but several butter knives and dessert forks, and the soup ladle were missing too.

Suspicion fell on Mary-Anne at first and then on one of the other girls, on account of the ladle and how the cook had beat the girl with it this one time. There were tears from both girls and snot making silver trails on the backs of their sleeves and protestations of innocence given up in broken words and sobs, and then those words turned to indignation and threats of notice being submitted.

The hullabaloo in the kitchen – for that is what he termed it – brought the head footman below stairs. When he saw the sheet and the cutlery arranged, he thought it must be the last Friday and he had overslept by some several days or had somehow overlooked the passage of time. The cook took him aside and set him straight on what was the substance of the matter.

'Six soup spoons, three butter knives, four dessert forks and the soup ladle.'

It is not uncommon for the rich to have things taken from them, under their very noses and by the very people who have been accorded a level of misplaced trust. Food had been going missing from the kitchen for some few weeks, and it was not the first time that this had happened. But Mrs Winchester had a prodigious memory for everything and she knew if a lamp in a particular room upstairs had been moved or was gone, or a silver letter opener in another room, or a pen. And now there were pieces of silver cutlery missing.

A search was quickly instituted, first through all the other drawers in the kitchen, and then through the rooms of the servants, for some of them were resident in the great house. Then in all the dark corners below stairs and under beds and behind cupboards and in any and every out-of-the-way place that could be thought of.

A hessian sack that had once held walnuts brought up from the orchards, was discovered stuffed behind the cook's stove, and wrapped in a linen napkin inside the hessian were the missing pieces from the cutlery drawer.

Where there should have been relief, there was none.

Mary-Anne sulked in the corner and muttered something about trust and knowing where she was valued most and how the cook had had it in for her ever since. She did not say ever since when, for that needed no saying.

The cook would have apologized for her wrongful accusations, except there was still the matter of who had stowed the hessian bundle behind the stove and until that had been resolved, no-one was above suspicion.

The spoons were returned to the cutlery drawer after a thorough clean, as were the butter knives and the dessert forks and even the ladle. Cassie was happier with things back to how they should be and her face fat again in twelve soupspoons instead of just six. But she took to keeping a more careful eye on everything and was in an idle moment to be seen watching the drawer in case any fork or knife or spoon should leap out and scurry behind the cook's stove, like in the nursery rhyme and 'the dish ran away with the spoon'.

The white cloth was put away until the last Friday when a fuller inspection was carried out and everything accounted for.

There the matter might have found rest, except that Mary-Anne was so bold as to take the matter upstairs one morning with the breakfast tray.

'Begging your pardon, Mrs Winchester, but there's been a hullabaloo in the kitchen.' She had borrowed the word from the head footman and saw no wrong in just borrowing. 'And I am accused of things that I did not ever do.'

Mrs Winchester nodded and asked if this was something concerning the six soupspoons, three butter knives, four dessert forks and the ladle, for if it was then, Mrs Winchester said, she was in agreement with Mary-Anne about her not being the light-fingered culprit responsible.

The head footman was given three more days to put an end to the issue of the stolen cutlery. He interviewed the staff, one at a time, the kitchen staff and then more generally the upstairs staff and even the orchard workers who were connected to the matter by virtue of the hessian walnut sack. Aside from the recovery of some plums that had been filched by one of the upstairs maids and which was dealt with separately, the head footman came up empty and had to report as much to Mrs Winchester.

'Try the new junior footman,' she said. 'And then make some small enquiry as to his circumstances at home, for there is ever a reason for such petty pilfering, a sick parent or sibling, or an unpaid rent, or some other pressing debt or account needing settled. I like the boy, Jack, and I would not see him gone from here. He must be made wiser by this lesson, of course, but that will be all that needs be.'

The boy was interviewed a second time and a confession more easily extracted by the certain knowledge that he was steeped in guilt. What had been taken before as a sign of nerves and only natural in one not used to the ways of the house upstairs, was seen now as a sure and definite mark of his culpability.

It transpired that it was all as Mrs Winchester had foreseen. The boy's mother was sick and could not rise from her bed and there was not money enough in the house to bring the doctor to her and so the boy had thought to help by the taking of a few pieces of silver. After all, Mrs Winchester never used but a quarter of the spoons and knives and forks, and the ladle was taken on account of the beating he had seen the cook give to the newer girl who had caught his eye and whose pretty face was in his head when he blew out the candle at night and closed his eyes and put his hands between his legs and dreamed.

The head footman made report of the whole interview to Mrs Winchester and she ordered that a doctor be sent to the boy's mother and the bill to be met by herself. Food also was dispatched to the boy's family and some small coin that might see them through their present difficulties. The mother of the boy was never given to understand who was her kind benefactor, for everything was done without name and without identity; but on the birth of her last child, she was heard to announce that the girl in her arms should be called Sarah.

As to the junior footman, he was taxed with extra duties in the house and that for a whole calendar month, until after the next Friday inspection. And he was watched, as hawks watch for the slightest wrong movement in long grass before swooping and their eyes sharp as needles, and the junior footman felt a pricking on the back of his neck for some several months afterwards and always when he was in the kitchen and the cook glaring at him. And at the end of each of those thirty days of working harder than he ever had before, he fell into sudden sleep and with no thought of any kitchen-maid or house girl, overcome as he was by a greater exhaustion.

He later learned of the doctor's visit to his mother and of the food that was sent to his family and to him it was no unfathomable mystery, though he said nothing to anyone about his suspicions, except that he wrote the words 'thank you' on a piece of brown wrapping paper and he slipped the paper under the door of Mrs Winchester's sitting-room.

Room 98

The Winchester Gun Club

It was him or me. That's how I saw it. Nothin personal on either side. He was just doin a job is all and the pretty price on my head was the bounty he was after. You can't be blamin a man for that. I just didn't see myself returnin to the four walls of no cell and all my thoughts caged and shrinkin to nothin, and the air so still and thick in there, with the last words of men who'd come and gone scratched into the stone beside the bed and difficult to read.

He was dogged, you unnerstan. Like he didn't know how to give up. Like nobody'd taught him that. He was trackin me for weeks, through all weathers and miles from where we started – holes in *my* shoes so it must have been the same for him. In open spaces, where the land was flat as tabletops and the sky wide and buzzards drawin tight circles in the unbroken blue, I saw him, far off. He looked small. Like a bug, like I could reach out and squish him between the press of my finger and thumb.

At night, I looked for the flicker of flame in the dark, and I envied him his campfire and his food warm and his coffee drunk from a tin cup. I breathed deep, standin downwind of him by several miles and hopin in vain to catch the faintest smell of that coffee of his. I had biscuits and a canteen of cold water I filled whenever I could and beef jerky that hurt my teeth and the muscles of my jaw with so much chewin.

It's funny, but knowin he was out there, I felt sort of safe, you know. Like sleepin in a bed and all the lights doused, but knowin there's someone in the next room – your mom or your pa maybe. I talked to him at a distance. Of course, he wouldn't have heard, but it was like he was company, and I told him things that I could never have told him face to face. I even gave him a name; I called him Clark, which was the name of someone I once knew.

Maybe that was my mistake, thinkin we could be friends if the circumstances was different, when in truth Clark was a mean critter and, with the bit between his teeth, he was huntin me down. I left him messages spelled out in the dirt. Small words that he might have found, or which might just as well have been wiped away by the wind or the tracks of a jackrabbit or the shuffle of a rattler. I don't know why I did that with the messages; I don't know if I thought that maybe he'd see me different and give up on what he was about. Stupid, it was.

The space between us each day became a little less than the day before and I knew it wouldn't be long till we was face to face and then it'd be him or me, like I said. Once, I thought I did catch the smell of his coffee, bitter and dark, carried on a tumbleweed wind; but maybe I was just wantin it so bad by then that I imagined I smelled it.

'Coffee sure smells good,' I hollered.

He was a deal nearer than I knew. 'Come git some then,' Clark yelled back, and I was, for just a moment, tempted to take him up on his offer.

Then we *was* face to face and nothin special in the day to say that this was it. I could see the dirt on his fingers and the gaps in his yellow teeth and his lank hair all grey and cut crooked. He was grinnin like the cat that has got the cream, or got a mouse caught 'neath its paw at least, and at first I thought I knew him and he was bein friendly. But he was holdin his gun ready. A rifle. A Yellow Boy Winchester. And I could see hc was calculatin his chances and maybe addin up the dollars he'd make by takin me in, dead or alive, but easier dead.

In the end it wasn't anything as I thought it would be. It wasn't him or me like I said. I shot Clark twice in the chest and he shot me twice and that was it. Maybe he scratched some last words in the dirt or hung them on the blowin air and let them carry on the wind, but if he did I never knew what they was; and there weren't no-one to hear my last words neither, no-one at all.

CHAPTER THIRTEEN

There were days when the ground in the Santa Clara Valley shook, as it did from time to time everywhere on the West Coast. They came without warning, those days, and they came suddenly and it was all over before it had begun, a small thunder under the feet, as when a horse passes at a gallop, or a team of horses, and everything shaking, and the Tiffany chandeliers in the great ballroom made a clink-clink music; and the bell made by Lester and Pack and hanging in the bell-tower swayed, and once it even rang and the house staff and the gardeners wondered at the noise and thought it was something dreamed and so not really heard at all.

The house suffered these earth-shakes when they came. Small cracks appeared in the walls and daylight leaked in, and the scent of plum blossom from the orchards crept into the house, and bees that had lost their way fizzed and sparked like new-lit fireworks and were later found dead on their backs in small spaces with dust on their wings. The cracks needed repaired and covered over, and all the rooms had to be inspected and the locks checked and the seals tested, and for days afterwards Mr John Hansen walked the corridors and passageways of the house with Mrs Winchester on his arm and their faces turned upwards searching for the smaller and smaller signs of damage.

'They are not happy,' she said sometimes and Mr John Hansen could only speculate as to who was not happy. He thought maybe she meant the angels and that was why their eyes were tipped heavenwards.

After these days had passed, and the thundering horses were calm once again and stepping forward on slippered hooves, after these days there was an uncomfortable silence laid over everything as if no-one was sure that it was really over, as if it was expected that there was more to be borne. Indeed, it was something the same *before* these ground shaking days too, or before the moments at least and maybe in this there was a warning after all: there was an unaccountable quiet when the hens took to their nests and made no sound, and the cattle lay down in the fields with their silent horned heads held low, and the junior footman insisted on stepping out from under the roof of the great house and there was a story he told of the sky falling and the whole glassy glint of heaven falling too and the stars sharp as knives or thrown stones, and he crept into the space beneath a carriage or a cart and would not be persuaded out from under until the shaking had come and then departed again.

Sometimes, when it was all over and breath could be drawn again, and birds had in ones and twos taken to the sky once more, and the cattle were on their feet and lumbering homewards, then complete rooms were seen to have been damaged so much that they had to be dismantled and rebuilt and the walls strengthened and the windows made straight again and a different design then to keep 'them' happy. And Mr John Hansen worked later at those times and he was closer to Mrs Winchester by being so much in her company, and by degrees over the years a new tenderness crept into their talk with one another.

'I had hoped it was you, Mr Hansen. When I heard the sound of footsteps on the stairs, I said to myself, that is surely Mr John Hansen. I am glad to see you well and rested for there's a greater deal of work to be done and I don't see how that might proceed without your saying that there's something amiss with my design or something right with it.'

On the table, as before and as always, lay sheets of paper that betrayed their age by the yellow that they were or their newness by the white. And every sheet bore the mark of ink in sketched lines and annotations in an increasingly spidery hand.

'It is room one hundred that concerns me today.'

Mr Hansen nodded. 'Is it in someway special for being such a rounded number, Mrs Winchester?'

She waved a hand in the air as if brushing away flies or dismissing an unsatisfactory thought. 'You know me better than that, Mr Hansen. It's just that I had hoped to have the room finished before the end of the week and now, with all these small repairs to cornices and balustrades and window sashes, well, I think we may be forced to run a little behind schedule and that leaves me ill at ease for I do not know what implications that might have.'

Mr John Hansen knew her well enough not to enquire as to what she meant and so he kept his attention steadfastly on the drawings and tried by turning the page this way and the other to make sense of what was written there.

'Perhaps the west wing might be left for a while and the workmen there brought to deal with the repairs, and you and your team could give your attention to room one hundred. I want to change something about the room. I know, I am such a flibbertigibbet in these matters, but it occurs to me that we might move the fireplace to another wall and the bed be where the fireplace currently is. Such an alteration might afford the person in the bed a more pleasant view when he awakens, for I see that the valley is all a-flicker and aflame with the plum blossom and the perfume from the trees blows up towards the house and enters the room through the open window and hangs in the air as though a woman has just left it.'

There was a new poetry in the things she said to Mr John Hansen and some things he didn't understand. He didn't know what a flibbertigibbet might be and had never heard the word used before. He supposed it was something to do with how particular she was in everything being just so.

'It'll take only half a day for the men in the west wing to make good what they are doing so that their work can be left. Then they can take up all the small and bigger repairs that must be carried out following the last quake, and then might a team and myself be about the business of making ready room one hundred.'

Mrs Winchester laid one hand on the top of his and in doing so she was reminded of an old dream and reminded, too, of a day when he had taken her hand in his to save her from falling and there were callouses on the palm of his hand and an uncommon warmth – leastways, she imagined it was uncommon, for William's hands had always been cold no matter the day or the hour.

'I do rely on you, John,' she said, and then she hurriedly withdrew her hand and moved onto other things, something about the orders stacking up at San Jose station and something about a photograph she had seen printed in a newspaper once and how she was expecting a copy of the photograph for room one hundred.

Then her eye was caught by something in the yard and she was silent a while before sudden laughter shook her and she called Mr John Hansen to the window to observe what was the source of her amusement.

'Do you see?' she said, directing one finger to a corner of the garden where stood an unhorsed carriage.

Mr John Hansen ventured to stand as close as propriety allowed and looked down the length of Mrs Winchester's crooked finger.

'Beneath the carriage, do you see?'

Mrs Winchester laughed again and, though there were whispers of grey and silver in her hair, her laughter was like that of a girl and so unexpected and still so new to Mr John Hansen.

'Do you see?'

'It is the junior footman,' said Mr Hansen and he too laughed.

'Do you think, Mr Hansen, that he has been there this whole time, since before the quake as you call it? Someone should go and tell him that it's safe to come out now. Send Bessie from the kitchen, one of the maids, I know he will come out if she asks him.'

Mr Hansen was close enough he could smell the German cologne on her skin, something astringent like lemons, and also something underneath, something a little sour and sweet at the same time.

He cleared his throat and swallowed, as if he might say something further. Seeming to think better of it, he remained silent.

'There's something else?' asked Mrs Winchester.

'No,' said Mr Hansen. 'There's nothing else.'

Mr John Hansen moved away and towards the door to see to the requests she had made about the workmen in the west wing, but he was stopped by Mrs Winchester who remained standing at the window seeming to still find amusement in the junior footman hiding under the unhitched carriage.

'I think that when room one hundred is completed we might have something of a celebration. It is, as you rightly point out, a well-rounded number and perhaps that betokens something in this world. I think you should take a few days' rest, time to be with Mrs Hansen and the children. They must consider that you are too much here and not enough with them. Yes, I think a few days should be granted to you. But first we must see to the room's latest alterations.'

It was as if she had read his thoughts, for it was this that he had briefly thought to speak of just now and had decided against. Mr John Hansen thanked Mrs Winchester for her consideration and left so quietly that she did not hear the fall of his foot on the stairs as he made his departure and for a while afterwards thought that he might still be standing outside her door.

Mrs Winchester remained at the window for some time, until Bessie the kitchen-maid stepped across the lawn and beckoned for the junior footman to come out from under the carriage. When the boy did not come forth at once, Mrs Winchester surmised that some bargain was being struck between them and this from the language of Bessie's hands and her body, and from the fact that when he did crawl out from under the carriage at last the girl made to offer the boy her lips and he did take her offer. Then the maid set to brushing the dirt and the straw from his coat and scolding him for his foolishness and laughing and hurrying him back towards the house and his duties there.

She stood by the window, remembering the touch of John's hand and smiling to herself.

Room 100

The Winchester Gun Club

Stories differ as stories will. It might have been The Kid, it might have been one of the others. I don't rightly know myself. That can happen in a gunfight. So much smoke and noise, and men shouting and cussing, and everything happening so fast. And afterwards stories get told and they change with each telling, and change again with each person telling the story.

It was up at Blazer's Mill, a sawmill and trading post on the Rio Tularosa. I'd sold up. Everything. The whole ranch and the house and outbuildings and a hundred head of cattle. I was at Blazer's Mill to collect the bank check for the sale. I was impatient to be gone. Itchy I was. There was trouble in the air and I could smell it.

They were there eating lunch. The whole gang of them. Beans and beef stew and cornbread on their plates. I could hear them laughing and boasting. I heard my name mentioned and it was The Kid who said he'd do for me if he ever got the chance.

A guy called Frank came out and sat with me on the sawmill steps. He did not seem unduly surprised to see me and he made things plain. He said as how I was outnumbered and how they were set on taking me in and nothing would sway them from their course. He might have said they'd run me in 'dead or alive' and he offered to take my guns from me there and then.

'Be a lot easier for everyone,' he said.

I didn't like the odds, but no more did I like the idea of them taking me without my guns. I'd heard stuff about what they could do, what they had already done. I'd heard said that The Kid had shot a man dead just for snoring too loudly, and another for cheating badly at cards, or just for kissing a girl The Kid liked. There were a hundred stories like that. I could hear Billy cussing louder than the rest and spitting, and it was my name he was against.

Frank went back in and soon after a few of the others came out, their weapons drawn and striding with purpose in my direction, one of them wearing a sugar-loaf sombrero hat, and with no more time for words the shooting began. I was hit in the stomach, and like I said, it might have been The Kid and it might have been someone else. I kept pumping bullets at them till my gun was empty. Hit a few of them, too, before making it to the old house and barricading the door from the inside.

I knew they'd not rest long. I readied myself for a fresh encounter.

I think it might have been Frank that spoke again, his voice sent like a flapping bird into the air, all holler and yell. He said I could still save myself. It didn't have to end this way, he said, didn't have to end with my last breath. My gut hurt like hell and my shirt was sticky with blood. I laughed at what Frank said.

Out of the window I could see them spread out, circling the house and gesturing to each other with their arms. One of them stuck his head up from behind a woodpile; he got off one shot, the smoke drifting from him like a ghost. I shot back and hit him in the eye. I think that gave them a fright. They pulled out sometime later.

It was quiet then. I could hear my breath coming short and fast. The sun crept down from the sky and a darkness fell on everything, and a slow creeping coldness.

It was a Winchester bullet that did for me. I know because I was firing a Winchester rifle myself. There's a picture of Billy the Kid, just the one, a 3x3 ferrotype. It's posed, a bit of a swagger in the way that he stands, a bit of a sneer, too, and his sugar-loaf sombrero set at a tilt. He has a holstered pistol on the jut of one hip and a Winchester carbine pushed to the front of the picture so it can't be missed. Could be it's the same rifle he shot me with, if it was The Kid who put the hole in my gut. Depends on the story you believe, depends who's telling the story.

CHAPTER FOURTEEN

Sometimes the nights were so cold they hurt and her fingers curled into the claws of dead birds and would not uncurl, and her knees ached so that walking was an effort even with a stick to lean on. Mrs Winchester was always leaving her stick in the place she'd last visited and sometimes forgetting where that was exactly; and she did not miss the lost stick till her knee buckled under her and she reached out to the wall for support or reached out for Mr John Hansen if he was near, reached out for John.

Mrs Winchester employed a young man whose only task was to tend to the fires in the house, for they were now in number too many for the maids to see to. The cold ashes had to be raked each morning and carried out from the house, and dry logs needed to be cut and stacked in metal-lined chests, and coal had to be brought up in buckets, and a fresh fire set each evening in those places Mrs Winchester stipulated.

During the day the fires could burn low and the windows of her rooms were thrown open and Mrs Winchester drank iced water or tea; as soon as the sun began to go down, the young man had to stoke the fires, especially those in the rooms that Mrs Winchester used and in the corridors in her part of the house and in some of the rooms she had arranged to visit that evening. Mrs Winchester had special gloves knitted and the ends of her fingers poked through so that there was no loss of nimbleness in keeping her joints warm. She wore long woolen stockings under heavy velvet dresses and thick cotton petticoats; but she was still cold despite a muffler, a fur collared jacket, and thick lined boots; and she rapped her stick on the floor to call the young man back and to give him more particular instructions regarding the closing of curtains so there was no space left for the cold to sneak in, and an extra log on the fire in her sitting-room, and a copper ash-pan to warm her bed.

Parts of the house were closed off during the coldest months and work slowed – but did not stop – and Mrs Winchester became irritable and restless. She spent more and more time at her desk, writing lists by the light of several oil lanterns or carbide gas lights, and making plans, and remaking plans, and writing letters – though it was some nights difficult to hold the pen and what she wrote suffered and was harder to read.

'My dear and dearest Lizbeth

I was so delighted to receive your last letter and your kindest invitation. I cannot believe that the little girl I first saw on the main street of San Jose has put away her dolls and her pinafore dresses, and is now grown to be a lady. It begins to make me feel old to think of you as you now are. I said as much to Mr John Hansen and he laughed and said I was talking foolish. I did forgive him that 'foolish' for John does sometimes forget himself these days and that, I think, is a sign of his age.

The annual orphanage picnic at the Winchester House was an excellent event this year and I thought of you then and wished you had been there. Then I wondered when last you were here and children bouncing on your knee and the sound of your laughter coming up to my window from the grounds below; or when last we took a turn about the gardens, just you and I, and Jack fetching us fresh lemonade, ice-cold and in tall glasses, and bees making the air buzz and birds stringing their songs from tree to tree in the apricot orchards; or when it was that you last accompanied me in my carriage around the town and shared with me all the small and silly news of the people there and the more serious news also. I confess that thinking about it, I could not say when last I saw you, Lizbeth, and so I missed you suddenly and wished to hear from you at once or sooner; and then your letter arrived, as if I had summoned it just by thinking of you.

Following this year's children's picnic and for three or four days afterwards, I saw a girl and a boy playing by themselves in the grounds. Sometimes they were there and then they weren't. She was always pushing the boy and laughing, and the boy sometimes ran away from her, though he did seem to invite her to run after him with his looking over his shoulder, and she did run after him and either she caught him or she ran beyond him. I think that caused some irritation in the boy or he pretended to be annoyed, and so they fell to wrestling together. Once, I think the wrestling became a kissing moment. When I sent our junior footman to enquire as to their names and who they might be, he said he could find no girl and no boy, nor any sign that anyone had been in the gardens. I do not know why I tell you this.

I told Jack of your news, Lizbeth, and he sends his best wishes and I think there was a break in his voice when he said it. I believe he was much moved to think of you so far from being a child now; he has a girl of his own and she has girls of her own and he does not see any of them nearly as much as he should.

If I close my eyes, I can picture you and picture him, the man you make such a fuss of in your letters, though I only have his name and the many small and insufficient things you have told me about him. I must hear more by return letter, or at least within the month, given that you will be much taken up with the preparations and then in the setting up of your new home. When you have time enough to pen another letter, I do wish for something more substantial on the young man and his particular better qualities.

As to the Winchester House, I can say as I always do that it keeps me busy enough and is more this year than it was last year and yet no nearer completion, which I do not bemoan for if it were complete I do not know what my life would then be, or John Hansen's life, or the lives of the men he does employ on my behalf with their hammers and their chisels and their handsaws and awls.

I have made some newer changes recently and have had installed several more fireplaces, for I do begin to feel the cold more than before. They say that the blood thins with age, but it is more especially my joints that suffer when it is cold and I must sometimes keep to my bed for several days at a time. The doctor has prescribed licorice and two teaspoons daily of flaxseed oil, and this he says will help with any inflammation.

All of which brings me to the import of my letter to you, Lizbeth, my child. I was, as I have said already, thrilled to receive your invitation. Such a lovely card and worded so sweetly and I knew the hand was yours in that. However, my dear, I am by doctor's orders confined to my room and my bed for the days ahead; just the usual complaints of age heretofore referred to, and so I must most sadly decline to attend the church and your wedding. I shall of course be there in spirit and singing and dancing and making such a fool of myself in fussing over the man who will be your husband and partner on the rest of your life's journey. Forgive me if you can. I send with this letter a small something for you to wear on your day in glory and I hope that in wearing it you will think just once of me.

Your dearest friend
Sarah Winchester'

The letter was addressed and the envelope sealed with wax and the whole attached to a richly decorated jewelry box and ready to be dispatched by messenger and delivered on the morning of Lizbeth's wedding.

The effort of writing the letter had taxed Mrs Winchester's energies and with its completion she had no more appetite for writing. Her fingers were twisted almost into knots and her eyes stung with so close an inspection of the point of her pen and for so long. The hour was well advanced and she was assured that John – Mr Hansen – had already departed for home, so she called instead for her footman. Then, resting on his arm, she made her usual patrol of the corridors, checking the fires in several rooms and seeing if she might be able to locate the beginnings of a draft that vexed her, and proceeding to the bell-tower for the midnight ringing of the bell, though this night she was a little after the hour before the bell was rung.

Then she left her footman by the tower and by a circuitous route and steps switching back on themselves and hidden doors in walls and one in the floor, she came to rooms one hundred and eight and one hundred and nine, side by side, and the wall between them as thin as paper almost, nearly as thin as thought so that words could easily pass between the two rooms. The first was prepared as for a boy, with pictures on the walls of popular heroes from the Wild West, the most prominent of whom were Buffalo Bill Cody, Kit Carson and Wyatt Earp. The adjoining room was similar in design, as though it was a mirror to the first, except that there was a little lace on the edge of the pillows and the bedspread was a warm rose color. There were pictures on the wall in this second room, too, but they were of Calamity Jane, Annie Oakley and Rose Dunn.

Mrs Winchester waited just outside the two rooms and her ears were sharp for the smallest sounds. The unsourced draft threaded between her legs and there was a familiar ache in her knee and she wondered in which room she had last had her walking stick. Then the whole place grew cold, and her cheeks nipped and her fingers hurt and she knew. She closed first one door and then the second and she locked them both.

It took the better part of a half hour for her to retrace her steps to where the footman was still waiting. She thought at first sight that he was changed into a spirit of himself for he was pale and, she thought, not so tall or so straight as he once was; in short, she discovered that her footman was old and she resolved to attend to the matter in the morning.

Room 108 & 109

The Winchester Gun Club

We'd been drinkin some but I still reckoned as I could shoot straighter then either boy. Course that irked 'em somewhat, same as when I beat 'em at arm wrestlin with one hand tied behind my back and they made me promise not to tell a soul and gave me two silver dollars each just to tie the deal, and I gave 'em both a kiss and my tongue in their mouths tastin of liquor then, too.

Dempsey, he was the worst, and he said he didn't agree, not about the shootin, not about anything, not ever. 'Girls is girls and boys is better.' Always his boast was bigger than the Mississippi river is wide. 'I could shoot the ears off a jackrabbit in racin flight,' he said.

His words was all spit and slur and I knew he was seein double by the way he was lookin at Cookie when he was really talkin to me, and his head was a little loose on his neck, like string puppets when they're slack, and he couldn't hold hisself straight.

'Could take out the eye of a sedge wren on the wing.'

We set up some playin cards. Stuck 'em to a fencepost with tree sap and spit, and then we stepped back, as far as fifty paces to start with and Cookie makin up the rules as we walked.

'Three shots each and Dempsey be aimin at the red card and Amy at the black and as near as the center of the card wins it.'

Dempsey had his dad's Winchester and I had my dad's Springfield breech-loader. We flipped a coin to see who'd shoot first and Dempsey disputed the call, like always, so I let him take the lead.

I don't think he could even see the fencepost never mind the card. He fired off three shots and I watched his bullets hittin the dirt a ways beyond the post. I felt sorry for him then, so when I fired off my three I made one of 'em hit one corner of his card, like he'd done better than just miss. My other two shots were bang center on my card, almost perfectly one on top of the other.

Cookie confirmed the score and we took another fifty paces back and shot again. Jesus, he was drunker than a skunk, and his shootin wilder than a bear after it's disturbed a nest of hornets. All over the place he was and I yelled at Cookie to watch out or Dempsey'd make the mistake of thinkin his skinny hide was the fencepost and his ass the ace of hearts.

He was gettin a bit ornery and spittin in the dirt all of the time, and he was pumpin his dad's Winchester rifle like it was the gun's fault he was missin the card. Cookie was jus laughin and I could feel the air all charged and prickly. I wasn't sure how to play it then.

'Fuck you, Amy Masterson,' Dempsey said. 'Jus fuck you, girl.'

I shrugged and said to him how it didn't matter none and how I was sure he was jus missin on account of he'd drunk more of his old man's hooch than me, which he had. I kissed him like before, maybe slower, and I stroked his cheek like I once seen a loose woman do with a drunk at the back of Sadie's Saloon.

Then I walked the hundred steps back to the fencepost and Cookie there wantin a kiss, too, and thinkin he deserved it more than Dempsey on account of he coulda caught one of Dempsey's wide-flying bullets, and I shrugged and thought he was maybe right about that. And that's how we was, me and Cookie, his arms wrapped around me and pullin me close and I thought maybe he'd been practicing since last time, with his kissing, and it was sort of nice, you know; then three shots, fired one after the other, and Dempsey was only tryin to scare us, of that I'm sure, only he couldn't hit a fence post when he was tryin to and I reckon he couldn't avoid hittin me and Cookie when he was tryin not to.

CHAPTER FIFTEEN

'I do rely on you, John,' said Mrs Winchester.

They were taking a turn about the upper floors of the house and discussing the layout for one of the rooms. Mr Hansen had drawn her attention to a problem with the stairs and the rise between each step and how much Mrs Winchester struggled to cope with this when she was troubled with her knee, which was often.

'Perhaps there is another way to achieve what I wish, John. Perhaps we could have two sets of stairs switching back on each other and thirteen steps with each set and so a shallower rise.'

Mr Hansen considered this for some moments before giving his agreement and suggesting how the staircases might be laid next to each other and the turn in the stairs navigated and how the extra balustrade might be fashioned, and how Mrs Winchester's original decorations might be extended to the extra staircase.

'You see, John, you see how necessary you are to all my plans for the house.'

They then fell to discussing the number of the doors, and the extra windows that might be incorporated, and the fancy that Mrs Winchester had for some English pottery, and a Victorian mahogany pedestal desk made in London that she had already ordered.

Mrs Winchester leaned more heavily on Mr Hansen's arm and he patted her hand and they proceeded at a slow and shuffling pace, so slow it was as though they were creeping and did not wish to be noticed.

'I have said it before, but I do not know how I would manage without you, John.'

Sometimes she allowed the formality of their relationship to relax. It was a small enough thing to do and afforded her more pleasure than anything else in her days. And when things were so relaxed, Mr Hansen smiled and stood a little straighter and he no longer patted her hand but stroked it in something that was nearer to a caress, nearer than either of them dared to admit but which neither of them objected to.

'When we are like this, and alone, you must call me Sarah,' she said to him.

'Sarah,' he said, as though he was testing the shape of her name in his mouth. Tasting it. 'Sarah.'

The next day, Mr Hansen did not appear at the Winchester House and it was half an hour after the time for his usual morning appointment with Mrs Winchester when a message was brought to her to say that he had kept to his bed and the doctor had been sent for – the same doctor whose house Mr Hansen had been building when Mrs Winchester had arrived in the Santa Clara Valley all those years ago and had in a moment turned everything on its head.

At first Mrs Sarah Winchester seemed to have lost her voice or her words. She read the message over several times, as if there might be some other hidden communication written between the lines or as if there was some code in what was actually written.

'John – Mr Hansen is sick?' she asked the boy who had delivered the message.

'He had a fall,' said the boy.

Again her speech deserted her for a moment. She got stiffly to her feet and, with the help of her stick, limped to the window and looked out across the valley in the direction where lay the house of John Hansen.

'Is it serious?' she enquired of the boy without turning to address him so that it was almost as though she was talking to herself or thinking out loud.

'He fell from his horse and there is some swelling in his leg and he clutches at his back and makes a face like he's sucking lemons.'

She might have been wondering how she was going to manage till his return, how she would oversee the continued building of the westernmost point of the house, and see to the finishing of the room at the top of the house that she thought of as room one hundred and twelve and which waited only for the delivery of Staffordshire pottery and the desk from London to be complete. But Mrs Winchester was not thinking of this; she was thinking of John and his hand stroking hers as they'd paced the stairs and the corridors and talked about everything and nothing. And she was thinking of the inflexion he gave to her name when he spoke it, almost as if it held music. Already she missed him and, as she was fond of saying, she did not know how she would manage without him.

'You say the doctor has been sent for?' she said to the boy.

The boy nodded.

Mrs Winchester returned to the table and began writing a note of reply. She held the pen a little awkwardly for her fingers were swollen, despite the licorice tea that the doctor had prescribed for her.

The boy did not know if he was dismissed or if he should wait. He shifted uncomfortably from one foot to the other and looked to the door as if he might make his escape sooner rather than later.

The only sound in the room was the scratch of Mrs Winchester's pen on the page, and her held breath until a word had been formed and then the release of that breath, and the quick snatch and suck of another breath, and held, till another word was on the page.

'Dear Mr John Hansen,

I am informed that you have suffered a fall and it is bad enough that you are in some pain and the doctor has been sent for. Rest assured that you are not to hurry back to work on any account, but must take the time until you are fully recovered. My thoughts are with you and your family at this time.

With my sincere good wishes for your return to full health

Mrs Sarah Winchester'

The boy was sent back with the note and told that he was to deliver it to Mrs Hansen and then to wait until the doctor had made his visit and to bring news back to her regarding how John – Mr Hansen – fared. She laid a Liberty Head five-dollar coin on the table and said it waited there for the boy's return.

The junior footman, who was no longer referred to as 'junior' but had not yet earned the label of 'senior' though he now walked everywhere in Jack's shoes and saw to all Jack's former duties, was sent for. Mrs Winchester gave instructions for the overseeing of the unpacking of the mahogany pedestal desk that had arrived that morning from London and its immediate installation in room one hundred and twelve and precisely where it should be in that room. The English Staffordshire pottery had also arrived, a creamware jug with blue transfer decoration and mention of Buffalo Bill's Wild West Show and its visit to London in 1887.

'Perfect,' she said.

Thereafter the work of the house continued as much as ever it did. The hammers and saws did not cease from their thumping and cutting; the fires were duly raked and reset; the kitchen was all a rattle of pans and plates and knives; trees in the orchards were pruned and the new movable beehives were shifted nearer the house for the winter; three carts were unloaded at the station at San Jose, the items stored in two of the lower rooms and everything logged and written down; orders were sent out and letters dispatched; and all the normal fuss at the Winchester House went on as normal, or as near to normal as might be allowed.

All as normal except in one respect: Mrs Winchester did not continue with her usual pursuits. She did not pen new designs on linen napkins or add any further amendments to the old; she wrote no more letters save later in the day she tried to pen something else to John, but when it was near to completion she tore it up and burned it on the fire and berated herself for her foolishness; she took no tour of the work in the house and trusted that the mahogany desk had been situated according as she had stipulated in room one hundred and twelve. Indeed, Mrs Winchester simply took to her own bed for the better part of the day – not because her twisted fingers hurt any more than usual, nor that her knee was particular sore or it was particular cold. She took to her bed because for the first time in years she felt suddenly and absolutely alone, and she knew then how she would do without Mr John Hansen, and feeling so alone she felt a little sorry for herself.

It was later in the afternoon that the boy returned to claim his Liberty Head five dollars. He had a further note pertaining to Mr Hansen. It was a brief note and to the point. It had been written by Mrs Hansen and said only that John was well, though a mild sedative had been given to help him sleep. It said that the doctor had advised Mr Hansen to keep to his bed for above five days to rest his back. The leg was not broken but he would feel the bruises more tomorrow than today. And that was all it said.

'Mr Hansen,' said Mrs Winchester, and what might be fathomed from that 'Mr Hansen' only she might say.

Mrs Winchester, when she had recovered her head, ordered several baskets of plums and apricots and some jars of preserved walnuts to be taken straightway to Mrs Hansen. Mrs Winchester was unable to hold the pen and was not prepared to admit as much to the boy or to the new footman who thought the boy must have mislaid the note and sent him back upstairs to check. Mrs Winchester said that the delivery of the baskets of fruit and the jars of walnuts would suffice for the time being.

Then Mrs Winchester returned to her bed until it was late and it had grown dark and cold and the curtains in her room had not been drawn so that flies had entered her room, and were bumping themselves on the glass shades of the oil lanterns and making such a nuisance of themselves that she rang for the footman to see to the duties that lately had been carried out by Mr Hansen.

She took some soup and ate alone so that her difficulty with the spoon was not noticed. Then she drank some tea and could not hold the cup by the handle, but clutched it by the bowl, which had the added benefit of affording some warmth to her hands.

When the hour was sufficiently late and much of the house slept, she ventured forth from her room and, slower than ever, made her way to the bell-tower and rang the bell as was usual and which would have been missed by the dreamers turning in their sleep and might very well have turned them out of their sleep had she not rung it.

Her later progress to the top of the house was painful and stumbling, even with her stick and the lower rise of the staircases already in place. She checked that everything was as she had demanded in room one hundred and twelve. The moon was full in the sky and this was just as well for she had not been able to carry an oil lantern or even a candle with her on her rounds.

The desk was in place, and on a low table sat a pot for making tea and the creamware milk jug, and over the back of the chair a buckskin jacket. On the walls were several black and white publicity pictures of Buffalo Bill and his 'Little Sure Shot' as well as an Indian feather headdress and a leather satchel bearing the tin badge of the Pony Express.

Mrs Winchester stood outside the room with the door open and the key in her hand. She waited till she was so cold that her teeth chittered and she could hardly hold the key. Then she closed the door and locked it and retraced her steps to the bell-tower before turning in for the night.

Though she slept, it was a fitful sleep, and in the dreams that were broken and broken again, she felt the loss of something or was ever looking under beds and in cupboards for something that was lost. In her dreams she did not know what it was she searched after; when she woke she thought it might have been Annie or William that she had felt the loss of, except that all her first waking thoughts were with Mr John Hansen.

Room 112

The Winchester Gun Club

May 9th 1887, London, Earl's Court show-ground. I was there at the opening. You never saw the like. The place was full. Later in the run, Queen Victoria attended two command performances for her Jubilee, and Edward, Prince of Wales was there, too. It was the talk of the town and everybody who was anybody wanted a ticket, and I was there at the opening with my brother, Henry.

We saw an attack on a Deadwood stage. I didn't know what a Deadwood stage was but there were Indians on horseback all beaded and feathered, and the air was shrill with their shrieking and whooping, and so many arrows dropping from the sky I thought it was a heavy rain, and guns cracking and horses falling stiff to the dirt. I was on the edge of my seat.

And then there was a Pony Express race and everything so yee-ha fast the whole thing was a blur and what the riders of those horses couldn't do from the back of a horse! And the US mail must go through, and it did.

Then the death of General George Armstrong Custer of the 7th Cavalry. The Indians called him 'Yellow-hair' and he met his end at The Battle of Little Big Horn and he met it again in the Earl's Court show-ground. And into the arena rode chief Sitting Bull, moving slow and the head of his horse bowed so low its breath disturbed the sand it walked over, and I did not know if I should clap or turn away.

But the star of the show, for me at least and for Henry, was 'Little Sure Shot'. Prettier than her picture, she rode into the performance area, the hooves of her horse making a small running rumble like thunder or drums, her hair flying behind her like a blowing flag and she was shooting into the sky. I think she smiled at me. I swear she did, and she waved, too, and Buffalo Bill took his hat off in a flourish and he stiffly bowed to his Annie Oakley.

She could shoot a fly at thirty paces, and split a playing card edge on, and knock the ash from a smoker's cigarette with a single shot. And the rifle she carried was a factory-made smooth bore Winchester 1873.

I saved up for two years and got one myself. Had it shipped over specially, packed in straw in a wooden box and I had to sign for it down at St Katharine's dock. I later posed for the camera with the gun across my arms and my face set serious, like I meant business. It was in Bourne and Shepherd's London studio and that photograph I set beside the picture of Annie Oakley on my wall.

Practice makes perfect, Annie had said somewhere, and I took her at her word. Weekends I'd walk out of the city and me and Henry would take turns shooting at a target carved into the trunk of a tree. Week after week and month upon month and no heed to the weather. Henry promised to pay for every shot that he made. We agreed on a price and I kept a tally of his account in a pocket notebook. It soon amounted to more than he could afford and I was beginning to make a noise over what he owed me. We fell out about it one dark sky Sunday and with my factory-made Winchester 1873 Henry shot me dead and tore the page from my pocket-book.

CHAPTER SIXTEEN

Mr John Hansen was off his work again. The fall from his horse a year before had not left him strong. There was a deeper grayness in him too, as though age had come upon him suddenly, and he was a shadow of himself or a ghost. He moved slowly now, as though each step was a great effort or a great pain; and he spoke in whispers, all his words reduced to few and full of wheeze and breath.

'It's time, John,' his wife said to him, and she said it to him often so that it had lost the gentleness that it once held and the words came out spat and jagged. 'It's time,' she said, by which she meant he should stop his work at the great house.

Of course, she was right. He knew that. But there was also a reason to keep going, something hidden, a reason for being there. He was less certain of what that was and could not have put it into words, but he kept going.

When he was there, in the great house, almost all his time was spent with Sarah – Mrs Winchester, if they were not alone. Some days they sat for hours in her sitting-room, their chairs close and touching and the words between them were all hers and she laid before him her plans for the further reaching of the house and all the rooms that were still to be. Some days she fussed over him and called him John and ordered tea and cake for them both; and she took his hand some days –

allowed herself to – and it was like something dreamed so that after it had happened and she had withdrawn her hand again, he was not sure it had been and nor was she.

'It's time,' said his wife when he could not pull himself from his bed, hard though he tried. The doctor had shook his head and said there was nothing to be done. John should rest was all the prescription he had and he shook his head again, knowing that a man who has worked all his days does not take easily to such medication.

Up at the Winchester House they sometimes walked as before, Mr John Hansen and Mrs Sarah Winchester, John and Sarah, walked along dead-end corridors, and down flights of stairs that had a shallow rise and went nowhere, and into rooms that still wanted finishing. She talked of what was needed here and what there, breathless and excited, and he listened, hearing her words as though they were a long way off, as though he was listening to her through a wall. He nodded and pretended he had heard every small detail, and they moved on to the next floor, seeming to creep as one creature; these days Mrs Sarah Winchester supported *him* and that was just fine.

Work progressed in the house, and sometimes they found themselves a long distance from Sarah's living-room, wandering in strange places, up staircases that they knew only from drawings she had made on linen napkins or into rooms that were familiar only as sketches on the backs of envelopes or down twisting passageways that they neither of them knew or recognized.

They laughed then and felt the small thrill of being lost together, like children when they hide under bedclothes and become so tangled that they are trapped and their wilder imaginations think they might never break free from those knotted blankets and a small and rising panic overtakes them. She took his hand then and said his name and once she kissed his cheek and held him close. Only the resumption of hammering and sawing in a nearer part of the building broke their reverie and they fell from each other as though they had been caught about some mischief.

'It's time!'

But for John it was not yet time and he could not tell his wife why it was not.

When he was not there, all those days stacked up against each other so that sometimes they were weeks, Mrs Winchester kept to her room and to her bed. Her meals were brought up to her and set at the dining table with all the usual ceremony and she sat alone and picked over her food, staring at the far end of the table as though there was something there that held her attention or something missing or lost.

These days, these missing-Mr-John-Hansen days when she did not really eat, the cook was cross and it were best to be out of her way, beyond the reach of her soup ladle, and her sharp tongue.

'Picks at her food like a bird, and a small chit of a bird, and what does that say to me who has worked her fingers to the bone making her meal?'

The cook was worried, too, though she never could have said it in so many words. Not just the cook: the footman, who had grown far beyond his once 'junior' and was now almost as sure as a man called Jack had been before he had returned east, this footman was also worried, and he frequently asked Mrs Winchester if she wished him to call for the doctor and he was certain that the doctor would not consider it any trouble to make good a visit to her just to be sure.

The boy who set the fires – and he was really now a man with a beard and thinning hair, – was worried too. He said that 'up there' was so airless and so dry, by which he meant in Mrs Winchester's rooms. He said she needed to open the curtains and windows so she could breathe and so he could, too. And he said when he saw her that she was pale as milk fresh pulled from the teat, and she was as thin as sticks.

'Is Mr John Hansen in today?' Mrs Winchester said to her maid. 'Send someone to see if he's on his way, I have matters to discuss with him pertaining to the building work on the seventh floor. There's something that troubles me about the work and only Mr Hansen can give me the necessary assurances that it will all be fine. See if he's here.'

The maid informed the footman and a boy was dispatched to the rise in the road to see if Mr John Hansen's cart was making its way across the valley and Mr John Hansen sitting up front huddled under a thick blanket and his head nodding and his hands holding the reins limply and a quiet clicking of his tongue to tell the horse to get a move on.

Then there was a squabble as to who should take the news upstairs or who should not. If Mr Hansen was on his way, then there would be a smile and a blessing from Mrs Winchester; if he was not, then might there be a scowl and was once a curse, and the color of the rest of that day was determined in that moment.

Once, on his return to work after a week's absence, he seemed in better spirits, as though the old Mr John Hansen inhabited himself again. He walked a little straighter and his voice was a little louder and he arrived at the house bearing gifts – a deep basket of apples picked from his own orchard, not windfall apples but plucked from the tree and wrapped in straw and each apple polished to a red glassy shine. He had them taken up to Mrs Winchester at first and her whole room smelled sweet and she kept them with her and smiled and asked him how he was and if he was better and, of course, she could see that he was.

'You do not need to bring me gifts when you come back to work, John. It's enough for me that you are well and you are here.'

All the windows were flung open and Mrs Winchester appeared flushed and was not so pale and she seemed to almost dance from room to room. The boy who set the fires took this knowledge back to the kitchen and the cook set aside her ladle and went at her cooking with a new vigor, and the footman's brow lost its crease and he went about his business with a lighter step, and all the house seemed to be singing and whistling, and even the hammering and the sawing seemed to be in tune.

But Mr John Hansen was off his work again soon enough and so the house was not singing or whistling and the hammers seemed to snap and bark and the saws cut the air into sharps and flats and there was a different broken music to everything.

'Send word to Mr John Hansen that he is not to concern himself with matters at the house, but must look to make himself better first,' said Mrs Winchester before she returned to her bed for the morning.

'It is time,' said John Hansen's wife. 'See how you are today, how you cannot even rise from the bed, and your face all pinched and punched with the pain of it. It's time, John Hansen, and it's God who tells you this in a hundred different ways, and you must listen to what He says.'

John nodded and tried to turn in his bed, but the effort was too great and his wife mistook his signals and helped him into a sitting position when it was sleep that he wished for.

'You have stood by her long enough, John. More than duty has been served. And we have a penny or two set by, enough that will take the pair of us to our graves, and now we are old we should sit back and measure the days and be looked after by our children as is the way of these things.'

John nodded again and closed his eyes.

'It is time, John.'

She was right, of course. It was time he called it a day. His wife was not alone in saying it, and they were all right, his grown-up children and his neighbors and some of the men he'd worked with before and they'd quit working and sat now with their feet up. It's time: that's what he felt on the days when he could not bring himself from his own bed, that it *was* time, time that he passed the responsibilities at the Winchester House to some other man; but there was no-one in particular that he thought to hand the job to. There was no-one that he had yet trained up, no-one he had prepared for the task. The truth is that he had thought to always be working there and always be deeper and deeper in Mrs Winchester's affections – Sarah.

'John?'

'It *is* time, wife,' he said, and he let her make a to-do over him and she was gentle again and laughing and saying how it would be from now on and what he had to look forward to and the days moving slow as molasses poured from a jug or slow as a river when it is lazy and meandering, and sweet as ripe apples those days and nothing to trouble either of them ever again.

Then, when he was strong enough, he was on his feet again, and some color had returned to him, his thoughts strayed back to the Winchester House and to Mrs Sarah Winchester. He pictured himself sitting beside her in her sitting-room and listening to her airy plans for the greater enlargement of her house, and sometimes she was touching his hand, taking his hand in hers, and he felt as though he was sitting on top of the world then, and once she kissed him – at least he thinks she did, and so in his head she did so over and over – and was that not God speaking also, he thought, though what exactly was being said Mr John Hansen could not decide.

'But you said, John. You said it is time. We agreed.'

He nodded and climbed stiffly up onto the front seat of his cart, gave the reins a light shake, clicked his tongue against the roof of his mouth, and the horse set off at a slow-plodding walk back along the track towards the Winchester House. And Mrs John Hansen shook her head and she sighed and she asked for God to please look after her husband this day.

Room 117

The Winchester Gun Club

He don't mind boys takin what's lyin in the grass, 'em as has fallen early, fallen before they's been picked. He don't mind boys takin 'em windfall apples. He says so every year, old man Tucker, sittin on his porch and a Winchester rifle laid across his knees and his cur curled at his feet.

'Jus don't be takin 'em apples as is still on the tree.'

He says *them* apples belongs to him, the pick of 'em does. *His* trees, *his* apples, he says, and the fruits of *his* labors is what he says them apples is. Only Bob don't see it that way. 'It's the tree what's done the laborin,' he says. All old man Tucker's been and done is sittin in the sun watchin the apples ripen, slow as summer days and weeks and months, and sometimes not watchin cos he's sleepin. 'Ain't no laborin in that,' Bob says, and I sees his point. Bob figures that sittin in the sun's the opposite of laborin.

So it's Bob's idea for us to raid old man Tucker's apple trees, one day when the man's back is turned. Bob plans the whole thing. Plans it like we was robbin a bank or a store, all whisper and lookin over his shoulder like he might be heard. And he's made a map of old man Tucker's yard, and he pushes the table to one side and spreads that map out on his kitchen floor. It's a map he drawed hisself and it's a good drawin. I'm impressed. It's got all the apple trees and red dot-apples on the green, and you can see the porch with the curl of a dog at the feet of old man Tucker, and the chair with old man Tucker asleep in it, his head tilted back and his eyes closed but his mouth open. Bob's even drawed a silver-spittle thread trailin from the old man's mouth and I seen it just like that once.

Bob tells us what's what and what will be. He's got it all worked out, the times and the positions.

I says I don't like it none.

Bob thinks I mean the drawin, which I don't cos as I says it was somethin good.

'I don't like the dog,' I says. I don't like nothin to do with dogs. And I sees Bob smilin then, like he's got somethin up his sleeve, which it turns out he has. He's been doin some experimentin with meat and sleepin powders. He shows us a small glass phial and he shakes it so we sees the powder inside. Somethin he stole from his grandpa's veterinary, he says, and he speaks in smaller whispers then, cos he lives with his grandpa now, see. Three years he's lived with him on account of Bob's ma bein in the ground since the day he was born and his pa bein away jus for now. And Bob tells us how old man Tucker's dog will be sleepin like a baby – only I still ain't so sure, cos I heard babies cryin fit to burst and I knows they's usually awake when they's should be sleepin.

Then Bob asks if maybe I's chicken or somethin, and I ain't chicken, no ways. So I agrees to go along with his plan. And we does it, jus like Bob said. Old man Tucker's cur gets a free meal, meat that Bob stole from his grandpa's fridge and it's been stuffed full of his grandpa's sleepin powder. 'Enough to fell a horse,' Bob says, 'or enough it could fell a cow, or a herd of cows, and then some.' And sure as eggs is eggs, old man Tucker's cur is felled and it's sleepin like no baby ever slept before. You could fart in its face and it wouldn't do no more'n sniff in its dreams.

And old man Tucker, well he's sleepin too, jus like in Bob's drawin, and I reckon Bob's put some powder in somethin the old man's been drinkin. The light is goin down and we sneaks about, hunched like the sky is pressin heavy on us from above, and we picks all the apples we can reach from old man Tucker's trees. Strippin 'em bare as near as. Bob's got old sacks, the smell of dead leaves on 'em, and we fills those sacks so they's hard to carry and lumpy with apples. And we gets a bit silly then. Laughin and singin, y'know. And that's our undoin, see. Cos old man Tucker wakes then and yells into the dark where we is and kicks his no-good cur and he pumps a shell into the chamber of his gun. And we's only laughin all the harder. And that's our greater undoin.

'I knows you, Bob Frankel,' hollers old man Tucker. 'I knows you anywheres, even in the dark, jus like your pa. And you'll get what's comin to you, boy, I'll see you do. You'll get jus what your no-good pa got. Cos there's a wall someplace with your name scratched above a metal-frame bed, and that bed in a prison cell dark as shoe-black and smellin of piss, and it's jus waitin.'

And then we ain't none of us laughin no more and I says we should take the sacks of apples and leave 'em on the old man's porch. And Bob spits into the grass and says he ain't afeard of old man Tucker and his threats.

'The apple don't never fall far from the tree, Bob Frankel, and I knows it's you out there.'

Then old man Tucker starts shootin and shootin into the dark, and jerkin the lever action of his rifle, and shootin again, and he misses more than he hits, but he hits, too.

CHAPTER SEVENTEEN

On the 18th April, 1906 at about 5.13 in the morning, the earth shook. The people of California were quite used to this, the juddering of the ground beneath their feet, just for a moment, and the shaking of clocks from their walls, or books falling from high shelves, or cutlery rattling in drawers and glasses leaping from tables, or church bells set to ringing for no reason. They lived with the threat that roof tiles might work themselves loose in ones and twos and be thrown down from the sky, or telegraph poles might one morning lean a little more crookedly than before or be fallen across the street and the day would be stopped and lost in the setting of things back to straight again. This sort of movement they were used to. But at 5.13 on the 18th April 1906, it was different.

Afterwards church ministers said it was as though the hand of the Old Testament God had crashed down on California in its sleep and the city of San Francisco woke and was startled and mightily crushed, and everywhere was destruction.

For a full minute the world shook, though at the time it didn't seem it would ever stop. It felt like the end times as foretold somewhere in scripture and for so many it was. Had the stars fallen from heaven, every one of them, it would have been no surprise but simply the fulfillment of some overlooked prophecy.

The wind roared as if it had teeth and shout in it, and strong men knelt and prayed, and women kept their children near, and buildings that had stood for years toppled like far-gone drunks or old men without their sticks. Mountains moved out of their place and leapt to be closer to each other, rivers bucked their paths, trees were uprooted everywhere, and there was devastation throughout the state. Afterwards, fires burned for days, and the people scurried hither and thither like ants when a nest is broken. The rest of the world woke and read about it in their newspapers, and everyone looked for answers to 'why?' and 'why now?' and 'why there?'

In San Jose the churches fell, not one or two, but four, church bells cracked, and churchmen rose up from the ruins and called on all the town's sinners to repent of their sins before God, and the people lifted up their voices with greater heart than before and the air was thicker with song and with prayers. Trains could not run, for in places the tracks were buckled and it was as though the flat land had been as water and had rippled outwards and everything had taken a new shape. At Agnews the State Insane Asylum collapsed and the mad were killed or unleashed on the community, and doctors and nurses lay with their limbs unnaturally splayed, looking like discarded and broken dolls in the rubble.

Mrs Sarah Winchester was awake. She had slept fitfully. The noise of the horses trampling in the stables had woken her perhaps, or the lowing of cattle in the fields, or the shifting and shrinking of the house as the air cooled. She afterwards told John it was the voices that woke her. A hundred or a thousand voices all raised against the name of Winchester and all crying out for vengeance for the wrong that was done to them. She told all this to John and it was the first that she had told anyone these things.

She opened the curtains just before 5.13 expecting to see the sun creeping into the new day, but everywhere it was dark and the moon bled in the sky. That is what she said to Mr John Hansen: 'It bled and the stars were not in the sky and I knew it was come.'

Then was a rushing sound in the Santa Clara Valley, as of a snarling wind or an army that runs at the enemy with every man yelling. The whole valley shook, and Mrs Winchester fell to the floor and all around her the house trembled as though it would fall also, and somewhere behind her floors collapsed and walls folded in on themselves and rooms that were complete were undone and what had taken years to construct was pulled apart.

'Oh, John, it was a warning. Don't you see? I have been too light in these last years, and too gay, and too taken up with… unserious things. So they have come to punish me and to warn me of my duty here.'

John Hansen had come as soon as he could and much against his wife's entreaties to stay at home on this terrible day.

'What reason would there be for you to be about on a day such as this? John, this is a day for being with your family and for prayers and for taking stock.'

But John Hansen was in earnest.

From a way off he could see that the Winchester House had suffered damage and much of the seventh floor was gone and a hundred windows that had once glinted in the sunlight were now blind and a hundred more squinted at him. The staff were gathered in consternation outside and the cook swore that she would not re-enter the building, 'not for love nor for any sum of money'. The greater worry was that Mrs Winchester was trapped in her bedroom and not yet rescued.

Mrs Sarah Winchester could not be easily reached by John Hansen and the rest of the workmen. A staircase had collapsed and doors had jammed themselves shut and nothing inside seemed to be where it should be.

She was badly shaken by the time that John secured her room and her safety, and all her words were afterwards set in that context and read as the ravings of one in shock and no sense to be given to what she said.

'Always there are voices and I lock them away in rooms and they are quiet again. But then there are new voices and so I must continue with the building of the house; and last night... last night a hundred or a thousand voices, more than could be contained in a room or a hall, shouted so loud that the house shook and fell, and I thought I should be made deaf with such a shouting or that the house would fall down on me and I should be buried here today.'

Mr John Hansen had Mrs Winchester carried to another part of the house and made comfortable there. Then he set about the business of putting things back into some kind of order and so did not have much time with Mrs Winchester but left her in the care of her maid.

All new work was suspended and men were dispatched to shore up walls or to dismantle whole floors or to assess how a crack might be repaired or a window straightened or a flight of stairs be unbuckled and made good again. The morning and much of the afternoon was whittled away in such matters and everywhere there was hammering and sawing again and the crashing and splitting of wood and the crumbling of stone as it fell.

Eventually the cook was persuaded back to her kitchen, though she kept looking at the walls and the ceiling, and hushing everyone to quiet around her so she could better listen to the house and what it might be saying to her, as if there were words and messages hidden in each creak and crack and groan.

The boy who set the fires, and who was lately become the man who set the fires, was given new instructions and new places to visit and new fires to set. Each chimney had to be inspected first and pronounced good and safe. The man who set the fires was lighter on his feet that day and for many a day after, wanting to be lighter than the boy he had been before, creeping as a thief creeps, moving on tip-toe and moving slow for fear that a heavier tread and a quicker one might bring further dislocation to the house and set in motion the falling of another floor, as with a tower of playing cards and the moving of one card can occasion the bringing down of the whole structure.

Later in the day, when the dust had settled, as they commonly say, Mr John Hansen stopped and took tea with Mrs Winchester in her new sitting-room. She was pale and agitated and her hands were like birds in her lap and their wings flapping in fright and never still.

He looked for something to say that might soothe her and assure her that all would now be well, but she kept her attention on the voices and the wrong she had done and the way that she might make amends and put things right again. Mr John Hansen made so bold as before and he put one hand over hers, to still those frighted birds, and he spoke softly to her and called her by her name.

'Sarah,' he said. Just that and no more, and yet everything was in that 'Sarah', all that had been between them of late and all that John felt for her and that had made him in earnest to be with her on this day when he should have been with his family.

For a moment everything was still, as though he had indeed brought calm to her thinking, as though this had been all that she had needed.

'Dear,' he further ventured.

She stiffened and there were tears on her cheek and she pushed his hand away, not ungently but firm. She got to her feet and began walking the floor.

'No more 'John', or walking arm in arm, or kisses where no-one can see, or wishing and dreaming, or you and I dancing in the ballroom in the middle of the day. No more. From here it must be 'Mr Hansen' again and 'Mr John Hansen' sometimes, and not alone together but always in the company of my maid, and no more waiting at windows for you to ride into the yard, and no more writing your name on scrap paper and burning it in the fire so only I know it. No, such way is madness and it does anger them to see me happy. I do not deserve to be so happy, not with a name such as Winchester. Don't you see?'

Mr John Hansen urged her to be seated again and to take tea with him, for where was the harm in drinking tea. She paced the floor and she wrung her hands and muttered under her breath, words that made less sense for being so broken and misheard.

'Please, Mrs Winchester, please be seated. Your tea grows cold.'

She stopped then and she looked at the man before her as if she did not know him, as though he was a stranger to her and they had just been introduced. Or maybe she looked through him, as though he wasn't really there, as if he might be a figment of her imagination or something less substantial than that.

'Please,' he said, indicating the empty chair opposite him.

Mrs Winchester sat down and was quiet for a moment. All was quiet, save for the fizzing of a bee at the closed window and that trapped bee yearning to be on the other side of the glass where sky was and orchard trees in blossom, even those that had fallen, and birds finding their voices once more and all the world finding its feet again.

'I had a daughter once,' said Mrs Winchester, and her voice was as small as a child's and wavering. 'Her name was Annie and she was all the world to me and all the world was there for her asking. Then I lost my Annie and she never can be found in this world again, except sometimes I think I hear her voice carried on the air, or there is a smell that catches up with me and it is the smell of her, or when I enter a room there is something that leaves it and I catch just a glimpse of that something and I think maybe it is the hem of Annie's dress or the heel of her shoe.'

Mr Hansen had not heard her talk of her child before, though he knew the story or such as it is when it is told below stairs and has more of the cook and the maid in it than the truth. He shifted uneasily in his chair and did not know what to say.

'Not so much lost, Mr Hansen, as taken from me and her father taken after. I am left alone now, Mr Hansen, and that is as it must be. And this house must continue to be built and new plans for new rooms drawn up and the voices in my head… the voices brought to quiet and to peace.'

At the end of what she had to say, Mrs Winchester sat a little straighter in her chair and a little taller for that; Mr John Hansen, as if for balance, sat a little smaller in his chair and his breath came in shorter and shorter gasps and he sipped his tea and did not know where to look or what to say.

'It is time, Mr Hansen.'

He nodded and did not move, not immediately.

On the 18th April, 1906 at about 5.13 in the morning the whole of the valley and the whole of the world shook and, when it was done with its shaking, California woke changed and it would never be the same again. Fires burned for several days and in the newspapers the number of the dead kept rising, and church bells were felled and silent, and there was singing and praying in the streets, and everywhere rats spread disease, and the mad spoke common sense and the sane were temporarily mad. And Mrs Sarah Winchester drank tea with her foreman for the last time and gave orders for the sealing up of the great ballroom; and when all that was done, Mrs John Hansen had a husband returned to her and he never was again at the Winchester House.

Room 125

The Winchester Gun Club

If it hadn't been a Winchester 1866 carbine, it would have been something else – a stolen Krnka breech-loader or a captured bolt-action Berdan Cossack rifle. I don't hold him responsible, the boy with his brass-plate Winchester repeater pointed at me. He was just doing a job, a man's job, and little wonder then that the boy's hands shook and his teeth chattered. He was probably more scared than I: after all, not only had we more numbers, but the Turks were dug in and going nowhere. I remember his moon-white face, and how he wasn't steady on his feet.

It was at Plevna, a place that was nothing and not known before this battle. Osman Pasha had lesser forces but they were well-armed thanks to American-manufactured rifles from the Winchester Repeating Arms Company.

The morning before the battle, Evgeny said he had a presentiment of disaster. He said he had dreamed of a great bear and it had stumbled upon a hornet's nest and straightway it set about tearing the nest into so many pieces as bears are wont to do. But in Evgeny's dream the hornets flew at the bear in such numbers and their stings were sore and so they drove the bear away and their nest was saved.

Oleg said he'd had a different dream and the girl in his dream had tits as soft as pillows and Oleg scratched at his crotch when he told us what he'd done with his dream harlot and we all laughed and thought no more of what Evgeny had said.

There was some singing before the battle, a thousand voices raised as one, and some slapping of backs and some joking in smaller circles. I knelt and clutched at my breast my copy of the Holy Book and I spoke with God and prayed for a safe end to the day and for goodness and virtue.

As we waited for our orders to advance, Pavel speculated on what we'd be enjoying for supper this evening, and Stepan said he'd be content if there was a bath to make himself clean and water hot as soup and maybe soap too and a girl to scrub his back. Yury said he'd give a day's wages for a bed to sleep in and clean sheets and blankets and his boots standing to attention by the bed and his clothes folded on the back of a chair. With Yury's talk of beds, Oleg was back to telling us about the woman with tits soft as pillows and he licked his fingers and made more of his lewd dream.

But the day held many surprises and the battle was not so easily won as we had expected. They had American rifles and their bullets flew past our heads as fast as hornets in a rage and sometimes they stung. I saw Oleg dropping to the ground with blood running from his mouth and his eyes closed as though he might be dreaming. Evgeny fell awkwardly as though he was dancing and he was the bear in his own dream. Maybe Pavel fell also, and I thought of the supper he had hoped for and now would never see.

Then I was of a sudden face to face with the fright-eyed Turk boy and his rifle pointed in my direction and his hands shaking. I think I smiled and would have spoken, except my words were slow in coming. And the boy pulled the trigger and his rifle jerked against his shoulder and jerked again, so hard I saw the boy wince and I knew there must be a bruise under his shirt, and I heard the angry fizzing of hornets past my ears and I thought that God was watching over me. I lifted my old Krnka rifle and careful was my aim and steady. And the boy swore at his bad shooting and he wrenched at the lever action again and fired again and again and again.

I do not blame the boy for the hornet sting that brought me down before I could fire my own rifle. He was just doing a job. It was not his fault. He wanted no more to be there on the front line of Plevna than I did. If he hadn't shot me, I would have shot him. But the name of Winchester is ever a curse in my mouth, even now, and in the mouths of thousands that died that day.

CHAPTER EIGHTEEN

The new man had no softness to him and he huffed and scowled when Mrs Winchester showed him her new sketches and her altered plans. He pointed out the short-comings with what she had put onto paper or onto cloth and he scratched his head and looked puzzled and at a loss as to how to proceed.

'You must ask Mr Hansen, he would know what to do,' she said, and that was all the mention she ever gave to Mr Hansen. It was something like a rebuke to the new man and he understood it as such.

At first he did precisely as Mrs Winchester instructed: he called on Mr and Mrs Hansen at the end of the day and presented them with Mrs Winchester's drawings, laid out the problem he had in carrying out what she wanted, and asked if Mr Hansen could help in any way.

John Hansen pored over each of the sketches with all the fierceness of study that he was wont to do before. Indeed, his scrutiny was all the greater for him not being there to oversee the work. But it was also as though he was looking for something in what Mrs Winchester had drawn, some hidden message in the angles and trajectories of this line or that, some word meant for only him and concealed in the twist of the staircase or the slant of the roof or the height of a column. But though there were no such messages, the fancy stayed with him, and he offered up a swift solution and sank a little further into quiet and reflection while his wife fussed over the new man.

The new man attended to everything that John Hansen told him. He considered the offered solution and nodded his head and stared into the drawing Mrs Winchester had made as if the solution that had just been given was somehow there all along and he had simply missed it. He learned much from these brief consultations and gradually he needed the help of Mr John Hansen less and less.

'You must ask Mr Hansen, he would know what to do,' said Mrs Winchester impatiently whenever the new man scratched his head and looked confused, but the new man slowly started solving the puzzle by himself. He sometimes took the drawing away to an empty room in the house and, pacing the floor, asked himself what Mr Hansen might do, spoke the words out loud as if he was with company; and sometimes the answer fell on him as sudden as a shot bird drops out of the sky. Other times he walked about for a day or so with the problem in his head and at moments when he least expected it, when he was about some other business and not really thinking of the problem at all, the solution would appear before him in all its brief gleaming simplicity. He took to always keeping a scrap of paper near him and the stub of a pencil in his pocket or by his bed, so that he might scribble the details down before they were nothing again and out of his reach.

On his return to work, he would knock on the door of Mrs Winchester's living-room and, when the maid answered, he said, in words that were as rough as stone and as sharp as bradawls and awls, that he wished to speak with her lady.

'I have no interest in what the solution is,' said Mrs Winchester. 'I am content that it can be carried out as I requested. And it must be thirteen steps, that I insist upon, and thirteen doors in the corridor, and thirteen windows, too.'

The new man had once made the mistake of asking why it should be exactly as she had drawn it, why it could not be a different number and so make more sense, or the door be in a different place, or the stairs turning anti-clockwise, or the fireplace set at another angle.

'It was never the custom of Mr Hansen to pose such questions. *He* understood.'

It was another rebuke, and something else, too, something that the new man did not understand. He nodded his head and drew breath and held it in the swollen purse of his cheeks before letting it go. Then he quietly got up from his chair and, with the drawing clutched in his hand and a newer puzzle in his head, left the room.

Over time, the new man learned what to say and what not to say. He more and more kept to himself the problems he saw in her designs and more and more he solved them in quiet moments when no-one was by. In this way the building work settled back into a regular pattern and proceeded pretty well as before – though after the great earthquake the house no longer reached upwards so ambitiously as once was the case, but spread further and further outwards, rooms crowding round rooms and a thousand windows flashing in the setting sun so that the Winchester House seemed sometimes to be aflame.

Mrs Winchester, dressed as always in mourning black, kept close company with no-one. Her maid, a surly and stunted woman who seldom spoke, sat in a stiff-backed chair near the door to the outer sitting-room. She was instructed to admit no-one unless given specific permission to do so by Mrs Winchester. She sat in a corner and worked on a piece of embroidery, picking and unpicking the stitches so that it never seemed to be much more than it was when it started, and so her head was always bent over her needle and thread; when there was a knock at the door, she lifted her head with a look on her face as one who does not at first know where they are or what has just happened. Then she answered the door and, keeping the visitor waiting outside, took the message through to Mrs Winchester sitting at table in the inner sitting-room.

'Excuse me ma'am, a gentleman at the door wishes that he might have a word or two with you.'

There was usually a card to let Mrs Winchester know the identity of the caller and from this she could sometimes infer the nature of the word or two that they wished to have with her and she could pre-empt the conversation by her response and so deflect the need for a meeting.

'It is the same gentleman as before and he begs his pardon in calling again but it is important.'

The card said it was the Reverend Ernesto Barrio who had called and he wished only to talk with Mrs Winchester, something about the proposal for a new church to replace the one that had been lost in the earthquake a year back.

Mrs Winchester made a small donation written as a check, and sent it back with her maid.

That would have been the end of the matter as it so often was when callers at the Winchester House came seeking some financial assistance for some worthy project or other, a new house for the poor, or a temperance shelter, or an extension to the asylum at Agnews. The donation was a little more than the Reverend Ernesto Barrio might have expected and so that should have been the happy end of it; but it was not.

'A word is all that I require, it's just that I have been visited in a dream and there's something I am charged to say to Mrs Winchester.'

This further message was relayed back to Mrs Winchester in as few words as the maid could break it down to.

'He has something to tell you. Something he dreamed. Wishes a word in person.'

Mrs Winchester sighed and waved her hand in the air and turned her attention back to the book she was reading.

The Reverend Ernesto Barrio was sent away.

It was about the same time the next day when the same message as before was delivered by the maid to Mrs Winchester seated in her inner sitting-room.

'It is the Reverend who called yesterday.'

Mrs Winchester looked up from her accounts, on which figures stood on top of each other and with everything carefully balanced until this interruption sent everything tumbling on the page. She set down the pen and unbent the fingers of her right hand, one at a time, using the fingers of her left hand to do so.

'Does he intend to call every day? Does he not have things to see to with the building of his new church? Does he need to be disturbing me so regularly?'

The maid was not sure if in these questions there was some communication that she was instructed to deliver to the young Reverend waiting at the door. She shuffled from foot to foot and looked flustered and a little befuddled.

'If it please you, ma'am,' she said, and neither of them knew what she intended by this.

The Reverend was sent away again, though this time the maid was gentle in her delivery of this directive and she thanked him for calling and she smiled at the young man and said how he might call again tomorrow if he had a mind to and that she at least would be pleased to see him. There were more words spoken by the maid then than had been spoken in a week of Sundays before and her customary surliness seemed to have unaccountably left her.

The Reverend Ernesto Barrio *did* call as the maid had suggested and he smiled and gave her his card, and she once more took his message in to Mrs Winchester.

She was busy arranging cut meadow flowers – Bailey's buckwheat, slender cotton weed, deerbrush and lupine – in a blue glass vase.

'It's the Reverend, ma'am.'

Mrs Winchester sighed and a small knot of irritation formed on her brow.

'Does he think it seemly and proper to be so pestering a gentlewoman? Has he forsaken his manners? Does he not understand that I have no wish to hear about his dreams or any of his Sunday sermons or to have his polite good-days? Does he not know how to behave?'

This time the maid was aware enough to perceive that there was no message in Mrs Winchester's questions. She did, instead, venture to speak further and this was so new an event that it caught the attention of Mrs Winchester far more than the calling card that the maid had placed on the table beside the other three.

'If it so please you, ma'am,' – again with her 'so please you' – 'I might enquire further on your behalf as to the import of his message.'

The maid spoke the words as though she had rehearsed them, as though she had been turning them over and over in her head since yesterday's visit and now had them to heart and had them right.

Mrs Winchester waved one gloved hand in the air and returned to the cutting of her flowers. From this dismissive gesture the maid decided that she could do as had been suggested, that she might ask of the Reverend Ernesto Barrio something of the nature of his message for Mrs Winchester.

The maid returned some short minutes later and she was, it seemed, back to her taciturn self.

'Annie,' was all that she said, but it was enough to bring Mrs Winchester up short. She set down her secateurs and took off her gloves and sat down to catch her breath.

After some short time had passed and Mrs Winchester had recovered herself, she nodded to the maid and so the Reverend Ernesto Barrio was admitted to the inner sitting-room and the maid told to wait beyond the door.

He was young, as the maid had said that he was, but he was younger than Mrs Winchester had calculated and at first she did not know what she should say. He was tall and a little stooped. His features were fine and sharp and angled as though he had been cut from stone.

'Mrs Winchester?'

She bowed her head and waited for him to continue.

'Manners dictate that I should first thank you for the donation to the rebuilding of our church, the Church of Five Wounds in San Jose. It is most generous of you. Second, I thank you for letting me speak with you today and my apologies for so pestering you on the matter these past few days.'

'To the point, Reverend Barrio, please,' said Mrs Winchester, and there was a shake in her voice.

He cleared his throat with a short cough, as though he was about to make a small speech, the folded fist of one hand to his mouth and his head bent forward like the craning neck of a blue heron when it thinks it might have a fish in its view.

'I have had a dream, Mrs Winchester.'

She gave no response to this, other than to seem interested in his continuing.

'The one dream, and it visits me night after night, and this dream only since coming here to San Jose. The dream is full of music and angels singing and bells ringing and all the host of Heaven lifted up in one great hosanna.'

He paused then, perhaps for the sake of heightening the dramatic intent of what came next, or perhaps because what he had said had come out of him in a breathless rush.

'And in the arms of one of the angels was a child and her name was Annie.'

Mrs Winchester sank back in her chair with her hand over her mouth, sucking the air and blowing it, as though she had been hit. The maid was called for and the Reverend Ernesto Barrio was hurried from the room. He made his apologies for so upsetting Mrs Winchester and left the house asking if he might call again another day.

The next day, and the days and weeks after, some further enquiries were secretly made as to the character of this new Reverend of the Church of Five Wounds, where he had completed his training and what was his experience before coming to San Jose. Letters were sent here, there and everywhere, and from such replies as were received Mrs Winchester was able to piece together the substance of the man. It was discovered that the Reverend Ernesto Barrio had with his story of angels and a dead child carried in the arms of one of those angels, and all of heaven singing and only the name that the child bore altered, approached several other wealthy widows in the state and each of them had, after hearing the story, made bigger and more generous their donations to the building of the new church; and it was learned, too, that not all the money collected went to the purchasing of wood and stone and nails, nor to the paying of craftsmen's wages or to the keeping of the poor.

Mrs Winchester was not so easily fooled as the Reverend Ernesto Barrio had supposed, and so the Church of Five Wounds received not a penny more of her charity, not even when, at Mrs Winchester's request behind closed doors, the Reverend Ernesto Barrio was removed and replaced by an older man who proved his goodness by his many visits to the poor.

It was at times like these that Mrs Winchester felt keenly the sacrifice she had made in letting Mr John Hansen go, and she missed him then the most, for without him there was no-one she could talk to about what had just happened – about what was in her head and her heart. She could not talk with her maid or her footman, and certainly not with the new man who so efficiently oversaw the continuing work on the Winchester House; and so she talked to no-one .

Room 130

The Winchester Gun Club

It was Ben's idea. He said he knew a place. He'd been watching it for weeks. It was a short way above the town. A knot of trees with their black fingers clawing the sky and thousands of red-winged blackbirds roosted there. Be like shooting fish in a barrel, Ben said.

I wasn't sure. My pop thought red-winged blackbirds were each one a gift from God, and all of nature the same. He'd have been mad if he had known.

We set out under the cover of Friday night. No moon was in the sky, just rolling clouds and a scowling dark. There was Ben and Fritz and Tilly and me. We slipped over back fences, quiet as shadows and as quick, not daring to step into the street out front where the yellow of porch-lights made pools of brightness that might reveal us. Ben led the way and he brought us after him with whispers and his free hand tugging at our sleeves if we lagged behind.

Up out of the town we crept, till we were clear of the houses and there was no more need for quiet. Tilly dared to ask why we were doing this. She said it seemed silly somehow. Pointless. Well, Ben threw a hissing fit. He said she was just a girl and she could go back if she was scared. Tilly said it wasn't that. Then Ben told her to 'fuck off', punching the air with his words. I laughed. I shouldn't have, but Ben saying those words, it seemed kind of silly. Like they didn't fit in his mouth. Like he was playing at being bigger than he was.

We might have stood there all night, except Fritz spoke. He said there was a storm coming and we'd better get a move on. He was right, too. The wind was picking up; 'carrying the moans of dead soldiers on the air' – that's what my mom would say if she was there. I don't know why ever she said that.

So we pressed on and walked a while in silence again, feeling the wind pushing us forward, and the sky seeming to fall on our heads. I thought of Chicken Licken and I laughed again, to myself this time.

It was just as Ben had described when we got there, except the noise of the trees as they thrashed about. Ben said we should load up and we'd fire on his count. Just fire into the air, he said, into the trees above our heads. We'd be sure to hit something, even Tilly would. There were thousands of them, the trees seeming to be full-leafed when they were really winter-bare.

Like fish in a barrel, Ben said again. And I was on the side of Tilly then and what she'd said before about not really knowing why we were there doing what we were doing.

Suddenly there was a jagged blue white flash of lightning and we fired as one, or nearly as one, into the sky, into the tree, and one or two birds fell heavy in the dark around us, and thunder rolled over us grumbling and groaning. We reloaded several times and got off several more shots before the rain began falling – great gobs of rain mixed with stinging hail and the air cold as clouds. Then there was a new sound, a beating sound, the noise of a thousand thousand feet scuffing out of church, and it was like the air was being sucked from where we were, and Tilly screamed, and Ben said 'fuck' again and this time I did not laugh.

We ran all the way back to town, as fast as we could in the dark of that breathless night, over the wind-knotted dead grass and the wet tangle of fallen ferns. Tilly lost her footing, as did Fritz and Ben. I must have fallen, too, and there was a flash of lightning in the dark and thunder drumming and Ben shouted out 'He's hit' and he meant me – but it wasn't lightning or thunder; it was a shot from a gun as I fell: Tilly's or Fritz's, Ben's or mine. And like Ben said, I was hit.

The strangest thing happened then, and I don't have an explanation for it. Suddenly there were things falling out of the storm-laden sky, small parcels of feathers and bones, red-winged blackbirds with their wings folded, and they fell onto the roofs of houses and onto the yellow-bright grass lawns out front. They fell everywhere. I thought again of Chicken Licken and the world coming to an end.

Ben kept saying I was all right and that I should 'fucking hang in there'. I wanted to laugh like before, but I couldn't. Tilly was sent to fetch the doctor. Fritz was kneeling beside me praying and crying at the same time, wiping snot and rain and tears onto the sleeve of his shirt.

I told Ben to tell my pop that I was sorry I'd taken his Winchester rifle without asking him. I made Ben swear to tell him, on his mother's life I made him swear, and not say about the birds we had shot, swear – and that was the last that I said.

CHAPTER NINETEEN

She was wont to talk to herself and to read out loud from a book or newspaper as she paced the floor of her room. This happened even more after Mr John Hansen left. Listening at keyholes, her maid noted that it was sometimes to him that she spoke.

'What shall it profit a man if he shall gain the whole world, and lose his own soul? What does that say to me, John, for I had the whole world once – twice, even – and I lost it all both times. And now I fear for my soul in case it might be lost also.'

'Not lost but given away the second time.'

'But you saw how the house suffered and what damage there was and how I now must oversee Mr Michael Harrower and his work in putting things back together again. And worse than houses can be broken and I would rather have given you away than have lost you as I lost those dear to me before.'

The listening maid did not always understand, except that the words held such a sadness in them, and so many words that the maid could not keep hold of them all but only recalled them in fragments.

'It grows warmer again in the Santa Clara Valley, and larkspur and lupins carpet one corner of the view from my window, and the orchards are everywhere in blossom again, and bees and hummingbirds stir, and last night I heard a whippoorwill song playing down at the bottom of the front garden. But still, John, I am troubled by aches and pains in my fingers, some days so badly that I am prevented from doing any small manual thing. Even to hold a pen does occasion me some hurt and I read only a page at a time unless the book can be propped up on the table and my maid charged with turning the page each time that I nod. My legs give me trouble too and I walk, if at all, only short distances, and so there are parts of the house that I have not seen in months and I must trust to this Mr Harrower in a way that sat easier when it was you, John.'

Sometimes there were whole speeches of which the maid could only understand part, though the sighs and silences between Mrs Winchester's words weighed heavy as heartbreak.

'I am informed that you do well enough in your dog days, John – I think they are called 'dog days' when there is nothing much done in them. I send you thanks for the first pick of your apples this year and I declare that they are the sweetest apples in the whole valley; and Mrs Hansen does write to me occasionally to let me know of how things are with you, how you now have the time to be with your grandchildren and what a noise and a commotion is in the house when they are there. You never spoke of your family before, when you were here, and I do now wish that you had, for there is a part of you that I did not have.'

There were indeed sometimes letters from Mrs Hansen, as Mrs Winchester said, and the maid was called upon to read them out to her and not once but several times, slowly enough that she could take in small details, though Mrs Winchester never wrote a reply.

'Last week, John, was the picnic for the children from the orphanage. I do not know how there can be so many lost children in this world. I kept to my room this year, but I watched from my window and it brought a lightness to my day to hear such trilling laughter, and the breathless holler and whoop of so many children. One child asked if she might be brought to see me, which I did allow. She had a clutch of blue and yellow meadow flowers, flax and gilia, and poppies already drooping limp. She made to offer these to me, but I could see that she would rather have kept them to herself. She said she wished to thank me, not just for the picnic but for the dolls in the orphanage, and for the baskets of plums in the autumn and the apricots in jars, and for the dresses in all sizes and in such pretty print patterns, and for the boys' shirts. I think she had been well-rehearsed in what she should say, but she delivered her lines so neatly that I was affected and could say nothing more than 'dear' and 'sweetness' and I held her to me in an embrace that was warm and soft and lingering.

'I am remembered of such an embrace.

'Afterwards she would not let go of my hand and we took a slow and faltering walk to the end of the corridor and back and she talked for the both of us about school and the books that she had read and Mrs Keble, her teacher, and what they would have for tea that night and how she could say her alphabet through from beginning to end and she was only six.'

Not a word sent back to Mrs Hansen, or even to John, not unless what she spoke in her room flew through the air and came to Mr John Hansen on the air as though in a dream.

'I sometimes wonder, John, how different things might have been with me and with the Winchester House if... but the hurt then is greater than the arthritis that plagues my fingers and my knees and so I do not think of it often.'

She spoke of dark things too.

'I read that the Winchester Repeating Arms Company does continue to prosper and I am not sure if that is a good thing or not. The money it has given me serves to keep this house growing and with so many to accommodate I do not see how that could be if the money did not come in. Yet the voices increase in number each day, John, and so I think it's something like a trap that I am caught in – a trap that we are all caught in, though only those of conscience will feel it as such. And it is a trap I wish I might be allowed to escape from.'

Sometimes the maid was so lost in what Mrs Winchester was saying that she shivered and felt as though she was not alone on her side of the door.

'Today the house is a little quieter and so I breathe a little easier and my head is clear and I close my eyes and hear almost no sound, save the crack and spit of wood in the fire and far off the burr of saws at work and the muffled thump of hammers hitting nails. That's as near to quiet as it gets here, as you well know, and I am grateful for these days, though the quiet would be so much easier to bear if you sat with me, John, knowing that when the bell chimes at two tonight there will be an end to the quiet and so many voices crowding into the house and all looking to find me and to torment me – at least I imagine I hear them.'

And the house *was* quieter, for the workmen were far off, employed at the far wings of the spreading house.

'John, I must tell you of some news and I think that you will be cross when you hear and think me foolish and not in full command of my wits. Last month, President Roosevelt himself made so good as to call at the Winchester House. I do not know of what his business was other than that I know he speaks well of the Winchester Repeating Arms Company and has done much to further the company's interests in his recommendations of the Winchester rifle.

'Unfortunately, the front of the house has been sealed off since the great quake, all the rooms and the great ballroom – yes, John, the ballroom where we danced before, or do I imagine that, too? And so I sent word that the President should make his entrance through the back of the house where the servants enter.

'I do not know if he took slight at this request or if time was against him and he was in a rush to be away on some matter of national business or if he changed his mind and thought better of his visit or if indeed it was the President at all and not some other prankster trying to work his way into my company for the better procurement of some charitable donation. Whatever it was, the man at the front door gave

his apologies to the air and left without so much as a card or a message
or any other polite word.

'I have ordered a specially engraved rifle to be boxed and delivered
to the Winchester House. I have instructed that Mr Louis Nimschke be
given the job of engraving the rifle for I do esteem his work to be of
the highest quality at the current time and as such it may be more of
an ornament than a rifle.'

The maid had seen such an order and the instruction that Mr
Nimschke should engrave a pretty hunting scene on the brass plate.
And knowing this much to be true she wondered at the truth of
everything that Mrs Winchester said when she was alone.

'What are we become, John, when Presidents wish to call on us and
make themselves known to us? I think William would have laughed
and said it was not before time and then he would have boasted of it
to all his friends. Instead, it is left to me, and the only person I would
tell is you, and I know you will have scold words for my not answering
the door in person and making something more of his visit. My only
defense is that it was unannounced and not what might be expected
from so fine a President as Mr Roosevelt.'

There *was* a visitor at the front door, and that was true also. And
maybe it was the President and maybe it wasn't. There was talk of it in
the kitchen and no-one was certain one way or the other.

'Enough; the day draws to an end and the sun sinks out of the sky
and I see you a little less clearly, John. The man who sets the fires is busy
in the other room; I can hear the scrape and scrape of his shovel and
the dull thump of a fresh log set to burn and, though he creeps from
place to place, I know he is near for he does have a habit of clearing his
throat in the manner of one who is always about to speak. Enough.'

The maid was by this time gone to her own room, for she had heard
the man who sets the fires coming up behind her and did not want to
be found eavesdropping on Mrs Winchester. She was engaged in her
own brief toilette and was talking to herself or talking with someone

she missed and who was not with her and maybe all people do that sometimes.

Room 133

The Winchester Gun Club

The nights before, he'd sit in the kitchen, his rifle in pieces on the table and he'd be polishing it like it was new. He'd be whistling sometimes and sometimes he'd tell us stories of other hunting trips he'd been on and how he'd once got him a bear as big as two men standing one on the other's shoulder, or once a wolf or a pack of ten, and he had a wolf-tooth necklace that he wore for three days before hunting and three days after just for luck.

The way he told those stories was all roar and fright and like there was drums beating, and between the kills he stretched time and held his breath as we held ours, so long that I was dizzy and almost faint, and Lily, too.

Pa was always the hero of his own stories. Me and my little sister would sit as near as we dared, listening to his every word, and I swear he was a little taller with each telling. And our mom would laugh and shake her head and we'd laugh, too, but only because she did.

'One day, son, it'll be your turn and I'll take you out with me.'

Each year it was the same: 'One day, son, it'll be your turn,' and I couldn't decide if that was what I wanted. I couldn't decide if it was a threat or the promise of something wonderful. How could I be the hero of my Pa's stories? I could not see how that would be.

There was a mark on the wall beside the range, a scratch made with the point of an iron nail in the stone, and he said that the day I measured up to that mark was the day I'd be ready. And he said when the time came he'd buy me a rifle of my own, an 1876 Winchester. He had an order for it down at Markey's Store.

'The 1876 Winchester rifle, first gun that Teddy Roosevelt ever owned, and if it's good enough for Teddy, then it's good enough for you.'

He was talking about the 26th President of the United States and the way he was talking it was like he was a close personal friend and I thought maybe they went hunting together sometimes.

'And maybe you'll bag yourself a deer and make your mom proud.'

Mom said I didn't have to bag no deer for her to be proud of me. It was enough if I did all my chores.

Then came the day and the mark on the kitchen wall was shrunk to my height and I asked my mom if she was sure and I asked her to check again. Pa was true to his word and he got me a rifle, the very same as the President's first gun, and it was engraved on the brass-yellow plate and fancy – a scene of running deer and a hunting dog and all made pretty by tooled scrolling leaves and ribbons. And he showed me how to take it apart and how to clean it and put it back together again. And he showed me how to load it with real bullets and I practiced using the lever action until he was satisfied and my hands hurt. He let me wear the wolf-tooth necklace the night before we went out into the woods and he said it'd maybe bring me luck.

I wasn't much for hunting, I soon decided. It wasn't like in Pa's stories. There were no drums drumming and no roar or fright. Just day upon day of time stretching to unbearable lengths. We were tracking something. Pa showed me the print of a mountain lion's paw – he said that was what it was – and he said how you could guess the size and weight of the animal from the impression it left in the dirt. He was excited; I pretended I was.

Then we came across a jackrabbit and it was sitting on its haunches in a clearing, its pricked ears alert to any sound, and Pa put one finger across his lips and pointed to where the target was. He showed me how to hold the gun against my shoulder and he said I should fix the jackrabbit in my sight and then, standing steady, I was to squeeze the trigger real slow.

The sound of the gun firing pained my ears and the smoke caught in the back of my throat and my shoulder hurt where the butt had kicked back into it. None of that seemed to matter to Pa for I had hit the jackrabbit in the head with my first shot and he said that I was a natural. He pulled me over to see my first kill and he dipped one finger into the black hole of the jackrabbit's wound and he smeared the warm and sticky blood on my cheeks saying how I was a real hunter now. I didn't feel brave or heroic, not like Pa in the stories he told, not seeing that jackrabbit kicking its last and the light going from the black glass of its eye.

Maybe it was something the mountain lion smelled: the blood of the dead jackrabbit that we carried tied to the end of a stick. Maybe it was the smell of the blood that brought the lion to our campsite that night, when the fire was low and sleep was on us. I woke with a start, some sound from Pa's stories in my head, the drumming and the roar and the fright that he had told us of. And Pa was shouting at me to stay where I was, screaming at me, and he was reaching for his gun and all my thoughts were spinning and the dark was snarling and toothed and Pa missed with his first shot and hit with his second and missed again with his third, and the dead weight of a mountain lion took all the breath from me and all I could think of was the look in the jackrabbit's eye when the life left it and the black hole in its head just like the hole in my side.

CHAPTER TWENTY

One morning there was a disturbance at the front of the house, in the drive, and a horse bolted taking with it a cartload of richly embroidered fabric brought from India and China, and the gardeners threw down their tools and hid behind the cypress hedge, and the cook burned the soup with so much looking out of the window to see what was what.

I was there, standing a little back from the gate, and I saw the horse kick and rear up on its back legs, as much as it could being so fixed to the cart. And I saw it bolt, the white in its eyes and the air all blown and snorting and the sweat turned to foam on its flanks, and the cart tipped over and lost all its contents, and people were running all ways to try and gain some control. It was all on account of the beetle-green automobile.

The arrival of an automobile, a French Renault, the same model that had some years previously won a Grand Prix race in Le Mans, was something to be noted by everyone who worked at the Winchester House. It had been in all the newspapers and the driver, an Austrian called Ferenc Szisz, had his picture on the front pages of the world's press, and so it had caught the attention of Mrs Winchester. Now a shiny green-bodied automobile, with brass headlamps and thick rubber tires, was hers and plans for a garage were quickly drawn up and Mr Harrower was given instructions that work was to begin right away and as a matter of some urgency. He scratched his head and looked puzzled; then he took the drawings Mrs Winchester had made and retired to an empty room to consider how the plans might best be implemented.

A local man, who professed some experience, was hired to drive the automobile and for some time he lived on the premises instructing several under-footmen in the workings of the Renault, in so far as he understood them, how the battery-operated engine might be ignited and how the automobile might be steered and the managing of the gears.

When Mrs Winchester was assured of the competency of her staff in handling the automobile, she ventured forth and was driven at a sedate pace once around the estate. The automobile was noisy and cattle in the fields set up a ruckus such as they might the day before a quake; and birds took to the air in shrill and piping alarm; and workers in the orchards stopped their work to stare and were not sure if the lady in the veil was really Mrs Winchester or some other maid sent out on a trial run in the green automobile.

The house was something bewildering strange to see and not like any house known to me. Like a whole town of houses it was, if every house in a town could be pushed up close to each other, closer than close and such that some houses were inside other houses. And not one shape but all shapes and so many windows that I wondered at how many people slept there and thought it must be an army of some considerable size.

The automobile broke down on the third day, some mechanical failing that baffled the footmen and also the man who knew only how to drive the automobile, and so Mrs Winchester had to be taken in horse and cart back to the great house. A letter was quickly dispatched to a mechanic in San Francisco and his services required for the fixing of the automobile. He was later persuaded, by virtue of the offer of an undisclosed but handsome income, to remain in the Santa Clara

Valley for the express purpose of being on hand to tend to the care and maintenance of all Mrs Winchester's automobiles, for there were others on order.

On one slow drive around the grounds almost a month later, it came to Mrs Winchester's attention that there was a girl waiting at the tall gates at the bottom of the main drive. This was not of itself unusual for sometimes railway men who were new to the area came over from San Jose to see the elaborate Victorian gardens and the strange house with its turrets and balconies and glass cupolas and the building stretching in all directions and so many windows that they could not be counted by one person. What was odd about the girl was that after some enquiry it was established that she had been seen at the gates every day for a week, or longer, as though she was waiting for something or someone.

Mrs Winchester sent a boy from the stables on an errand to see who the girl might be and what the matter of her waiting by the front gates was. Once before, there had been a visit from a relative, a nephew or cousin from back east, and he had called at the Winchester House and had asked if he might speak with Mrs Winchester. She merely sent a servant to the door with a check written out in the young man's name and he was never seen again. Mrs Winchester supposed the matter of the girl at the gates was something similar.

A boy was made to ask after me. He was a scruffy sticks-for-bones boy and he did not speak with any manners and so I would not give him my name, but said simply that I had business there. He naturally asked what my business might be, and I said it was none of his to know. Then I added that I was there to see that a man I loved was settled in the life that came after this life.

The boy from the stables was somewhat confused by what the girl at the gates told him, and what he then delivered to Mrs Winchester, by way of the footman, made little sense.

'The girl has no name or will not give her name. She says she is there only to be near him, but she will not say who she wishes to be near or why, except that he is gone from this world but is not yet comfortably in the next but is somewhere between here and there.'

Mrs Winchester nodded, as if she understood, and she ordered that food be taken to the girl at the gates, some bread and cheese, and fruit from the orchards. And something to drink, some lemonade perhaps or water.

She sent me food and something to drink. I would not touch anything that had come from her. I do not think he would have wanted me to. Not from anyone who bore the name of Winchester.

When the girl was seen again at the gates some days later, an invitation was extended to her to approach the house where she might be better accommodated. The girl shook her head and would not speak more to the boy from the stables or to one of the under-footmen who was afterwards dispatched to make good the same offer.

Business at the house continued as before and little thought was given to the girl except that food was sometimes taken down to her and once a blanket was sent against the cold that the day had become.

I did not take her offer of a blanket either. Not anything from her. It did not feel right.

A week later, Mrs Winchester was again in the Renault and this time with a certain purpose, and the girl was once again seen at the gates. She seemed paler and her hair was unbrushed and she was as one who has not slept at all or well.

And today she stopped her car and spoke with me through the window. She looked into my eyes and maybe she looked through me and into my very soul, for I felt some sort of connection that I had not expected. It seemed to me that she was as steeped in grief and loss as I was and I almost felt for her. She said only one word and it was enough.

Mrs Winchester had the automobile stop for a moment, just where she might observe the girl at some small distance. She muttered something under her breath then, and the driver could not be sure but he reported on his return that Mrs Winchester had said only one word and she had said 'Sorry'.

The automobile had then proceeded on its further journey to a meandering river that cut through Mrs Winchester's property and wound through the length of the Santa Clara Valley. She instructed the driver to bring the car to a halt where the river was wide and she sent him to the water's edge with a large pewter ewer. He was to fill the ewer with water from the river and return it to her. Mrs Winchester had the ewer set at her feet and then she covered its mouth with a thick piece of damask cloth, after which they returned to the house without again passing the front gates or the girl.

The ewer of water was taken immediately to room 135 in the Winchester House and set on the table, in the center as though it was a thing of importance in the room. Then Mrs Winchester, who had overseen the whole operation, retired to her sitting-room where she put pen to paper. Her hands were tight and sore and so she held the pen even more awkwardly than usual and though the note she wrote was brief, it took her a longer time to write for she was anxious that every letter be clear and precise, even though when it was complete it looked like a well-schooled child might have written it and not a lady of some breeding and learning.

The note was then taken to the girl waiting at the gates, but as it had not been sealed it was read first by the footman, and then by a kitchen-maid on its way to the errand boy from the stables who was charged with delivery of the note – and he, too, made to examine the note when he was sure he could not be seen from the house. Reading what Mrs Winchester had so carefully and so painstakingly written threw no light on the matter. The note simply said: 'It will be soon now.'

The same boy as before and a note brought from Mrs Winchester and I asked if the boy had read what it said. He nodded and looked quickly over his shoulder as if he might be seen making such a confession. Then he looked back

to me and I made him tell me what the note said, rather than my taking of it
from him. The boy unfolded the paper and read, 'It will be soon.'

That night, at the ringing of the midnight bell, Mrs Winchester took
the recently installed Otis electric elevator to the third floor. She crept
along a winding stretch of corridor and climbed a flight of shallow
steps that took her to a door that required she dip her head to enter.
Then, by means of a hidden sliding panel, she seemed to disappear,
only to reappear some minutes later back at the entrance to the
corridor. Then she doubled back on herself again and made her way to
room 135 where the ewer of water had earlier been placed on the table.

I heard the distant ringing of a bell.

The fire had been lit and so it was warm in room 135 and the walls
danced and the shadows were not still. Mrs Winchester sat at the table,
as though to catch her breath. She rested her stick against her chair and
she stared out of the window and into the starless dark.

About her the house settled and every small crack and grumble of the
wood was made audible in the quiet of the hour. At the furthest reach
of the house a team of craftsmen were at work laying a complicated
parquet floor to a pattern drawn up by Mrs Winchester. They worked
by gas light and oil lantern. The sound of their hammers and gouges
and saws, did not reach to where Mrs Winchester sat. She seemed to be
waiting for something, as the girl at the gates had waited.

'Sorry,' she said at last, and such a weeping was in that word and
such a remembering.

As the hour grew later still, a coldness stole into the room, and
despite the fire, Mrs Winchester became aware of the strange chill.
She pushed against the table and got up from the chair. She took her
stick and exited the room in silence. She shut the door behind her and
locked it. The key she took with her and she returned, by way of the
electric elevator, to the bell-tower. It was two o'clock when she pressed
a button that activated a mechanism for the automatic ringing of the

bell. Then Mrs Winchester made her way back to her bedroom, but she did not sleep.

I heard a bell ringing, the same as before, and faintly, and I could feel something then, and it was like the air rippled and then not the air but something in me, and all at once I felt alone, and completely alone, and I had not quite felt that before. And a weeping overtook me, and a letting go of everything, so that when I was done I took a deeper breath, as one who drinks long enough to quench a dry thirst and then after breathes. 'It is done,' I said, and maybe I said the words aloud, and they were light words and heavy words; and it was then as though a greater weight had been taken from me, and I turned away from the gates of the Winchester House and took the first of many steps back to where I had come from.

Room 135

The Winchester Gun Club

Do you know what I miss more than anything else? More than her touch or the sound of birdsong or the sun warm on my closed eyelids or the smell of cornbread fresh from the oven or coffee fresh from the pot? Do you know what it is? So simple, you might not believe it: I miss the taste of water, cool and clear, and scooped in the cup of one hand, scooped from a running river, and lifted to dry lips. That's what I miss more than all the rest.

It's not that I don't miss those other things. I do. I have a memory of those things and I hold those memories close to me. I can recall lying in Belle's bed on a Sunday morning and her parents not knowing I was there and Belle kissing my neck and her hand down the front of my pants and birdsong drifting in through the open window and the sun up and warm on my face and I'm pretending to be asleep and the sound of Belle's mom in the kitchen and the smells of cornbread and coffee hanging in the air. All of that and more I recall. But the taste of water on my tongue and swallowing it sharp and clean, that memory escapes me.

Oh, I have the words, and I can replay those words in my head, but they are only thoughts when I do that and thoughts are so far from the real taste and touch of cool water. I kneel on the floor of this darkened room, and I make believe I am kneeling at the edge of the Little Applegate River and birch trees at my back, and fern and creeping snowberry if you look close, and bearberry, too. I lean forward, listening for the memory of water running over stones and the small wind shaking the trees and birds knitting skeins of song and trailing those songs from one tree to the next and through all of the river woodland. And twitch-gone scritch-scratch squirrels hiding from my gaze, and deer sleeping in the dappled shade, and bear tracks to be found in the soft ground, and beaver swimming in circles at a bend in the river. And I reach one hand out to where there would be water if this was more than imagining, and I scoop up air and bring it to my mouth.

That's how it was late on a Sunday morning, and I'd snuck out of Belle's bed without her parents discovering me, the fifth Sunday in a row that had happened, and I was taking the long way home through the trees. I could smell Belle still on my fingers and I was walking taller than tall. The sound of the river was like a music to my thoughts and it called me to its side. I was kneeling by the river's edge and scooping up water to cool the back of my neck and to slake my thirst, and that's when he came upon me.

He was of the Takelma people and their name means 'those along the river'. I figured he was young and lost on account of the Takelma had been shifted to a coastal reservation years back, further back than memory and only now in story. Maybe he was there looking for his beginning, as is sometimes the way of people who are displaced. I don't know who was the more afraid, except he raised his rifle and before I could swallow the water in my mouth he shot me through the head.

And it's the taste of water, and the cool and the clear and the running, that is what I miss. More than Belle kissing my neck and her hand down the front of my pants and the sun on me and the noise of Belle's pa singing church songs and her ma busy in the kitchen and the smell of cornbread coming through to wake me and Belle, and the smell of coffee, too. And it's the taste of water, plain and simple, that I long for.

CHAPTER TWENTY-ONE

Some of the servants and the staff stayed in rooms up at the great house. Some stayed in leased property on the edge of San Jose and travelled in each day, bringing the gossip of the town with them.

Those that stayed at the Winchester House were forbidden to drink and to gamble. There'd been an incident with some of the gardeners involving cards and a claim of cheating and a fight had followed, and one man was so badly beaten that the doctor declared he'd never seen the like. The man was off his work for more than a month, and when he returned, he walked crooked and there was a scar across one eye.

Mrs Winchester got to hear about most things in time and, on learning of the crippled gardener, decreed that there was to be no drinking in the house and no cards. She even ordered the bricking up of her own wine cellar and all the passages leading to it were also sealed and covered over.

Once, a bottle of Jule's Bourbon was smuggled into the house and the junior footmen met in the maids' room and they drank till they were silly. Mrs Winchester heard about this, too, but she pretended not to. Then, a week or so later, a workman lost his job and she gave no explanation, but everyone knew.

Outside of the Winchester House and its estate, it was a different matter. In one bar in particular, members of the household staff frequently met on a Friday night and they drank and 'lived it up'. They talked too, as is the way when drink loosens tongues, and some of the things they said grew taller in the telling and so they were not much believed by those who did not work at the house.

'She's mad. Like Sinny Boulder's mad. She talks to shadows and dances with ghosts. Lies with them too, I have no doubt.'

Sinny Boulder had been but recently committed to the state asylum at Agnews. She'd lost a child just like Mrs Winchester, and it had untied her wits and she spoke in riddles and to walls and tables. There was no doubting but that Sinny was mad. But with Mrs Winchester, opinion was divided. There was always someone to jump to her defense.

'She ain't mad. No more mad than anyone who has more money than sense to know what to do with it. She's just lonely, is all. I talks to myself when I'm alone and feeling down. That don't make me mad.'

Others were more careful and said nothing. They thought Mrs Winchester had spies everywhere and they valued their positions too highly at the Winchester House and so they said nothing or little.

Sometimes newspaper men came to the town and asked lots of questions and put stories together from what they heard. Some of their stories reached the papers and fueled the idea that Mrs Winchester was a rich eccentric. Reports of the great stained glass windows that came from Austria and took a day to be transported from San Jose train station to the Winchester House got some coverage, as did the silver inlaid doors all the way from Germany and the crates of rich blown colored glass packed in tissue and straw and sent from Venice, Italy.

But mostly lips were tight and sealed when it was known there was a newspaper man around.

'She's just lonely, is all, and we all been lonely at sometime or other.'

Gossip travelled the other way more easily. News from the town was taken into the Winchester House each day and passed from lip to ear in all its corners and corridors. A railwayman had been found in bed with the sheriff's wife and he was caught leaving town in his underwear and the sheriff shot him rather than take him in, shot him twice in the leg and with a warning to the intruder to be in another town far from here before morning or there'd be worse to follow. A simple smiling chit of a girl in the asylum called Mayline had given birth to twins and she would not say who the father was. An Indian had been seen in the dark, rustling cattle on the furthest edge of the valley, and Old Man Goober said that his herd was short by at least ten steers.

Then news of Mr John Hansen ran ahead of a note to Mrs Winchester sent from Mrs Hansen. He'd been sick and in a fever for some several days and the doctor had been with him and the doctor had left the Hansen house shaking his head at the grown-up Hansen children all gathered there.

There was some discussion in the kitchen of the Winchester House about who should take the news upstairs to Mrs Winchester. Eventually, Mr Harrower took on the job.

Mrs Winchester admitted Mr Harrower to her sitting-room and eyed the man with some sharpness, expecting that he was about to point to some failing in her most recent plans for an outside staircase that would make passage from the second to the third floor a little easier. But, looking at the man, she could see that there was something else that troubled him.

'You should ask Mr Hansen,' she said. 'He will know what to do.'

'Begging your pardon, ma'am, but I do not think that Mr Hansen will ever more know what to do.'

Mrs Winchester at first thought Mr Harrower was being somehow impertinent. She got up from her seat and, leaning heavily on her stick, she paced to the window.

'I do not think I understand your meaning, Mr Harrower. Or if I do, I am not sure I care for it. Make yourself plain.'

Mr Harrower took in a breath, as he was wont to do, and held it in the ball of his cheeks before letting it out slowly. Then he shook himself and stood a little straighter and made to speak again.

'What I mean to say, Mrs Winchester, is that I have news regarding Mr Hansen.'

He made a brief pause then, not sure how to proceed, for the plain speaking that Mrs Winchester had urged on him, did seem to him a little uncomfortable and he knew enough that he wanted to soften the thing he had to say.

'Regarding Mr Hansen?' prompted Mrs Winchester.

'He has been not himself these past few days, ma'am, and he is himself no more or ever shall be again.'

Mrs Winchester stamped the floor with her stick, a habit she had only recently developed as a way of signaling her impatience at the man before her.

'That is to say, Mrs Winchester, Mr John Hansen passed away in the night.'

There was a knock at the door at that moment and a note was delivered to Mrs Winchester's maid and after a whispered exchange at the door the note was taken and put into the gloved hand of Mrs Winchester.

'You must read it to me, girl,' said Mrs Winchester.

The girl broke the biscuit-wax seal on the note and unfolded the paper. There were few words written on the page. The girl looked at Mr Harrower as though she might find assistance there, then she held the paper closer to her face and stammered over the short message.

'Dear Mrs Winchester, John would want you to know that his last thoughts in this world included you. Yours most sincerely, Mary Hansen.'

Mrs Winchester waved Mr Harrower and the maid from the room, like she was shooing birds or cats. Then she was alone and grief overcame her of a sudden and she threw a Tiffany jewel lamp, smashing it against the wall, and she tore her own lace veil, and collapsed to the floor and wept.

The funeral was a quiet affair, but a place was reserved at the front of the church for Mrs Winchester and her maid. A delay was put on the occasion in the hope that she was merely late, but eventually the minister suggested that they should make a start and Mrs Mary Hansen gave her consent for proceedings to commence.

Mid-way through the ceremony, Mrs Winchester was helped out of her Renault automobile and into the church. Heads were bowed in mumbled prayer and she crept so slowly from the door to the front pews that many did not notice her entrance and on the final 'amen' the people looked up to see a lady in a black dress and veil suddenly standing next to Mary Hansen at the front of the church; it was the first that Mrs Winchester had been seen in the town for some years and some later said that it wasn't really her at all but a maid dressed up in her stead.

'Is he really gone?' whispered Mrs Winchester.

Mary Hansen took her arm and pressed it gently by way of an answer. Then Mrs Winchester was suddenly weaker than before and she had to be helped into a seat where she sat in silence for the rest of the service.

By the grave the minister intoned from the Holy Book, and the sun slipped out of sight behind a dark cloud, and the birds seemed to stop their singing, and in the street the men removed their hats and the women touched their hearts and counted their blessings.

'Then shall the dust return to the earth as it was: and the spirit shall return to God who gave it.'

They each dropped a handful of dirt onto the coffin lid, making a deep and irregular drumbeat, and then in ones and twos they departed the grave, stopping to share some small words of condolence with Mary Hansen.

Though it was not proper or seemly, Mrs Winchester was the last to leave the graveside, standing alone for some time and speaking in whispers behind her veil. She was helped back to her automobile at last. She had no words of comfort for Mrs Mary Hansen, which she later regretted.

For a week following the burial Mrs Winchester would not speak, but kept to her room with strict instructions that she was not to be disturbed, not for anything. The curtains were drawn shut and the fires untended and cold. She would not eat either, and the cook saw her best efforts returned to the kitchen untouched.

'She eats less than a bird. This hasn't even been picked at, see?' The ladle was in the cook's hand again and the kitchen was a quiet and serious place and no-one dared to cross her in anything or even look at her.

In whispers small as mouse breaths, everyone talked of Mrs Winchester's visit to the church and the funeral of Mr John Hansen, and how she was more lonely than ever now that he was gone. Of course, the stories they told grew in the retelling and there was all the romantic speculation of what had been before Mr John Hansen had retired from the work at the Winchester House, but though they were just stories found at the bottom of whiskey glasses they were never really so far from the truth.

A week after he was laid in the ground, Mrs Winchester sent a seven-page letter to Mrs Mary Hansen. It cost her in tears to write such a long letter for her fingers were twisted into claws and she had not yet given her approval for the fires in her rooms to be relit. It is between Mrs Hansen and Mrs Winchester what was written in that letter, those parts that could be read. Suffice it to be recorded that Mrs Mary Hansen did, after receiving the letter, send one or two of Mr John Hansen's personal things up to the house for Mrs Winchester's safe-keeping: a sealed letter he had earlier written to Mrs Winchester and which had never been sent, a shirt he had but recently worn so that the smell of him was still held in the cloth, and a pipe that he was wont to smoke of a 'dog day' evening as the sun went down and he sat on the porch facing the direction of the Winchester House, and he would not have those moments broken for anything.

Room 137

The Winchester Gun Club

I do not say that life was perfect before they came, but it was better in many ways. They brought disease with them and so many in the tribe died. They brought whiskey also and it burned the throats of our young men and sent them crazy. And then they brought their guns, sticks that flamed and smoked, and killed more than any spear or arrow ever did before.

Their coming was not foretold by the storyteller. Not anywhere in the tales he told of black birds and so many they blotted out the sun with their wings, or the rains drying up so that the crops in the fields turned all to dust. Nothing about men pale as smoke and all the bad they would bring with them. Nothing about the beast that smiles with one face and wearing the other steals the land from under our feet and more than just the land.

One there was and he was called Daniel. I do not know the meaning of this name except that it appears in the important writings of these white people, and Daniel was someone who lay down with lions and was not harmed because his god protected him. And this other Daniel – Daniel in name but a godless Daniel – he came to our village and he brought gifts for the chiefs and he laughed to show he meant no harm, his head nodding like a pet bird that is kept on a string.

He was the first of many, but he was the worst. I saw how he looked at our women, licking his lips as though he was thirsty and scratching at his cock without shame, preferring the youngest that we had. And when we were all drunk on his fire-water, and sleep had come to the village, it was godless-Daniel, our guest, who lay in my daughter's bed behind my back. And she for shame did not after say a word for she was to be the wife of a chief's son before three more moons had been in the sky.

When a pale-skinned bastard child was born, my daughter was shunned and I rode with her to the house where godless-Daniel lived. I told him we must talk and he invited me inside. The walls of his house were made of stone that could not breathe so that the air was hot and thick and smelled of things that are old or dead. Godless-Daniel offered me whiskey and we sat together on the wooden floor. Outside, my daughter was sick with a fever, and my grandchild cried for the milk that was not in my daughter's breasts, and like that they waited.

I told godless-Daniel he had done me a great wrong, and all my words were spat and short. I said he must make everything right again and I smacked the cupped palm of one hand with the fist of the other.

He offered me more whiskey and he was smiling and I could see that he did not understand.

'She is yours now,' I said, but the words were my words and godless-Daniel did not know them. I made show of what I meant in the movements of my hands and my face, but still he shrugged his shoulders and shook his head and looked stupid.

I took him outside to show him the child that was his and that, I think, made things a little clearer. He was paler then, his face not like smoke but like clouds that do not carry rain. He looked as a rabbit looks when it runs from the fox, eyes wide and his ears sharp. He ran his fingers through his hair and blew out the air in his cheeks. He said 'fuck' and 'shit', which I know are not good words for him to say. Then he went back into his stone house and he fetched his Winchester rifle, which I thought he meant to make a gift of to me, his new father.

Godless-Daniel was the first and the worst, though there were others mean of heart and spirit who came after him. He shot me twice and then he shot my daughter, his should-have-been wife, and lastly he shot his own child; and he left us in the dirt where we fell, so the birds could pick at our flesh, and the wind whistling through our bones ever after and making a sad song that carried across the whole of our shrinking world.

CHAPTER TWENTY-TWO

The war in Europe troubled everyone soon enough. Some of the younger men joined up and some of the girls wanted to be trained as nurses. There was even a little excitement mixed in with the worry and the threat. Mrs Winchester invested generously in Liberty Bonds and she agreed to cut the number in her employ by a quarter and she let some of the younger staff go.

'I do not understand why there should be so much killing,' said Mrs Winchester's maid one morning. It was delivered with all the lightness as though she was merely making remark of the weather. She was speaking to no-one in particular but it was said in the hearing of Mrs Winchester.

'What are you talking about?' asked Mrs Winchester.

'Begging your pardon ma'am, I have been reading your newspaper this morning, before bringing it to your table. We have all been reading it. 57,000 casualties in one day. There is surely a madness in this?'

Nancy, the maid, was referring to a battle in Northern France and the lives of British troops thrown away in that battle. Mrs Winchester reached for the newspaper and found confirmation in print for what Nancy had said.

'I lost my father some years back,' Nancy said. 'He was old and it was his time. Some nights, when I am home, I still think I hear him moving about the room where he drew his last breath and I am comforted that maybe he is home and comfortable. Do you think the ghosts of those 57,000 men will forever be wandering and lost in the battlefields in France?'

Nancy was being uncommonly and unaccountably bold and Mrs Winchester did not deign to give the girl an answer but waved her away from the table.

'Begging your pardon, ma'am.'

Mrs Winchester sighed and she could not eat her breakfast, not with the thought of so many dead troubling her. The maid was later scolded for her words by the cook and thereafter the newspaper was always delivered a little after breakfast was over and was not to be a topic for conversation between the maid and Mrs Winchester, not unless Mrs Winchester did of herself instigate such a conversation.

Mr Harrower met with Mrs Winchester in the second half of the morning as was their arrangement. He gave a short report without interruption on the progress of building work and he itemized a short inventory of the goods still to be unloaded from a train waiting at the station at San Jose. Mrs Winchester had stopped ordering articles from Europe and so everything came east from New York and Washington.

'Do you own a gun, Mr Harrower?' said Mrs Winchester when he had finished.

'I do not understand your question, ma'am.'

Mrs Winchester stamped the floor with her stick. 'It is a plain enough question, Mr Harrower. Do you or do you not own a gun?'

Mr Harrower scratched at his head and blew air out from his cheeks. 'I own a Winchester model 1910 ma'am. I bought it new from Crennan's store. Cost me almost thirty dollars. But I ain't fired it at nothing more than a desert cottontail or a black-tailed jackrabbit for the pot.'

Mrs Winchester seemed to consider what Mr Harrower had said before responding.

'Thank you, Mr Harrower.'

'Yes, ma'am,' he said and, thinking his business concluded, he turned to go but was halted in his tracks when Mrs Winchester continued.

'I have been thinking lately about the things that are done in our time on this earth. It must be all the talk of war that has made me so gloomy and the cost it has been to us even here. I wonder, Mr Harrower, if you think what we do, or what is done in our name, is important?'

Once more Mr Harrower was at a loss as to her meaning and again he scratched his head and sucked in air and blew it free again. He'd heard a question in what she had said but he was not quite sure what the question was.

'I think we must always strive to do good in what we do, Mrs Winchester,' he ventured.

His answer seemed to be sufficient, for she nodded and seemed once again to give his words her most careful consideration. He would have gone then but he did not want to make the same mistake as before so he waited to be dismissed.

They stood facing one another without speaking for some minutes. The sound of horses being unharnessed in the yard leaked in through the open window, and the curtains shifted in a cooler draft, and a butterfly suddenly entered the room, drifting through the air like a thrown rag cloth or a piece of torn paper carried on a draft, and it settled on the rim of a teacup that waited still to be cleared away from the table by the maid. The butterfly opened its wings in a flash of orange and black, and then it folded its glory away again. This small display took their attention for a moment.

'It is a milkweed butterfly, Mr Harrower. Beautiful, don't you think? They come here in summer and brighten the air almost as much as the meadow flowers brighten the fields. But they are poisonous to predators due to the milkweed plant they feed on when at the larval stage.'

'Yes, ma'am.'

The butterfly edged around the rim of the cup and opened and closed its wings again in a handclap of color.

'Do you know, Mr Harrower, that the Greek word for butterfly is 'psyche' which means 'soul', and there is a belief amongst some people that butterflies are the souls of the dead that must wait before passing through purgatory and then ascending into Heaven?'

'I think we commonly call it a monarch butterfly,' said Mr Harrower.

'Indeed. Please to take it to the window and set it free again.'

Mr Harrower did as he was bid, holding the butterfly carefully in the cage of his cupped fingers, and on its gently tossed release the butterfly took to the air and ascended upwards as though there might be some small truth in what Mrs Winchester had said about butterflies and souls.

'Before you leave, Mr Harrower, I would ask of you a small favor.'

'Yes ma'am.'

Mrs Winchester took a seat at the table and indicated that Mr Harrower should sit down too.

'I have been thinking of late, as I mentioned, about what we do in our time here. We are in agreement, I think, concerning the good we must strive after in our short lives. I wonder if you also think, Mr Harrower, that a wrong can be righted by a life of self-denial and good deeds.'

Mr Harrower performed the expected scratching of his head yet again and the huffing and puffing of his cheeks. 'I think, ma'am, you should be talking to a more learned man than I am. Maybe there is a minister you can be asking these questions of and maybe he would be able to give you more of an answer than I.'

She did not this time seem to consider what he had said but continued as if he had not spoken at all. 'Even if it is a family wrong, Mr Harrower, and not really a wrong of one's own, and even if that wrong continues to this day and is not righted but merely balanced by the good that a person does. Do you think this may be enough, Mr Harrower?'

Mr Harrower was reduced to animal noises, grunts and moans, that seemed to neither offer agreement nor disagreement with what Mrs Winchester had asked him.

'I would ask that you deliver a check to a certain charity in San Jose,' she went on, though this matter of a check did not seem to Mr Harrower to be related to anything else that she had said. 'It must be done in secret and no-one is to know who is the giver of this bounty. Do you think you could assist me in this matter?'

Mr Harrower was not sufficiently recovered to be able to say anything so he made some more noises in the back of his throat and nodded, and he scratched his head again, even though there was no problem to solve in what Mrs Winchester had just said.

'Thank you, Mr Harrower. I think that will be all for now.'

When he had gone, Mrs Winchester got to her feet once more and, with the aid of her stick and dragging her feet, she shuffled over to the open window with its view out across the orchards and all the flowers in bloom in the fields and the souls of the dead flitting from place to place all over the valley floor.

'I think Plato had something to say about bees and souls also,' she said. 'Something about bees being the wandering let-loose souls of quiet sober people. I think I should like to be a bee for they are ever busy and do only good in the world.'

She stood a while at the open window and the sun was warm on her face, but it was not sufficient to lift the gloomy disposition of her thoughts.

'Is it enough to be sorry, if sorry is a feeling that runs through everything that you think or do?' she said.

There was no-one to hear what she said and even had there been it is not certain that they would have understood. With no-one to hear there was no answer except what was in her own head and so she remained gloomy for the rest of the day and into the next.

Room 144

The Winchester Gun Club

I don't blame him. He was just one against so many. Trapped in a corner and no other way out. He had no choice and so I do not blame him. None of us do. None of the innocents who were on the edge of things and our doors bolted shut and the whole family cowering beneath tables and behind chairs; same for all the families in the street.

His name was Ed and no doubt somewhere down the line of his palm there is a break in his lifeline and he'll get his. Not that I'm saying he deserves as much. Like I said, there's no sense of wrong in what he did, not in me. But a man like that, having done what he done, well, there's a price to be paid and those that will make him pay it one way or another.

I saw a cat once. Aunt Lucy's cat. I forget its name. That's something that happens on this side of the darkness, things begin to slowly fade. Some things do. Names and dates, they fade. And Aunt Lucy's nameless cat was caught out in the open and two curs snarling and showing the snap and nip of their teeth and nothing to save that cat except Aunt Lucy who came running at the commotion. She put herself between the dogs, and she scooped up that hiss-spit cat and its claws were out and she was badly scratched. Blood on her dress, that I remember, and the cat held tight and covered so the dogs wouldn't get it. The man called Ed, the man in the street, he was cornered the same, only there was no Aunt Lucy to save him.

I don't know what it was he done. There was talk before the shooting. Something about a woman and Ed's hand under her skirts and that was wrong, even though I saw the minister do the same once with Mrs Bridgewater. In the back of the church I saw it, late on a Sunday, and I'd gone there to fetch the hat I'd left on my seat that morning. It was dark inside and I don't think I was seen or heard. The minister was breathing hard and fast, like a horse when it's been well ridden, and Mrs Bridgewater, her skirts lifted, was making mewling noises like a baby when it's playing. But Ed doing it, putting his hand under a woman's skirts, that was somehow different, and I think all the difference that there might have been was that he was seen.

There were six men rode into town and word of their coming riding ahead of them. Six men with their eyes hard as flint and their trigger fingers itchy. That's what my mama said. Itchy as ant bites. And so we were under the table, waiting for Ed to be shot dead and the six men to leave town afterwards.

'He don't stand a chance,' my mama said, and my dad just shrugged and shook his head as if it wasn't his business.

And that's why I don't blame Ed, none of us do. He didn't have no choice. Leastways, that's how I see it. And he came out shooting and pumping his rifle and shooting again, quick as quick. Quick as jackrabbit legs when it's running from a prairie fox. And bullets flying all ways, fizzing like wasps when a nest is disturbed. No knowing where all them wasps went to, but six mean curs stung dead in the street and mama stung, too, and little Thomas and me, and who knows who else in all the other houses with their curtains shut and their doors bolted.

I don't blame Ed… but I have to blame somebody. It was a Winchester 1873 that Ed held and he had a name for it scratched on the rifle butt, but I forget that name just like I forget the name of Aunt Lucy's cat.

CHAPTER TWENTY-THREE

The doctor was more and more at the Winchester House and he was not the old doctor but a new fresh-faced young doctor with a polished shine to his shoes and a smart new suit and his hair all slicked back. He talked of opera and ballet with some confidence and was a bright companion over tea or coffee. Yet Mrs Winchester could not help but regard him as a boy, a pleasant enough boy, but a boy all the same. His name was Doctor Ellis Wright.

He had ideas about her arthritis too. New treatments that he said would be far more effective than licorice tea.

'No, no, we prescribe bee venom now.'

Mrs Winchester laughed, thinking he had made a joke, but he was in earnest.

'There was a lady in Madison County and she had a most painful time of it with her knees and her elbows and nothing made any difference to her. Then one day she was stung on one knee by five orange rump bumblebees and within but a few short days all her pain was gone from her knee and was not gone from anywhere else. That was more than three years ago and she still has an absence of pain in her knee. Indeed, she has allowed other bees caught in glass jars to sting her elbows and her other knee and she does swear by the treatment.'

Mrs Winchester enjoyed his conversation up to a point, and his good company, but she did not regard his medical expertise with anything other than concealed scorn.

'I have a fondness for bees, Doctor Wright. I have said before that they do only good in this world and I was corrected in this when a maid showed me a bee sting she had suffered and it was angry and red for days. Now you mean to tell me that there is some good in bee stings also?'

She was polite enough to endure in principle the young doctor's new ideas on treatment, but she kept to her licorice tea and a diet devoid of tomatoes and potatoes and she rubbed a home-produced concoction made from ground sunflower petals and pine needles into her joints.

'There are papers written on the subject, Mrs Winchester, and they are discussed at length in the corridors of our capital's universities and colleges, and the use of bee venom is now common practice on the East Coast where I did my training.'

Some days the conversation could be tiresome.

'Recommend to me something I might read,' said Mrs Winchester, 'something to divert my attention from all this lingering talk of war and the cost to the country. I am sure that will help with what ails me.' And with such as that she hoped to detain the doctor a little longer and at the same time distract him from his talk of bee venom injections and their miraculous healing properties.

One day she had a fall on the stairs and though her leg was not broken, she was told by the doctor to keep the weight off it for several days just to give the swelling in her leg time to go down and for the bruising to lighten. She ordered coffee to be served to the doctor and the smell of fresh roasting beans scented the house for the rest of the day.

'Coffee, too, may be considered a medicine, for it is a pleasant antidote to headaches and is a great restorative.'

'Talk to me of music, Doctor Wright, for I used to play the piano when I was younger.'

The doctor took an especial interest in this piece of information and suggested that Mrs Winchester should resume her interest in piano playing, for it was thought to stimulate the action of the joints and so might help offset the advance of her arthritis.

An hour or two of the young man's company was about as much as she could take at any one time; his obsessive concern for her arthritis when it surfaced brought a tedium to his conversation and so he was then quickly told to go.

After he had left, Mrs Winchester went about the business of her day, the bruising of her leg and the doctor's injunction to rest notwithstanding. She drew maps for her personal use, maps that took her to different parts of the house with the avoidance of too many stairs. In this way she was able to keep an eye on what was going on and to make her presence still felt in the house. She came upon some of the servants by surprise and watched how they went about their duties and watched the time that they took to do this or that small task. Then she suggested that they might do everything in a different order and so save on the time that they had taken.

It was so for the maids in the kitchen as it was for the workmen laying floors and for the plumber fixing leaks and for the mechanic servicing her three cars and for the stable-hands looking after her horses. The stories of her being suddenly in the shadow of this servant or that workman were passed around table and because she was so generous in the remuneration of all her employees, they were rarely lazy or not about their various tasks.

'Is there a young woman in your life, Doctor Wright?' Mrs Winchester made so bold as to enquire. She had hoped that there might be and that perhaps he might bring the young lady the next time he called. Mrs Winchester hoped for a cultured companion to share her interest in glass ornament or rich brocade or dress design, someone she might make something of. A sister to replace the one that was lost to her by being so far away, or a daughter who would be grown by now and so grown that she would be an educated woman and a good companion. Unfortunately, there was no such young lady and so Mrs Winchester brought their meeting to a close.

'I might ask before departing if you have given any consideration to the matter of the bee venom injections, Mrs Winchester.'

Mrs Winchester explained that she had written to a doctor friend of hers in New Haven and was awaiting his reply on the subject.

With the new young doctor in attendance so often, speculation below stairs increased as to what might be wrong with Mrs Winchester. It was her own maid, Nancy, who set things straight. 'It is ever the one thing,' she declared. 'The mistress is lonely and wants for company.'

Of course, news of Nancy's diagnosis reached Mrs Winchester's ears, though no-one below stairs could ever say how. Mrs Winchester put the maid right on her pronouncement.

'It is quite the opposite,' she told her. 'I yearn to be alone and for silence. I have not been alone for years and everyone is always talking at once. Now I am old I had thought that there might be a softening of the voices and not so many as before and maybe only the one voice that I miss, or another that I have not heard in more than thirty years, or a child's voice, and I might hear each one speaking as clearly as you might hear a bell that is rung. Not lonely and craving the company of young men who are still wet behind the ears, as you think. The doctor diverts my attention away from all the noises in my head, for a little while, and then he is just another voice in the room and I am tired then.'

Nancy did not make any sense of what Mrs Winchester said to her. When she tried to repeat what she had been told, it made even less sense and comparison was made between Mrs Winchester and madhouse Sinny – the same who talked in riddles, and for the price of a

Liberty Walking half dollar an hour might be spent in Sinny's company to some small amusement.

'Listen,' said Mrs Winchester when next the young doctor called.

The doctor tilted his head and listened.

'Tell me what you hear, tell me everything,' she said.

He listed all the sounds that were in the house, the hammering and the sanding and the dropping of tools. He heard the shifting of wood in the warming day, small clicks and cracks, and the running of water in the pipes. He made note of the sounds the fire made in the room where they were and the noise of the curtains dragging on the floor in a draft from the open window, and outside the snorting of horses in the stables and the clink of harness, and the chatter and song of birds, and the wind moving in the trees.

'Smaller than all of those,' said Mrs Winchester.

The young doctor thought she was playing a game so he listened again and he held his breath to better hear the small and smaller sounds.

'I hear the sound of bees passing the window and the fall and rise of your veil with each of your breaths. And I hear the blood in my own ears and it is rushing like a small and quick wind. And I hear my own thoughts jostling for attention.'

She did not really think that he heard bees as he said he did.

'And I hear something more, under everything. I hear quiet.'

He did not hear voices, or he did not say that he did. He did not hear the clamor of voices that broke her sleep more frequently and had of late grown more and more urgent with their shouting and their claims against her.

'Do the good deeds in this world amount to anything in the next?' she said.

The doctor was wrong-footed and he did not know what to say or why the question had been asked.

He reached out and took her pulse and laid a hand over her forehead to feel for any rise in her temperature and tapped her knee with a small wooden hammer so that she gave out an involuntary kick.

'I am not sleeping well,' she said.

Doctor Wright accepted that this was explanation enough for the strangeness of her questions and the listening he'd had to do. He suggested that she have a regular and light meal before retiring, a little something to eat, with honey from the bee.

Again with the bees, she thought.

'I have known that to help in some cases. Or maybe to wet the head with cold water followed by warm. If this does not work, then I might prescribe a bromide drop.'

She thanked him for his time and for his kind consideration. She paid him in coin and bade him a good-day.

When he was gone she heaved a sigh of relief and lay down on her bed and slept but briefly.

Room 152

The Winchester Gun Club

If at the last it ended just as Jenny said it would, perhaps that was only to be expected. Wasn't she always saying that my luck would run out one day? Didn't she say it over and over and the flat of her hand on my chest and pleading with her eyes?

'A man ain't nothing more than his reputation,' I told her.

'That's your pa talking, that is,' she scolded.

She was right, of course. She was right about most things. I can see my pa when I close my eyes, can hear the ghost of his voice saying those same words about reputation, one hand patting the Colt pistol holstered on his left hip.

'It doesn't have to be like that for you,' Jenny insisted. ' It can be different. Not always running from place to place and looking back over your shoulder just in case, and never settling to anything. It can be different if you'll let it.'

Jenny. Hair like grain stalks that have given up the grain. Eyes blue as an Iowa sky in summer and as wide, and every man itching to lay their hands on her and wondering why she was with me – the likes of me, they mean.

Like I said, she was right most of the time. But I'd done things, see. I'd done things I couldn't tell Jenny about. In my past I had, before I met her, and that's why there was always someone waiting to take me down, looking to stand a little taller because they'd be standing on my shoulders. That's how they saw it. That's how it was. And I understood that – even though I wished it could be different.

'You got *reasons* now,' Jenny said. 'Reasons for being something else.'

Jenny was stroking the new swollen roundness of her belly and she took my hand and laid it there so I could feel the baby moving inside her. I can still feel the little punch and kick against the palm of my hand, like a small shot of electricity, soft and urgent both at the same time.

'You got reasons,' she said again.

One day Jenny is just a girl in my bed and asking for nothing and kissing me like a girl and laughing at me and playing coy. The next she's a little thicker about the middle and her breasts are women's breasts and she'll be a mother soon. Always changing, never just one thing or the other, never staying the same.

It's different for men. I think it is. That's why I did what I did. Even with Jenny begging me not to go, begging me with her 'reasons'.

'It's who I am,' I told her, my voice all bluster and bluff. 'It's who I'll always be.'

It was him or me. He was just a kid looking to make his name. That's the way it is, the way it always is. That's how it had been for me once. In a fair fight I reckon I'd have taken him down easy. I think he knew that and so he was hiding a long ways off. Beyond the range of my pa's Colt pistol that hung then on my own left hip. The kid had a rifle, a Winchester repeater, the 'Yellow Boy' brass all glimmer and gleam. I didn't stand a chance.

CHAPTER TWENTY-FOUR

'My mom's sick, as you know,' said Mrs Winchester's second-best maid. The hour was late and she was in her cotton underskirts and not decent but lying in the bed of the head footman, even though he was so much older.

'But *she* knows. Mrs Winchester knows. About my mom. I don't understand how that is. We do not ever talk, which is to say that she does all the talking and I listen; I nod to show I'm listening and I make a soft clucking noise in my mouth which is taken to mean anything she likes it to mean. But I'm not so forward as to be making conversation with her, or in giving her to listen to the bits and pieces of my life. And yet she says that she knows that my mom's sick.'

The head footman kissed the neck of the girl in his bed and his kisses meandered to behind her ear and he whispered her name – Frances – and he made a small and soft moaning sound somewhere in the back of his mouth, all of which Mrs Winchester's second-best maid, brushed away with a careless shrug, as a person might do if they were bothered by a fly or a wasp.

'She says that she hopes my mom's better today, says it as warm as if we might be friends or neighbors and passing the time of day over our washing or our tending to the vegetable patch in our gardens. She says that she hopes the improvement in the weather has brought my mom some respite from her symptoms. I do not know what this 'respite' is, but I remain silent in Mrs Winchester's company, except I think I said a quiet 'yes ma'am' then, which is allowed.'

Thomas, the head footman, edged a little closer to the girl and patted the back of her hand. He stroked her cheek and shifted her tumbled and tousled hair away from the nape of her neck.

'I do not think she knows I am there some days, or she forgets who I am. Not my name, for there's no need that Mrs Winchester should remember something so small as my name, but in her head I am some other person.'

Thomas whispered the girl's name again and he kissed her neck once more, softer than before, and the girl, Frances, did not this time move from him but continued with her words running and skipping ahead of herself, continued with her prattling; Thomas took some encouragement from this to put his hand on her breast, light as a butterfly-touch.

'She talks and I listen, that's how it is, and sometimes it's as though she talks to herself or to someone else. And no different when I am not there, when I am in the other room with the door closed, still she talks, even though she is alone. I hear her talking.'

Thomas nodded his head and made a noise that might give Frances to think he was listening, which he wasn't, not unless his ears being sharp to the pauses in her speaking, or his hearing for the breath between her words, not unless these might be called listening. He nuzzled her neck and pressed his hand against her breast with more confidence.

'I know it's not proper that I listen when she's alone, but I do and I think that anyone else would do the same. I stand a little closer to the door and I try to look busy in case she comes forth and catches me idle, and I listen through the door to every word she says. There's someone she talks to and she calls him William and she's sometimes cross with him and she scolds, but then she's quickly sorry for what she has said. I do not know anyone called William, not unless the boy in the stables who is Will or Willie and his Sunday-name may be William, but what Mrs Winchester says to *her* William is not what would be said to a stable-boy, leastways not said by any lady such as has money and standing.'

Thomas fingered the white ribbon fastenings on Frances's bodice, his fingers creeping slow and soft as mice, and he untied the first ribbon, and then the second and the third, and Mrs Winchester's second-best maid did not seem to notice the advances he made.

'She says she's sorry then and she asks forgiveness, from this man called William who is not there except in her head. I think maybe it's a memory that she talks with, for I have sometimes been alone and talked with a boy who once was sweet to me and sweet on me, and I did him a wrong before, and I wish now that I had been different then. Maybe this William is something the same with Mrs Winchester and is only a memory that she talks with and a regret.'

Thomas peeled her underclothes from her shoulders and the whisper of cotton falling from her was a smaller sound underneath Frances's talking, scarcely noticed, except that Thomas noticed. Frances was naked from the waist up then and Thomas let his hands explore the warm small of her back and his lips moved from her neck to her shoulders.

'Not always a William, but sometimes and more often there's someone who seems to hold a higher place in Mrs Winchester's thinking and his name is John. Mmmm... and when she talks with him, with John, there's a different sound to her voice... and the nearest I can come to describe it is that she seems to be singing under her breath. She calls him 'dear John' and 'dearest' and she asks him how he is and she talks through her recent plans for the house and she looks for his opinion of some small detail in her designs. His name is John... and I think there was a John here before... a John Hansen maybe, and I do not know if it might be the same John that she now has a conversation with.'

Thomas discovered a quickness in France's breath and her words began to come less easily and she sighed between the things she wanted to say, but she went on with what she was saying for there was a purpose to her speech and she was moving towards something of importance to her and Thomas.

'She asks this William and this John the same questions... she asks if a person who appears good may really be good... and she asks if the good that a person does... she asks if that will amount to something... in the final reckoning... What do you think?'

Frances turned to Thomas and she stopped him with a look. She held him with her eye and he was arrested in his fondling of her breasts and his kissing of her nipples. He'd heard the question in her voice but he had not heard the words. He knew something hung on this moment and his further progress with her was in the balance.

'Do you think a person can appear good and yet be something else?' said Frances.

Thomas nodded and he made a noise somewhere in his throat, same as before, a noise that might let her to believe that the question was not an easy one and he was giving some thought to what she had asked him.

Frances reframed the question and Thomas might have wished then that he had been quick enough to have given answer to the earlier version. 'Are *you* as good a person as you pretend to be or does your goodness hide some darker you?'

Frances was not the first girl in the household that Thomas had bedded. Indeed, she was not the second or the third, and each of them in turn had thought that there might be something more honorable in him than proved to be. If the kitchen gossip was to be believed, he had made such promises as would turn a girl's head and then afterwards he had found some inconsequential reason to end all his many liaisons, one after the other. He therefore had a reputation and Frances was wise to this.

'I think a man's goodness is something that is not easy to determine,' he said quickly. 'And it is so for a woman's goodness. Mrs Winchester has more money than can be imagined and she wants for nothing. She gives donations to this cause and every which other cause, and she does so without her name needing to be attached to the giving. This does appear to be good and Mrs Winchester does appear to be a good person. But if I had her money, I do not doubt but that it would be easy to do something the same.'

Frances pulled her slipped bodice back over shoulders and covered herself again and by this Thomas discerned that he had failed to give the girl the answer she had hoped for. The advantage would be lost if he did not come up with something else.

'Are *you* good?' he said, and he withdrew from her a little and it was, he thought, a clever move in a game he had played before and had always won.

'And do you think that doing wrong in this world means there's a price to be paid in the next?' she said without attending to the question he had asked.

Thomas nodded again. He had underestimated this girl, this second-best maid. He brushed his hair back from his face and sighed.

'Are you talking Judgment Day and matters of the soul?' he said. 'I think it's the minister you should be in bed with if these are the questions that bother you.' There was a feigned petulance in his play now.

'She knows my mom's sick, Mrs Winchester knows, and she gives me two gold five-dollar coins, shiny and glinting and new, and she presses them into my palm and says I should get Doctor Wright to visit my mom and if it's more than the ten dollars, I should tell her. And she says I am to take some of this year's Hansen apples as a gift from her to my mom, which is thoughtful and kind. I think that makes her good.'

The head footman slowly reached for a packet of Lucky Strike cigarettes by his bed and a box of matches. He made a show of lighting up and not attending to what the girl was saying.

'Mrs Winchester then says as how I should be careful and I know she means with you even though she does not say your name. She says something about the heart and what she says makes no sense to me at first, something about how the heart is made heavy by the loving of the wrong man and how a life might be shaped or mis-shaped by the man that one chooses to love. All her talk of love does at least confirm in me that she's talking about you.'

The head footman drew on the cigarette and took the smoke deep into him before letting it out slow. He had a glint in his eyes, and he would have smiled then but with an effort he kept his face straight. He had seen the way to his further advantage and how it might be gained, for the second-best maid had revealed herself in what she had said.

'Love,' Thomas said, and there was no more meaning in it than the simple saying of the word, and he said no more, just the one word like a pebble dropped into water, and he waited for the ripples of that dropped word to spread outwards.

Frances leaned into him then, and she laid a hand on his chest as if to measure the beating of his heart and she looked into his eyes for she had heard that they are the windows to the soul and she wanted to know this man and what he was.

'This woman that I do not talk with, Mrs Winchester, and she talks to me like she knows me, like we could be the same, and she says something about regrets and things lost and things found again afterwards, found long afterwards and when it is almost too late, and though I do not understand what she says, not much of it, I think she says what she says out of goodness.'

Mrs Winchester's second-best maid leaned in a little closer still. She kissed the head footman and then pulled away. She got up from the bed and began dressing again, fastening the ribbons of her bodice, straightening her cotton petticoats and pulling her dress over her head.

The head footman watched her, not smiling anymore, and he gripped his cigarette a little tighter, and he pretended that her going did not matter, but it did.

Somewhere else in the house, Mrs Winchester was sitting at a table. She held a pen in her hand and she wanted to write a letter and it was important, but she could not lift the pen to the ink, nor then the pen to the paper, so she sat and waited for the knot in her fingers to loosen and the pain to slacken its grip on her.

'If she lives and she can be found, there might be an answer and an end to all my suffering,' said Mrs Winchester. 'Do you see, John? And the distance that was between us once, and is a distance still, it is somehow different for now I can speak freely what is in my heart, John, and so it feels like we are closer than when you lived.'

Mrs Winchester stopped her talking a moment and she tilted her head to better hear something. Not the faint far-off hammer and thump of the night-shift builders at work, or the house shifting in the cooling air, or the sound of water in the pipes or the small thunder of gas in the lamps. She heard the second-best maid, Frances, stealing through the house somewhere below stairs, walking on tip-toe from the head footman's room back to her own room. Mrs Winchester smiled to herself and nodded as if in answer to a question that had been asked and answered.

Room 156

The Winchester Gun Club

Pinning a tin badge on his shirt changes a man. Makes him stand a little taller in front of the mirror, his chin a little more square and his nose a little straighter. Not just in his own eyes, but in the eyes of others too. Men passing him in the street tips their hats; and ladies plays with their hair and dip their heads and wish him a good morning, and the way they look at him they wish him more than a good morning, if you get my meaning.

It changes a man is what I'm saying. Makes him walk different, aware of his new-won importance. Like he owns the whole town now and what he says goes. I seen it do that to Thomas Smithy. Knowed him all my days, knows everything about him what with growing up alongside him, and all the mischief we done together and more than just the mischief, by which I mean the bad. And now he's the sheriff and he pretends like he don't know me on account of I seen the color of the man, the real color.

They says a man can change, and maybe that's so. But Thomas Smithy ain't fooling me with his polished boots and a clean shave. Didn't we once get so drunk, me and him, and Lucy whose pa runs the general stores? Didn't we get so drunk that we took advantage and Lucy crying afterwards and we woke up all sorry and ashamed, saying we was, and the three of us swore to keep it a secret between only us?

And now Lucy smiles at Thomas Smithy and acts all coy and Thomas wishes her a good-day and pretends he don't know she's got a mole shaped like a bird on her left breast.

And I knows who it was as shot that Indian boy up by the hollow; seven years and some back it was, a bullet to his head, and Thomas was as surprised as anyone when he hit his target. Was his grandpa's old Winchester he had and he didn't think it could shoot so straight at that distance. He just meant to frighten the boy. That's what he said, and we swore then, him and me, and another secret to be kept. Now he's the law round here and he don't give me the time of day.

I don't know how Thomas Smithy can forget what he done, what we done. I still sees that dead Indian. No older than we was at the time, and him laying as still as though he was a picture in a book. Now he's a picture in my head and my hands sweat when I thinks of him and I looks over my shoulder in case it's obvious to everyone what I is thinking.

And I drinks myself into broken sleep most nights and when I wakes I don't rightly know where I am, not straightaway. Sometimes I'm sleeping outside Lucy's house and I writes 'sorry' in the dirt just where she might see. Sometimes I sleep outside the sheriff's office, so as he might find me in the morning when he wakes and be reminded of who he is at heart; sometimes curled up in a cell and the door ain't locked and I can leave as soon as I'm sober and I thinks then maybe he does recall what we was to each other once and what we still is.

But all of that is just cold remembering. Words is all it is now, coming to me out of the darkness. And maybe all of that's an explanation for what he done, too. Maybe the bad was just eating away inside him, same as it was me. And he was scared it would all come out, all slurred and whiskey breath, and my finger pointing at him and calling his heart black and the silver star on his shirt all tarnished and dull. Maybe that's why he rode me out of town that drunk black night and why he carried his grandpa's Winchester rifle in one hand, the first time he had touched it for seven years, and loaded it with three bullets. And he says to me then as things is different now and we ain't boys no more and there ain't room for me in his town – calls it 'his' town.

It was mercifully quick when it came and I'm grateful for that. It was a sort of release, too. See, I don't think of that Indian boy no more, or if I thinks of him it ain't in pictures exactly and so I don't see him laying in the dirt still as stone. All I sees now is Thomas Smithy, a shine to his boots and his chin all smooth and square, and his black heart hidden behind a tin silver star, and I see him walking away, always walking away, and carrying his grandpa's rifle, empty now, and he don't even wait to watch my last breath leave me.

CHAPTER TWENTY-FIVE

'Is there a letter come for me today? Have you checked? Send word to the station and have them look again, to be sure. Yes, a letter. It is expected.'

Mrs Winchester fretted through the start of each day, and she stamped her stick on the floor, and she sighed, and she kept shifting the curtain at her window to better see into the yard outside, to see if there might be a message delivered late from the station. Her daily interview with Thomas, the head footman, seemed to have fallen into a pattern of worry and restlessness, and it started the same today as it had every day for the past six months.

'Are you certain?' she said. 'No, not something about shoes or slippers from Joseph Byers, or something from Culliford's Dye House in Brooklyn, or from the Gallerie Colbert in Paris, or Oxford Street in London. No, it is another letter that I enquire after, one from a Mr Archibald Lean in New England.'

When nothing arrived at the house, Mrs Winchester ordered that a horse be saddled and a rider dispatched to the station at San Jose to check again.

The head footman nodded and said, 'Right away, ma'am.'

It was the same rider each morning and he was dressed and ready on the stroke of nine, and the horse was brought up from the stables, the iron bit rattling against its teeth and the brass rings of the saddle and harness making a jangling music out of the horse's slow pacing. The rider mounted the horse in the yard, just where Mrs Winchester could see him, and then he rode out at a gallop, and the horse kicked up dirt and dust in thin clouds, and a small rolling storm thunder it made in the drumming of its hooves, and there was an urgency in everything even though it had been the same display for months.

And the rider had, over time, come to be known and expected beyond the reach of the Winchester House. Townspeople on the road stopped to wave, called after him and cheered. Some set their watches by his passing, and others asked for the blessing of luck, with muttered prayers under their breath for no reason other than the urgency they read in the rider's haste betokened worry. He did not stop, not ever, but kicked his heels and urged the horse forward, all the way to the station at San Jose, arriving dirty, breathless and sweating – as did the horse.

At the station stood a man who watched each day for the rider coming. He was a railroad man and he held a glass of cold water in one hand and a short typed inventory of the parcels and letters and telegrams that were for Mrs Winchester and had just been unloaded from the first train of the day. The letters bore the stamp of east coast furniture dealers, glass manufacturers, and fabric stores.

Before the rider dismounted, the railroad man shook his head and shrugged his shoulders, spilling some of the cool water onto his shoes. He wasn't sure he knew what Mrs Winchester was looking for, but he had come to know that it was not something from the usual wholesalers: a catalogue of new dresses, or a company bill, or a note on any of her orders. He held aloft the typed inventory note, waving it like a flag of surrender or hope.

Once, there was an envelope marked with a black border and the railroad man wondered if that was what Mrs Winchester was waiting for. He would not allow the rider to dismount on that day, but sent him back by return with the black-edged letter tucked into the rider's coat.

However different this letter was from the usual round of business communications, it had, when it was opened, transpired to be not anything that Mrs Winchester had expected; it contained news of the death of her former head footman, Jack, her very first footman. With the simple card that gave notice of his passing, was a brief letter from Jack's eldest daughter saying how fondly her father had always talked of Mrs Winchester.

An order for flowers was sent and a note of apology explaining that Mrs Sarah Winchester regretted but that she could not travel east to attend the funeral on account of her poorer health and her doctor's advice that such a journey would only weaken her further. She said she was sorry and she enclosed the gift of a check with the promise of a monthly pension to keep Jack's family looked after.

The next day, the rider was dispatched the same as every day for months before, and the people on the road that he passed cheered and waved, and prayers were muttered and invocations voiced against all misfortune. He arrived back at the station at San Jose, out of breath, his face smeared with dirt. The railroad man looked disappointed, and he shook his head and he shrugged his shoulders and he spilled water on his shoes again.

'If it wasn't that, then I'm damned if I know what it could be.'

Mrs Winchester's second-best maid, Frances, who was second now only in title, had some idea of what Mrs Winchester waited for, but she had learned the better part of discretion since that night almost a year back when she had briefly been in the head footman's bed – the ninth of the servants to have been in such a position. She had learned to keep what she knew about Mrs Winchester to herself.

For her part, Mrs Winchester had gradually come to further trust her second-best maid and to rely on her for things of importance. So it was that Mrs Winchester had, on the morning that she'd heard the maid leaving the head footman's bed, asked if she could write something for her, so that the quality of the girl's handwriting might be judged.

Following on from this request, Frances was given writing exercises to improve her hand and these were conducted in secret in Mrs Winchester's sitting-room where the girl's efforts could be overseen and favorable comments passed on the progress that she made from one day to the next. As a reward for each little improvement in the loop and kick and slant of her letters, Mrs Winchester pressed on Frances a silver Peace dollar and arranged for another lesson the following morning or afternoon.

This was how it had been for some several months. Frances put in extra hours of practice when she was alone in her room, her tongue gripped between her tight lips and her brow crumpled with concentration and effort. By degrees she came to have a passable good hand so that Mrs Winchester began to make use of her through the dictation of short letters to set out the details of some order for curtain fabric, or some particular requirement for a porcelain dinner service, or some stitched addition or alteration to a yellow dress that she had sent for, or some necessary stipulation to a box of lilac scented soap that she had requested.

One morning, Frances was relieved of her household duties for the day and asked to make herself available for the duration in Mrs Winchester's sitting-room once again. This time the letter she had to write was not brief, and though it was a business letter of some sort, it pertained to no such thing as orders for household goods or millinery finery or items of personal toilette. The letter was addressed to a Mr Archibald Lean in New England.

The letter was several pages long and Mrs Winchester stopped in her dictation several times over the course of the morning so that Frances might rest her grip and flex her fingers and her wrist. Sometimes lemonade was ordered, or tea and biscuits, or a light meal. Mrs Winchester read over what Frances had written, while the girl ate something or slaked her thirst or rubbed the cramp from the heel of her hand. Then, after a suitable length of time had elapsed, Frances was asked if she thought she could continue and Mrs Winchester resumed her dictation where she had left off.

What Frances kept to herself was the substance of the letter she wrote that day and the name and address of the person to whom it had been sent. So it was that Mrs Winchester's second-best maid was the only person who really knew anything of what Mrs Winchester waited on and why she made enquiry each morning as to whether or not a letter had been delivered to her at San Jose.

At last, almost six months after the sending of the letter to New England, and the man at the station felt sure he had the missive that Mrs Winchester looked for, even though the plainly addressed white envelope he waved in the air betrayed nothing of what it held.

'It's a letter and it's different from all the rest,' he said. 'Not a bill or an advertisement from a glove-maker's store or a letter from a window manufacturer, and it does not have a black border to it. And it smells different, too, smells of dust and old books and a little of Dr Thomas's Eclectric Oil liniment, a faint aroma of menthol and camphor. I think this might be the letter that she has been expecting. It must be.'

He handed over the letter to the man astride the horse and immediately checked the time on his pocket watch and nodded to himself. When he looked up again at the messenger, he was a little surprised to see that he was still there. The messenger turned the letter over and over in his hand. He held it near to his face, as though a closer inspection of the envelope might reveal something more than the station man had noticed. He inhaled the scent of camphor and menthol and he coughed. Then he shook himself into a decision, tucked the letter into the inside pocket of his coat and turned the horse around.

The head footman did the same when the letter was passed on to him: he turned it over and over, and he scrutinized the name and the address, holding it close to his face or up to the light, and he noted how the name and the address sat square on the envelope as though there were faint pencil lines to help it all sit straight.

Mrs Winchester pressed a coin into the head footman's hand – 'For the rider' – and waved him away so that she might be alone when she read the letter. She waited till he had closed the door behind him and until his footsteps were a fainter and fainter sound.

The letter had few words and so she read it several times before sending for her maid.

'A reply from Mr Archibald Lean of New England,' she said, holding it out for Frances to read.

Dear Mrs Winchester

Thank you for your most recent and most detailed letter. I have, with close reference to your precise instructions, done exactly as you directed. My investigations and enquiries have revealed that the person you seek still lives and I have enclosed the details of the place and the street where the person resides. I await your further instructions in this matter and enclose an itemized bill for my services thus far.

Yours sincerely

Mr Archibald Lean

Frances read the letter to herself, one finger tracing under each word in turn and running to the end of each line. Then, satisfied that she had the contents to heart, she folded the letter into the envelope again and passed it back to Mrs Winchester without a word or any other sign to show that she had understood.

'I think we might write a reply,' said Mrs Winchester, by which 'we' she meant the maid writing under her dictation as before. There was an agitation that crept up on Mrs Winchester, even as it was kept from her words: her stick clicked against the floor as though she was tapping out a tune, and her hand holding the letter in its envelope shook, and her breath came quicker and shorter.

Frances ensured that the door to the sitting-room was properly closed. She opened a drawer in the table and took out a small stack of paper and the pen and ink. Then she arranged everything on the table, methodically as she had learned to do, and she took a seat, her back straight and her feet placed squarely on the floor, the point of the pen poised above the opened bottle of ink.

*

When the second letter was written, and addressed once again to Mr Archibald Lean, it was sealed and handed to the head footman and an order given for a horse to be saddled up and for a rider – the same rider as before – to take the letter to the station at San Jose so that it might be put aboard the very next train east.

The rider had to be pulled out of sleep to carry out Mrs Winchester's errand. He yawned and spat in the dirt and mounted the horse. Then he set off at a gallop and did not look back, not even at the people by the side of the road or the farmers in the fields who wondered at the rider being about his business in such a hurry at this later hour of the day.

The railroad man at San Jose station was also surprised to be told that the rider was asking for him. The new letter was passed from the rider to the railroad man who checked the time on his pocket watch and nodded to himself and turned the letter over and over in his hand as if he might learn something from such a performance. Then he took it inside the station, made a record of it in his book, and passed it to the mailman on the train that was waiting to depart.

Thus the pattern of the days that had been in place for almost six months and might have been broken with the arrival of the looked-for letter, was not really broken, and it came to be within a week or two that the horse was each morning saddled at Mrs Winchester's orders, and the rider was called on as before, called on early to make the journey to the station at San Jose in search of another letter from a Mr Archibald Lean of New England.

And Mrs Winchester stamped her stick on the floor without knowing that she did, and she sighed impatiently, and the arthritis in her fingers tightened so that every movement was a hurt and there were stubborn tears in her eyes behind her veil.

And again she waited.

Room 159

The Winchester Gun Club

The railroad men was in town and everywhere you went they was talked about. Respectable women in Hal's store shook their heads, and narrowed their eyes, and exchanged whispered gossip about what was going on: men seen drunk in the street of a morning, cussing the birds in the sky, and pissing their pants in front of children without any shame.

Some of the flightier girls in town had other things to say. One of the railroad workers was particularly handsome and others were passable; and anyways, they had more money than sense, every one of them, and they didn't mind how they spent it. Sam Mitchell's dress store did its best trade ever, and his window was empty and it never was before. He took on extra seamstresses to keep up with the demand.

There was fights, of course. Mostly fists, and Sheriff Douty had his hands full and no room in his cells for the month the railmen was in town. The judge handed out fines each new day like he was handing out good mornings on a busy street, and the railmen paid without complaint.

On Friday nights throughout the year, I could be found in a back room of Millie's Saloon, playing cards with some of the farm-boys and Doctor Benjamin. It was an arrangement we had. The pot was never so big as it would break the bank, but it was a way of passing the time, and we'd share a few laughs and drink till we was past being drunk. Saturdays we slept it off and swore we'd give the whole thing a miss the next Friday, but never did.

Well, with the railmen being in town, things was a little different. They moved extra tables into Millie's back room and the cards that was played was a mite more serious and the money that was there for the taking was more than could be made in a year by such as me and Doc Benjamin sitting with the farm-boys. They was almost giving it away, those railroad men, seeing their cards through the bottom of a whiskey bottle and not knowing if they saw a six or an eight and that made it easy. One Friday night I took in more than sixty dollars and everybody was laughing and the Doc took almost the same.

On the ride home that night, I was singing and my horse moving at a walk and the sun was coming up and my pockets was heavier than pockets should be. I thought Elizabeth would be pleased and I was thinking of the new dress she could buy and maybe a new mirror and some perfumed soap – smelling of lilacs. I wasn't thinking of nothing else, not really minding the time or the shadows at the side of the road and how they was alive.

He was a railroad man. I knew that straight off, even though he had a kerchief tied across his mouth and his chin, and his hat pulled low so I could scarcely see his eyes. He was alone and he spoke his words all growl and grit. He called me 'mister' and he said how I should get off my horse, moving real slow and real careful, and no-one was to get hurt. He had a rifle in his hands and he was pointing it at me. I didn't have a choice, only I was still thinking of Elizabeth in a new yellow dress and smelling of lilacs and seeing herself in the mirror and knowing she was the prettiest woman this side of the mountains, and maybe the drink was making me a little stupid, too – railmen stupid. I tightened my hold of the reins and kicked my horse in her side and it was like she was expecting it all along and like the wind she took off.

He shot me in the back, three shots reeled off one after the other with his lever-action Winchester. Three shots and three hits, and I fell from my horse, my pockets spilling silver dollars everywhere into the dirt, railroad dollars.

CHAPTER TWENTY-SIX

Mr Archibald Lean of New England made all the arrangements as per the instructions given in Mrs Winchester's sixth and seventh letters. He booked the train tickets and the rooms in hotels and sent regular telegrams to inform Mrs Winchester of the progress he had made, the dates and the times, and all the conditions of the visit and so forth. 'All being well,' he wrote at the end of each communication.

But Mrs Winchester was not well. She was visited by the young doctor, Ellis Wright, almost daily and, though she still thought him a boy, and was always suspicious of his modern thinking and his strange prescriptions, she allowed herself to be directed by him in matters of her health. She did not give consent to the use of bee venom, but in all matters else she did take heed of what he had to say.

There were days when she kept to her bed and she conducted all her business from there through the intermediaries of her footman and Frances, who was now her best and only maid. She asked for reports on the house and how it progressed; she gave orders for specific alterations to rooms under construction and saw the foreman several times a week to make clear her plans, drawing pictures in the air with the wave of her hand when she could no longer hold a pen; she asked, each day, whether there was a letter or some other communication come from Mr Archibald Lean, and she sent the rider to the station at San Jose to check; she met with the cook once or twice a week to discuss the menu and to put into place the particular dietary recommendations of the young doctor, for there was some new research to suggest that what was eaten might help in the management of this or that ailment; she dictated letters to Frances, speaking in a voice that was the ghost of itself, grown thin and full of air and lacking in sound; and she asked after the gardens and the orchards and her cars and the plans for the orphanage picnic and any other small thing that pertained to her estate.

Mr Archibald Lean had negotiated the visit and every small detail had been attended to. He had also agreed to accompany the person on the journey west. No expense was spared, as was the express wish of Mrs Winchester, and so he had made free with the lady's money in everything: the best seats on the train, the best rooms in the hotels and the best cars to bring them to the station on the morning of departure. The person he had agreed to take to the Winchester House in the Santa Clara Valley was made presentable by many visits to the finest clothes stores, and new shoes were procured, several pairs, and hats and gloves, and all manner of accessories that were the fashion of the day for one so advanced in years, as was this person.

'When is it they are expected?' Mrs Winchester asked Frances, and that became the start and finish of each day; before rising and before retiring she had a conference with the maid and each meeting began or ended with that question.

On days when she rose from her bed, she had to be helped into her clothes and her hair brushed and all the finer points of her toilette carried out with Frances' assistance. Then she had to be helped to the window so that she might look out and know what kind of a day it was.

Sometimes she requested that a car be made ready and sometimes she was well enough and able to make it to the Otis electric elevator and could then, with her arrival on the ground floor, be carried into the back seat of her Pierce Arrow limousine and driven slowly once around the estate. She tapped her stick on the floor of the car if she wished for the driver to stop so that she could better observe some activity in the orchards or so that she might enquire of the workers as to how last year's crop measured against the year before's, and what they thought this year's should bring. She tapped her stick where once she had stamped it like a heavy foot; she tapped it, and sometimes she tapped it so softly that she was not heard, and then when she was at last heard she had forgotten why she had wished for the car to stop.

Mr Archibald Lean paced up and down the station platform, continually looking at his watch and checking the time against the station clock. A man at the entrance caught his eye and shook his head, by which signal he knew that the person of importance had not yet arrived. He consulted with the stationmaster to ascertain how long it might be before the train's departure and made so bold as to suggest a short delay and offered some remuneration for the trouble that this delay would cause the man.

'Timetables is timetables, sir,' the stationmaster said. 'They is to be kept to in all instances except by some greater emergency or catastrophe or some problem on the line. More than my job's worth to hold up the train just because a gentleman requests it, begging your pardon.'

Mr Archibald Lean asked to know the time of a later train and the stationmaster, with all the ceremony better accorded with the handling of some sacred object or holy relic, withdrew from his inner coat pocket a folded paper timetable for the gentleman's examination.

Some days Mrs Winchester, leaning on the support of her maid or her footman, took a walk about the corridors of the house and made some inspection of a particular room before its completion and the locking of the door. She kept the keys to all her locked rooms in the safe alongside newspaper cuttings and old letters and small articles of clothing, and other such items of importance to her. There were hundreds of keys, all different and all thrown into a box which itself had a key and was locked.

'This is my most treasured possession,' she told Frances one day, withdrawing a small velvet box from the safe. The box had lost all its color and was now grey. She took it back to her room and placed it on the table. 'My most treasured,' she said again, as though for dramatic impact, though more likely she had forgotten that she'd already said as much to the maid.

Frances expected the box contained some special piece of jewelry. She'd heard about diamonds that were the size of a child's closed fist, some of them blue and worth a king's ransom. She'd thought the box would hold something of that nature, a ring or a bracelet of precious stones or a brooch. She was a little disappointed when it was opened and a thin and limp lock of hair bound in a faded ribbon was all that was inside.

Mrs Winchester lifted her veil, and she held the lock of hair to her nose and breathed in. There was no longer any smell to the hair or to the ribbon, but Mrs Winchester imagined there was.

'Annie,' said Mrs Winchester, and she bid the maid come a little closer and she laid one hand on the girl's head and stroked her hair and called her 'Annie' and there were tears in her eyes.

'Do you think…?' began Mrs Winchester.

It was a question she began more and more often, to Frances, and the foreman and the footman, even to the cook on a single occasion, and not once did she come to the finish of her question so that there was much speculation below stairs about what it might be.

A telegram was sent by the firm of Mr Archibald Lean to confirm that the train was at last departed with its full complement of passengers and the time of its expected arrival at San Jose was affirmed and the need for the limousine to be prompt was made clear in the gentlest of words. 'I look forward to our meeting face to face, all being well.'

The journey west was not so slow as it had been more than thirty-five years before when Mrs Winchester had made the trip. Nor was it so uncomfortable or so tiring. Mr Archibald Lean sat alone at a low table and he reread all the letters sent to him by Mrs Winchester, read them to ensure that he had tended to all her specific requests in the planning and execution of her business. He made careful calculation of the monies she had sent him over the course of the past year and offset this against the costs he had been put to in arranging everything. Arriving at a final figure of profit he nodded approval and ran over all the numbers again just to be certain that he had not missed anything.

Mr Archibald's companion did not make an appearance on the journey but kept to the small cabin that had been booked for the purpose of privacy and which had been arranged to offer all manner of comfort, and settled so as to accommodate all the conditions negotiated prior to the agreement to the undertaking. The blinds were drawn against the wide-open expanse of prairie that lay on the other side of the glass, and the kicked-up dust and the rolling tumbleweed, and the searing blue sky and the unkind sun. Iced tea was on order and delivered to the cabin on the hour, every hour; and fresh fruit in slices and dusted over with powdered sugar, and jellies in all flavors, and soft bread and mashed potatoes and poached fish without bones or skin; and warm water to wash in and clean towels and soap smelling of lavender.

'When is it they are expected?' said Mrs Winchester.

The weeks that it had been, were shrunk to days and then to hours, and Mrs Winchester grew more tired. A particular dress had been picked out, and a timetable for tea and refreshments drawn up and a tour of the house and the grounds planned ahead of time and then dinner was to be served. Come the day, though, and Mrs Winchester could not rise from her bed.

The young doctor shook his head and closed his black bag and he pressed Mrs Winchester's hand and told her to rest and not to over-excite herself.

'When is it they are expected?'

It was no longer enough to give, in answer to the question, the time of their arrival at San Jose station, the time according to the railroad timetable, which was as reliable as clock time ever is. Mrs Winchester wanted to know more definitely the matter of how many hours and minutes before they would be there by her bed and talking with her.

The black and grey Pierce Arrow limousine picked up Mr Archibald Lean and one other passenger from the station. The train was late or early by a few minutes, but it did not really matter. On the drive to the Winchester House, the driver pointed out this or that feature of the town and the estate as he had been scripted to do, drawing particular attention to the places that had seen some benefit from having Mrs Winchester as their neighbor. Girls from the orphanage, identified by their pinafores and green stockings, pointed to the limousine and, taking the veiled passenger inside to be Mrs Winchester, waved and smiled and made much of the car's passing. Gentlemen on the road made the same mistake and doffed their hats to Mr Archibald Lean's companion, and ladies waved also.

Soon the passengers in the limousine saw the Winchester House in its sprawling entirety. It wasn't like a house at all, but a jumble of houses all competing with each other in style and extravagance. All the words the driver used to describe it fell far short of the reality. It wasn't enough to say, as he did, that the number of windows, turrets, towers and cupolas was 'vast'. He tried harder to explain how many rooms there were. ' No-one knows how many. There might be a thousand or more,' he said, as if they were *his* rooms and this was *his* senseless boast. 'Certainly more,' he said, and, 'A world without end.' Words failed him.

The sighting of the car when it was still a long way off was reported to the footman and then to the once second-best maid who took the news to Mrs Winchester in her bed. The young doctor was on hand to offer camphor and peppermint smelling salts so that Mrs Winchester might be prevented from fainting.

'Do you think she is with them?' Mrs Winchester said, but her words were so small and her breath so heavy that no sense could be made of what she had uttered.

She beckoned for Frances to stand a little closer, and she took her hand and said again, 'Do you think she is with them?'

Frances patted Mrs Winchester's hand and nodded without understanding what she had been asked.

The arrival of the car was witnessed by Mrs Winchester and her bedroom attendants; noise of the car and the driver issuing instructions how entry to the house might be gained, reached Mrs Winchester and the rest through the open window of her bedroom.

'The front doors have not been opened since the great earthquake of 1906, not for the doctor or any of her relatives, not even for the President Roosevelt. This way,' said the driver, leading them to a side entrance.

The sound of the Otis electric elevator, the scream and screech of its winding mechanism and the stop and start of its engine, heralded the approach of the expected visitors and Mrs Winchester waved the doctor away, and the footman, and asked only that her maid remain by her side.

Mr Archibald Lean, a thin man with a shock of dark hair long and fashioned like a girl's, and an extravagant waxed mustache, bowed and made the official introductions of himself and of the lady who stood in his shadow. The name of the lady meant nothing to Mrs Winchester, except that it had been mentioned in Mr Lean's letters to her these past few months.

Mrs Winchester shook the hand of Mr Archibald Lean and thanked him for his services and sent him away to the other room where he might find refreshment and anything else he required.

There was an awkwardness in those first moments. Frances drew up a chair near to the bed for the visitor to sit in and then she stepped back into the shadows. The visitor was dressed from head to toe in black, as though she was in deeper mourning for some personal loss. She was short and shrunken and beneath the veil her cheeks were sunken and hollow and her skin pale. She moved as though on tip-toe or as though her shoes hurt her feet, her back was bent so she was crooked, and her arms hung loose so that they did not seem to belong to her. She accepted the offer of the chair and sat down.

'Perhaps you wish something to drink or something to eat after your journey?'

Frances translated Mrs Winchester's breathy whisper into words.

The visitor took a long time to respond before she shook her head and folded her hands one inside the other in her lap.

'It has been a long time,' said Mrs Winchester.

Her words floated in the air, like smoke or mist, and the maid was not sure if what was said was heard by the visitor or understood.

'Is she with you?' said Mrs Winchester. 'You would not have come all this way to tell me she was not. Is there an Annie with you and does she wait for me on the other side? What does she say to me today? Speak with her and tell me.'

The visitor shifted in her chair. Her bones cracked and she moaned a little and made to clear her throat as though in preparation for speech. Then there was a breathy silence between them and no words.

Outside, the day was busy and the sounds of the gardeners at work and the stable-hands and the mechanic checking over the car and the rider returned from the station with the letters that were for Mrs Winchester, all of the sounds of that day leaked into the room where they were; still there was a silence of sorts.

'Not William or John, not John today, but Annie. What does she have to say to me?'

There was a quiet desperation in Mrs Winchester's voice and tears on her grey cheek and an agitation in all her small movements, her hands not at rest but fluttering like the wings of cooped hens when there is a fox loose among them, her lips all a tremble and her breath coming broken, and something grabbed at.

'What does she say?'

The visitor cleared her throat again and this time there *was* a speech, if three words might be taken for such. 'Enough is enough,' said the visitor, and as before, thirty-five years and some before, there was a wealth of meaning in what was said and Mrs Winchester was able to take what she wanted from it. The muscles of her face relaxed and her hands stilled and her breathing became even and shallow and soft.

They sat in a silence for some time. The visitor lifted her veil and reached out and took Mrs Winchester's hand in hers. There was no difference in the thin or the grey or the lines of age in those hands she clasped, no difference from her own hands. They sat like this for an hour or more before the meeting was thought to be at an end and the visitor lowered her veil again and quietly departed, accompanied by Mr Archibald Lean, the two of them driven back to the station in San Jose and this time the driver of the limousine silent.

Room 161

The Winchester Gun Club

What must a man do when his wife and his children are slain and all his neighbors' wives and their children, too? What must a man do if he is to be counted a man in this life or the next?

The village was in darkness and that is how we knew on our return that something was not right. I went ahead of the rest, soft on my feet and moving swift like the shadow of a hawk in flight cast on the ground. So it was that I came upon them. Many looked as though they were sleeping, except they were stiller than any sleeper. My son's eyes were staring and fat black flies crawled forth from his open breathless mouth. I carried the bodies of my wife and children into the tipi and arranged them for the next world and then set the whole to flame. That brought the others and they did the same for their own families. There was such weeping.

Afterwards, I stood by the running river. I do not know how long I stood there or why. When I heard chanting and raised voices, I understood that there was a council come together to decide what to do. Only then did I leave the water's edge and take my seat with the other men.

There was much talk of hate and revenge and what we might do to the women of the men who had raided our village and what we might do to *their* children also. There were pictures drawn in the dirt with the point of a stick and I cannot put into words what were those pictures except that they spoke to the darkness in our hearts.

One among us spoke up then, and his words were hummingbird words, and he said the spirits of our own women and our own children were near and talk such as this was not what they should hear on their way to the spirit place. I left the council then, afraid of hurting the men who were my brothers by what I had to say. There were three others who understood how I felt and they left with me.

In the hills and just before that first morning came up, I made time to be alone. I sat facing towards where the sun would be, waiting for the day to begin. I closed my eyes and passed into the spirit place where everything is without substance and where it is like being in a dream and there is no such thing as day or night, only being. I called out for my wife and, though she was made of air, she did come before me and danced for me one last time, her movements like water running. There was blood on her dress and there were tears on her cheek. She did not speak but her thoughts were my thoughts and so we understood each other. 'It will not be long,' I thought, 'and we shall be together in the next life. I swear it.'

So began the year of hate and our faces painted each new day and oaths sworn and sworn again. Many were the lives that we took and we were as beasts or as men who are crazy and do not care anymore for their time in this world. We left eagle feathers in the hair of their dead women and we stripped them of their clothes and laid their dead children at their feet. I know that white men wept as we had wept and I know that they were filled up with hate as we were. There was no satisfaction in that, but there was something.

We moved through the country, never staying in the one place for long, and soon there were soldiers on our trail and men with hard hearts and few wits. We knew there would be an end to what we were doing. Their numbers were greater than ours and their weapons better.

Besides, our thirst was almost quenched and we looked back on all that we had done and we did not know if this was what it was to be a man.

Then at last the sun came up on the day when I knew I would be with my wife again. There was no fear in me, only a sense of peace. They came upon us, thinking we were unawares, and they emptied their quick-shot rifles into us, so many bullets that they might have killed a hundred of us instead of just four.

Now, I am adrift in the spirit place, and I search for the woman who was my wife once and will be my wife again, and I call her name, Willamette, which is in meaning 'Running Water' and I do not know if she hears me.

CHAPTER TWENTY-SEVEN

The young doctor remained in attendance for the hours immediately following the departure of Mr Archibald Lean and the female visitor that came with him. He anticipated that there would be some further need of his skills before the night was done and so he checked on Mrs Winchester every hour, checking her pulse, temperature and breathing.

Mrs Winchester slept, or if she woke it was as though she dreamed and she spoke in sound that held few words and little sense. The maid called Frances mopped at Mrs Winchester's brow with a cool damp cloth and she soothed her with words of comfort, such as she could find, and she held her lady's hand in hers and prayed.

'Is it Annie?' said Mrs Winchester when she seemed briefly to surface out of dream. 'Is it you?' she said, her voice suddenly bell-clear. 'Is it really you?'

Mrs Winchester's maid smiled and nodded, and it did not feel like a lie to say that it *was* her, and besides, she could be anything Mrs Winchester wanted. Hadn't she learned to write like a lady just to please her?

Mrs Winchester could not eat and she had to be helped to drink, small sips of water with honey and lemon and a teaspoon of medicinal brandy. The young doctor held her wrist and he counted, looking off into nowhere so that all his concentration was on the faint butterfly-fluttering pulse under the tips of his fingers. He counted twice to be sure, then he penciled a record of the figure in a small notebook and shook his head again and retired to the next room.

It was dark soon enough and an oil lantern had to be lit and set by the bed and Frances said that she would sit with Mrs Winchester in case she was needed. The window was closed and the curtains pulled to.

'I wonder, ma'am, if it would be proper for you to undertake a little dictation at this time?' Frances said, her voice not her full voice but speaking as though she was at prayer.

She opened the drawer in the bedside table and took out some sheets of paper and a pen and some ink. She arranged these on the larger table and by the light of the lantern she began to write, stopping every small while to rehearse in speech what she would pen, and trying by such rehearsal to sound the same as Mrs Winchester whenever she did command her to write.

What she wrote was a letter of recommendation such as Mrs Winchester might have written had she not slept or been lost in some sedative delirium. She signed the letter, too, for Mrs Winchester had schooled her in that also. Then she slipped the letter into an envelope and used Mrs Winchester's wax seal to fix the letter shut.

'Have I been good enough?' Mrs Winchester said, and Frances hurried to her side and assured her that she had been most kind and thoughtful and generous with everyone.

'But is it enough?'

Frances did not know what Mrs Winchester meant and so she simply said that yes, it was surely enough, and this seemed to still the agitation in Mrs Winchester and she slipped back into sleep.

At around midnight, as near as Frances was able to estimate it, she tiptoed out of Mrs Winchester's bedroom and crept downstairs to the electric bell-pull. Somewhere in the house the noise of hammers fell silent for a moment and the burr-sound of saws paused and it was as though the whole house held its breath and listened. The bell rang as usual. It is what Frances had done every night for a year, on Mrs Winchester's instructions. She rang the bell twice, and the hammers fell again and the saws resumed their cutting and the whole house breathed once more. Frances ascended the stairs again and crept unnoticed back into Mrs Winchester's bedroom.

'Annie?' said Mrs Winchester.

An hour later the doctor was summoned into the room. There was a new edge to Mrs Winchester's breathing, a stopping and a starting that was different, and the maid was alarmed.

'It is nearly time,' said Doctor Ellis Wright. 'I have seen this before. It is what we doctors are used to seeing.'

He calculated her pulse again and laid the back of his hand against Mrs Winchester's cheek. Frances thought it an action of some boldness, as well some tenderness. She wished for the young doctor to offer her some such comfort for it seemed genuine to her.

At around half-past one, the night being at its coldest moment, Mrs Winchester breathed her quiet last. As if some silent messenger had immediately carried the news through the house, the night-shift workmen gave up on what they were doing, nails not fully hammered home were left, and wood half-cut was set aside, and men buttoned their shirts and sat back on their heels and sighed without fully knowing what had just happened.

The next morning the day-shift did not turn up for work, though no word of Mrs Winchester's death had yet leaked out; and the servants below stairs, having discussed the matter in hushed whispers over breakfast, began packing their things and making preparations to leave; and the gardeners ceased their picking of ripe fruit, apricots and plums; and the mechanic wrapped his tools in oiled cloth and covered Mrs Winchester's cars in sheet tarpaulin; and the stable-boy released the horses into the paddock and they walked soberly and did not run or kick or make a sound; and the rider who was used to being dispatched to the station at San Jose every morning, shrugged his shoulders and kicked a stone down the length of the drive and stopped to talk to a girl he normally passed at a gallop; and the young doctor, who had slept the rest of the night on a sofa in the smaller sitting-room, got to his heavy feet and picked up his black Gladstone bag and quietly left.

Frances, had, by this time, already made good her departure, unseen and unheard, clutching her letter of recommendation from Mrs Winchester, and a purse that was not small and contained all the silver Peace dollars she had earned, and a valise with all her worldly goods. She was crying as she left.

The head footman, over the next few days, made all the necessary preparations for the transportation of Mrs Winchester's body to her home in New Haven. A letter detailing Mrs Winchester's last wishes had been entrusted to his safe-keeping some years before so that he would know exactly what was to be done.

It was quiet in the house when everyone was gone, the same quiet as attends a theatre after a great and splendid performance, the quiet that is more than just an absence of sound but has in it the sense of something missing or lost or ended. There was nothing of any substance in that quiet, no sound save that which is made with the shrinking and expanding of wood, or the slow deepening of cracks in the plaster, or the wind whispering through gaps in the walls, sighing beneath doors, at the windows, and water sometimes gargling in the pipes, and mice making homes in the cupboards and making almost no sound at all. In all the rooms and corridors of the Winchester House there was no other sound.

Epilogue

Once there were voices. In my head and not in my head. I am sure there were, though the years are many on me now and maybe I misremember. Now there is but the one voice and that is my own and even that has no sound, for I have forgotten what it is to speak out loud in a room and to hear my voice caught between four walls, or set free on the air in a street and added to all those other street-voices, for all hearing is hard now.

What I do recall is that day when she first visited me and the things that I said to her on that day and how I wished her harm and did a wicked thing then. I talked of curses and a hundred voices raised against her and against her name, a thousand voices, and all on account of the business that made her who she is or who she was. I would have sooner seen her dead on that day than to have seen her before me with her purse of gold -- tainted gold – and her face all questions and searching for some small word from her husband and the girl she had lost. I forget the name of the girl, but I pretended that there was a word from them both and that word was 'sorry' by which I knew she could take a whole room full of meaning or more than a roomful.

I sent her west then, on a mad crusade, and I thought it might break her and soon enough one day I'd read about her passing in the newspaper and reading that would cheer me. There was a debt she owed me, you see, in my reckoning there was, and I would have had it paid in her blood or her death as my son had paid with his.

It was a little after that 'go-west-day' that the voices left me, and of a sudden. At first it was as a blessing, and I could sleep and dream and there was no need for the sedative help of whiskey or port, and I could hold my breath to better hear what people in this world were saying in private and not wanting to be heard, wind-whispers and leaf-whispers and prayers said in the muffled dark and I could hear all these if I was by, and I did not need to have my head in my hands against the hurt of so many voices talking at once. It was a kind of peace, at first, and so I rejoiced. I took myself out of the city one day and into a field that was far away from everything, and I lay down on a blanket in that field and just listened, to the wind moving around me, and the grass speaking in whispers, and the sweep of butterfly wings, the buzz-saw of bees and the thrill of birdsong.

But then I came to miss the voices, for hadn't they been with me always? Hadn't they? And there was one above the rest that I had hoped to hear and not hearing any might mean that all hope of that was lost. I took myself to a graveyard one black-blind night, and I lay down on the gravestone of a woman who was recently buried and I pressed my ear to the stone to see if I might hear something, some small moaning, or a voice lifted in angel song, or making some speech about the end that she had met and some spat complaint about the time that had been stolen from her. I heard nothing; nothing more than the digging of star-nosed moles in the velvet dark or the far-off cry of a saw-whet owl or the softer scraping of cicada beetles. There was no voice other than my own.

I was miserable then, as miserable as she was, and my loss was all the greater for being borne in that new silence that I cursed, and I hated her more than before for her part in that loss.

He was all my world, and no other to hold that place in my affection, for his father was a drunk and he had no knowledge that he was a father and I had no knowing where the father was and no care to know either. My boy was enough and everything, and his Sunday-name was Frederick but he was always Freddie. He was what a boy ever is, and he was always running from his mother, dragging her behind him at first to see this leap-squat frog or that dead mouse or some other such small wonder. Then, when a mother could not be dragged, he ran with other boys and I do not know the mischief he got up to then, though I was forever stitching tears in his clothes, wrapping bandages about small wounds and scolding his silliness.

I could not stay angry with him for long and maybe I did spoil the boy a little, if by spoiling is meant that I loved him overmuch. I saw something of the father in the boy as he grew towards being a man, something of the father that I had loved once but briefly. The kiss-curl of his hair above a square brow was the same, and the blue of his eyes like a New Haven sky in full summer, and the cut of his chin, sharp as a knife or a sword. But he was a good boy, too, even though it is his mother that does say it now and that mother old and looking back through the dark and misted glass of so many years.

Then there was a girl, or a dozen girls, and that is always the way, and a boy does not love his mother so much then. There was one who was above the rest in his affection, and her name was Sarah, which has no bearing on the hate I felt towards Mrs Sarah Winchester and is only a matter of some small coincidence. And this Sarah, *his* Sarah, was the center of all my boy's thinking, and he saw pretty where I saw plain, and he heard sweetness in her singing when I heard cracks, and he said enough was enough, and he told me I didn't know her like he did.

But he was not alone in setting his heart on this Sarah, not alone in making small gifts to her of ribbons and rings and a peridot gold brooch that was more than he could pay for. Sarah had the choice of some four or five young men and so there were sometimes fights among them and Freddie came home with his knuckles bruised and his lip split and blood making small roses on his shirt and a boast that the other young man, his rival, carried home worse injuries, which was no comfort to me.

I warned him then, as is the duty of a mother. 'She is trouble,' I said, which only made him turn the more against me and turn all the more towards her.

'Enough is enough,' he said again.

'Take care,' I said, but I do not think he was listening, for he thought all my words were spite and spurn.

So we arrive at the darker day, the day that is my black day and his, and a day that we both would have back to begin again if we could, to begin again and end different from how it did. One of the other boys, thinking himself a man, brought a gun to the fight and it was a Winchester 'Yellow Boy' rifle, all brassy and glint and glister, and he warned Freddie off and threatened him with that rifle.

And foolish, foolish child, for Freddie did not read the hate and the hurt in that boy with the rifle, did not have the proper measure of him, and thought it all an idle boast – till the bullets bit and not one bite but another and another, six in quick succession, all thanks to the pump action design that had made the rifle famous. And Freddie was dead and all my world dead, too. Except that she came to see me one day, Mrs Sarah Winchester, and her being before me was a fan to my hate and so I took my revenge.

I told her it was what the voices commanded and I sent her west on a fool's errand, and I waited for her to die, and all those years between then and now I have waited and grown old and deaf in all that waiting, my ears ever straining to hear the voices that were lost to me and wishing to hear Freddie's voice above all the others, and wishing to hear *her* voice too, for hearing her voice would let me know that she was dead.

Then a Mr Archibald Lean comes calling and he wishes to see me, and he shows me a letter from Mrs Sarah Winchester and in the letter she asks if I might make a visit to her house in the West and the offer is made of more money than an old person could spend in the years that are left to her.

He is a nice man, this Mr Archibald Lean. He reminds me of Freddie, or how I imagine Freddie might have been if he had been given a few more years and a chance in life. So I agree to what he asks and I agree to see Mrs Winchester one further time.

The journey there is tiring and I do not think that Mr Archibald Lean knows yet that I am deaf. He talked to me and I lost his words in watching the movement of his lips for he talked too fast; and he took my arm when we mounted and dismounted the train and I could see he was talking again and passing some pleasantry on the weather or the day or the time of year.

I saw no reason to tell anyone of my disability, but kept quiet and with my veil covering my face. There was a car that picked us up at San Jose station and the drive to the Winchester House was a long one, during which I thought of what I had done to this woman whose greater sin was in marrying a man called William Wirt Winchester.

The house was a sight, a sprawling mess of windows and doors and rooms, all jut and jar, and everything in a state of chaos, and builders hard at work on laying floors and putting up walls or constructing staircases.

Mrs Winchester was not well and had kept to her bed. I was taken in and given a seat close to her. I could see that she suffered and it is what I wanted to see, what I had come all that way to see and to spit in her face at last for taking my boy – and then a voice said enough was enough. And my heart softened .

There were things that she said and some of them I read on her lips and some I read from the maid's lips, for I think the girl sometimes repeated what Mrs Winchester had spoken. But much of what passed in that room passed in a thick and muffled silence.

There was a moment when Mrs Winchester seemed to ask me a question. I think I could imagine what she wanted to hear, for her questions must have also been my questions, but all I could say was 'enough is enough' – and sorry I might have said also, for I meant to, the same sorry that I had said before, long before, except this time there were no voices in my head and that 'sorry' I might have spoken was all my own.

Today the word is of her passing, in all the newspapers, and looking at the date and the time I see that she lasted only a few hours after we parted. It is a day I have waited on for so long, but now it is here I am not cheered as I expected to be, for I *am* sorry. I say it out loud, as I did in Mrs Winchester's bedroom, but I do not hear the sound that it makes just as I didn't then.

Acknowledgements

Thanks to the late Helen Lamb who pushed and pushed for me to get an agent for the book. Thanks to my agent, Duncan McAra, who had immediate faith in the text. Also thanks to Jean Findlay at *Scotland Street Press* for taking a chance on this. Thanks to the 'Demon Beaters of Lumb' and Stephen May and the 'Fiction in Progress' writers group who have all supported me with the project. Thanks to Clio Gray for help in the initial edit and to David Robinson for the final edit. Finally, special thanks to Daniel and Holly who gave me the idea and to the rest of my family who have had less of me through the writing and publishing process.